WESTERN ISLES LIBRARIES

Readers are requested to take great care of the item while in their possession, and to point out any defects that they may notice in them to the librarian.

This item should be returned on or before the latest date stamped below, but an extension of the period of loan may be granted when desired.

TEENAGE

Date of return	Date of return	Date of return
- 2 DEC 2011		
2 7 DEC 2012	W	
- 9 JAN 2014		
1 8 FEB 2014		
2 3 APR 2015		
1 2 SEP 2018		

meadowside 🍃
fiction books

First published in 2009
by Meadowside Children's Books
185 Fleet Street, London, EC4A 2HS
www.meadowsidebooks.com

JAKE HIGHFIELD

CHAOS
2
UNLEASHED

SCHOOLBOY
OPERATIVE
FUGITIVE

ALEC SILLIFANT

meadowside *fiction*

For Brandon, Jake, Alec, Jamie

Having fun is the first priority but after that
the harder things to achieve in life are always
the ones most worth having

A WALK IN THE PARK

As usual the intelligence had been accurate. Four guards patrolled the perimeter, each covering one side of the fenced industrial site, armed with assault weapons and reporting in at half-hourly intervals.

Chaos's mouth twitched into a smile as the guard on the north fence made a half-hearted report into the radio microphone pinned to his lapel. "Tango One, twenty-three hundred hours. Situation Black, repeat, Situation Black, over." Lying in wait in the undergrowth he knew he now had thirty minutes to complete his mission.

As he carefully lifted himself from his lying position, a pile of leaves to his side was disturbed. In the still air of the autumn night, the rustling seemed to amplify amongst the trees like a round of applause. The guard spun, his lethal firearm raised at the darkness before him. Chaos froze in his half-crouched pose, unsure if he had been seen or not, but no challenge was issued. The guard continued to scan the wood, trying to pinpoint the location and source of the sound.

Chaos controlled his breathing, forcing it into a slow, steady rhythm. He ignored the tightening grip of pain that pulled at his thigh muscles as he held like a statue.

He knew he could not afford to give the guard's eyes the slightest twitch of movement to catch onto.

A hedgehog appeared from the shadow of a tree, oblivious to the tense situation or its role in it. The noise from its movement brought the guard's attention and gun swinging round in its direction. Chaos mentally swore at the stupid creature as it plodded casually up to the back of his right hand and decided that this would be a great place to stop and sniff around.

The guard let out a throaty chuckle, relaxed and lowered his rifle. "Hello, little fella," he said in an almost sing-song voice. "You gave me a bit of a scare."

Chaos watched the guard with the intensity of a tiger watching its prey. Then the guard began to walk towards the hedgehog. 'Just my luck to get Private Tree-hugger,' he thought as the guard carefully crept forwards in an obvious attempt not to scare the small beast away.

As he reached down to scoop the hedgehog up, the guard froze as he realised he was looking into the eyes of another human. For a split second he didn't know what to do. His mind ran through a catalogue of reactions but before he could select one, Chaos saved the guard from having to make a decision with the use of his wrist gun.

The unconscious guard was a dead weight. As he was too big to drag into cover easily, Chaos decided to leave him where he fell. The unkempt grass would keep him hidden. Besides, he counted on being long gone before the man was discovered and it would be eight hours before the tranquilliser dart wore off. Scrambling over to the fence, Chaos made quick work of the metal lattice with bolt cutters. He was soon through the perimeter, scurrying between the maze of storerooms and offices that littered the site in a random design.

He used the cover offered by walls and shadows to hide him from prying CCTV cameras that swept the grounds; avoiding the glare of security lights that shot pools of light in ineffective directions. It was easy work to move undetected through such sloppy defences and Chaos was soon crouched by a fire door.

From a pocket Chaos pulled out a matt black box the size of a pack of playing cards. It had what looked like a blank credit card attached to it by a flat wire connector. He slipped the card into the card reader by the door handle and flicked a switch on the box. Numbers flickered across a small LCD screen. They blurred too fast for his eyes to follow, so Chaos turned his attention to the immediate area, checking for any sign of movement.

Everything so far was just as he had been told it would be: the lax security, the weakness in the system at the fire door; but he kept alert nonetheless. He knew from experience he could never be sure of anything. Even in an apparently safe situation there was no knowing when another 'hedgehog' might show up to make things more interesting.

A click and the rattling buzz of a latch being held open by electro-magnets drew his attention back to the door. He snatched the card out of the lock, pulled at the door and slipped inside. With deliberate care, he picked up a crumpled cigarette end and jammed the door onto it, leaving it slightly open giving him a quick escape route, should he need it. He checked his watch. He knew he had eighteen minutes remaining before the four patrolling guards would report in again, or at least three of them would. He would have to speed up his progress.

However, speed and haste were two different things, as he had been told numerous times during training. Before he dared venture deeper into the facility he had to check that his box of tricks had taken care of the building's internal security. Chaos looked up at a movement sensor hanging high up on the wall next to the ceiling. Clever as the electronic gadget was, it, like all equipment, could go wrong. In the final analysis a crude test was the only way to be one hundred per cent sure.

"Here goes nothing," he muttered and waved his arms high above his head. The red light on the sensor blinked on and off rapidly but no alarm was triggered. Beneath his black ski mask, Chaos grinned, giving the pocket where the card reader was stowed again a congratulatory pat.

He'd spent much of the day before memorising the blueprint of the building's layout and the route he would take, so Chaos made no delay in reaching the door of the room he required. The name plate, Dr Watkinson confirmed he had the right place and after quickly forcing the inadequate lock, he was inside the office.

The room was sparsely furnished, as Chaos had expected. Other than the small desk, with a solitary phone, and a chair under the only window, the office was clear of any clutter at all. No pot plants, no filing cabinets, not a single framed photo of a loved one. In contrast to this, each available centimetre of wall space was floor-to-ceiling bookshelves, packed tightly with journals on weighty scientific topics. Chaos remembered from studying Watkinson's file that he was a paranoid technophobe, especially when it came to computers, and the absence of one on his desk supported this.

It was this mistrust of computer technology that meant Chaos had been sent into the field. Normally, the Academy Tech Department hackers would gather all the required information remotely, sliding unnoticed into computer files to lift the electronic data that was needed. But Watkinson's mistrust of the internet and his not totally unfounded belief that all computers were easy prey to spyware meant he employed the old ways of pen and paper to back up his own memory. That was what Chaos was here to download, in a similarly old-fashioned method.

Details for his mission had been exact right down to which carpet tile needed to be lifted to access the floor safe. With time running out, Chaos was more than pleased to be armed with these facts. He located the safe and reached for another piece of kit. He found himself wondering with amusement what Dr Watkinson would make of such advanced computerised wizardry being operated in his office without his permission.

Placing a small LCD screen on the safe door, he flicked a switch and was given a high resolution, three dimensional picture of the inside workings of the safe's locking mechanism. Chaos's hands moved deftly over the combination wheel as the screen fed him the diagram of complicated tumblers falling into place. Within a minute the safe was open and Chaos was photographing the information he needed from the papers laid out on the office floor.

Chaos checked his watch; six minutes remained until the perimeter guards would check in by radio again. The papers had been replaced; the safe had been relocked and covered with the carpet tile, which just left him with one job to do. He reached into a pouch on his belt and from it produced a can of spray paint. 'Time to give Dr Watkinson an art attack,' he thought to himself, grinning as he shook the can before spraying across the packed shelves of books.

"See, Dr Watkinson, even these low-tech back-up files aren't completely safe from corruption," muttered Chaos as he scrawled the three letters of a well-known animal rights group in a rough design in day-glo yellow across a large block of book spines.

The cry of "Stop right there!" from the office doorway genuinely made Chaos jump. Instinctively and without turning, he slowly raised his hands, still holding the condemning evidence of the spray can.

Chaos heard the familiar sound of a weapon being cocked. "Turn around and identify yourself!" barked his unwelcome discoverer.

He did as he was told, checking his watch with a quick glance as he did so. There were still three minutes before the perimeter guards would report in. If he could get out of this situation quickly enough he could be on his way before things got too hot. Chaos looked at his captor and noted the slight red swelling on the man's neck. He realised this was the perimeter guard he'd knocked out on his way in. Something was wrong. He should have been down for at least eight hours.

The guard kept his gun trained on the intruder as he read the luminous vandalism. "A-L-F. You one of those animal rights freaks?" he barked.

"Is the hedgehog alright?" asked Chaos calmly in a mocking tone.

"You're in it deep, mate," warned the guard. Chaos

could see the man was intent on keeping his finger on the assault rifle's trigger as he fumbled with his other hand to reach his radio microphone. "Tango One. Situation Red. Repeat, Situation Red. Intruder, Sector Seven. Over." The radio replied with a static hiss.

Chaos realised the guard hadn't reported in until this point. Maybe he was trying to save face? Trying to get the situation under control before anyone found out, avoid the embarrassment of having been taken out on the job...especially by some soft animal rights activist. Whether this was true or not didn't matter, but it would explain the lack of howling alarms and the absence of running personnel.

"Tango One," tried the guard again. Then again even louder, as if shouting into the radio would make a difference to the blocked signal.

"Do you want me to have a go?" asked Chaos, purposely putting more pressure on the already stressed guard. "I'm quite good with electronics."

"Shut it, you!" The man abandoned the radio and gripped the weapon with both hands again. "One move from you and I'll decorate the rest of the office with your guts!"

Chaos nodded slowly to show he understood and that he was 'shutting it', pronto.

"Take your mask off!" ordered the guard. "Slowly!"

Chaos reached down with his right hand and pulled the black ski mask up high enough to reveal his face.

The guard's expression and shoulders dropped simultaneously as he visibly lost the nervous tension in the rest of his body. "Jesus, you're just a—"

Chaos knew a cue for action when he heard one.

Before the armed man could react to his lightning movement, he won the second battle of reflexes that night. His heavy boot collided with the side of the guard's knee forcing the joint against its normal movement axis. The complex structure of bones snapped with a sickening crack.

The guard folded to the side as his damaged leg could no longer support his weight. As he gave out a high pitched scream, the pain reflex that etched itself across his face also tightened his trigger finger. Bullets sprayed from his gun, cutting an arc as guard and gun fell toward the floor, first drilling the ceiling then ripping pages from the books. Finally they bit into and shattered the office window into a rain of silver fragments.

Chaos kicked the fallen guard's gun across the office floor to keep it out of his grasp. He could see at that present moment the guard's hands were only concerned with clamping his shattered leg, as if merely by being there they could heal the damaged limb.

An alarm howled out into the night air and Chaos slid his ski mask back down. Underneath it he was grinning like a cat that had been locked in an aquarium. Leaping through the destroyed window he rolled onto the concrete below and into the building's shadow, his heart banging like a hammer.

'At last this mission is getting interesting,' thought Chaos. 'Time for a game of evade and escape.' He laughed to himself and then muttered, "Ninety-nine, one hundred, here I come, ready or not."

Chaos sprinted forward and melted into the night.

Three Years Earlier

RECRUITMENT DRIVE

Jake sat in the small office and grinned as the man behind the desk wiped the sweat from his bald head with a tatty greyed handkerchief. He flicked through the loose pages of a file. Stress was eating away at the overweight man.

"What are we going to do with you, Jake?" he said slowly without lifting his head from his reading. "I'm really at a loss this time."

"Don't worry about it, Mr Humpty—"

"Humphrey," corrected the bald man, fixing Jake with a stare that was more plea than threat.

"Yeah, right," repeated Jake, his dark brown eyes not wavering from the challenge. "I wouldn't worry about it, Mr Humpty. Something always comes up at the last minute."

Mr Humphrey lost what little control he had left and leapt to his feet. "There is no last minute this time, Jake." He tried to shout but it came out more like a squeak of panic. "We've run out of options! Look, look," he added, flicking through the papers in the file. "I've tried everything I can to help you but you always do something—"

"To mess it up?"

15

Mr Humphrey stood like a statue for a second before letting out a deep sigh, obviously trying to let his years of experience get a grip on his composure. "I know you've had problems, Jake. All the kids here have but you...you seem to wallow in it, revel in it."

Jake stood up from his seat; at eleven years old and five foot four in height he was already two inches taller than his case worker. He knew this made Humpty feel uneasy and he often played on the fact. He pulled a sheet of paper from the file and read from it. "What about Mr and Mrs Rank? Maybe they'd be willing to give me another chance?"

Mr Humphrey snatched the paper from Jake's hand. "Another chance to give them high blood pressure, I suppose. Since they fostered you, they have removed their names from the fostering programme."

"Shame," smiled Jake. "They were such nice people."

"Too nice for you—" began Humphrey before he was able to stop himself. "I'm sorry Jake, I didn't mean that. Please sit down."

As Jake retook his seat he could see a flicker of relief on the face of Mr Humphrey as he regained the height advantage. "What now then? Am I doomed to spend the rest of my days here?" Jake said, indifferently.

Mr Humphrey let a rare smile break through his stressed face. "You don't exactly spend most of your days here anyway, do you Jake? Between running away and spending time in police custody, I think you're more familiar with the outside world than I am."

"You should get out of the office more, widen your experience; or," added Jake with a smirk, "at least try to heighten it anyway."

Mr Humphrey ignored Jake's smart comment, occupying himself instead with straightening and closing Jake's file.

"The fact of the matter, I'm afraid," he said eventually, looking at Jake with what appeared to be genuine sorrow, "is that it's out of my hands now."

"What do you mean?" said Jake, sitting up in his seat and taking full notice for the first time since he'd been called into the oppressive office.

Mr Humphrey lifted Jake's file and banged the edge of it on the desk a couple of times to tidy the substantial contents before laying it flat once more. "You are not my problem anymore, Jake. You're being transferred."

"Transferred," said Jake, swallowing. "Where to?"

There was a short loud knock on the office door.

"Come in," snapped Mr Humphrey loudly.

The door was pushed open by a tall, thin man in a dark suit. Everything about the man said 'tidy and in order', from the tip of the perfectly cut hair to the shine on his black shoes. With two strides the man was in the office and at Jake's side.

"Mr Humphrey?" asked the man, holding out his hand in greeting.

"Yes," replied the bald man, shaking the offered hand, "and you must be?"

"Packard. Sorry I'm a bit late. Terrible trouble with the traffic, but speeding only causes accidents, doesn't it?"

"Quite true, Mr Packard," smiled Humphrey, seemingly pleased to be in the presence of someone who didn't reek of trouble, like most of the people he had to deal with. Jake could sense the unease the short man felt at the other man's six-foot-plus stature.

Packard turned and looked at Jake. "And you must

be Jake," he said, ruffling his hand through Jake's thick, brown hair.

Jake pulled his head back, sneering with disgust. He had a horrible feeling in the pit of his stomach that the last two years spent bending Humpty to his will were about to be thrown away and he was going to have to start all over again on this...this, touchy-feely prat. Jake stared as defiantly as he could, directly into Packard's eyes, firing the first shot in the war he had silently declared on this new enemy.

Packard absorbed the hard look and continued to smile without flinching. "I can understand you not trusting me, Jake, but soon you and I will be the best of pals. What do you say, hey?"

Jake opened his mouth to voice his opinion on the subject but Mr Humphrey, well aware of Jake's ability to use colourful language, intervened quickly. "Well, here's his file, Mr Packard. I've arranged to have his belongings packed and ready for collection on your way out." He thrust the bulging brown card folder into the man's hand. "I hope...I'm sure you'll have better luck getting through to Jake than I did." Humphrey glanced down at his desk, unable to hold the look of either of the other two people present in his office.

Jake couldn't help taking pride in Humphrey's genuinely upset look, brought on by the man's deep feeling of failure. It gave him a sense of confidence for his new job of work, namely Packard.

"Well," laughed Packard. "I'll try my best." He paused and looked at Jake again. "Actually *we'll* try our best, won't we, Jakey boy?" he said, ruffling his hair again.

Jake jerked away from the hand so violently he almost fell

out of his seat. "My name's Jake," he hissed, vehemently.

"See that?" Packard chortled. "We're already on first name terms."

He held out his hand once again. "Nice to meet you, Mr Humphrey, and sorry about the fleeting visit. I'm running a bit late. Still, you never know, we may meet again; hopefully then we'll have more time to get to know each other better?"

Mr Humphrey smiled vaguely in reply before turning to Jake. "Good luck, Jake," he said, almost offering his hand but stopping himself at the last second, realising the futility of the gesture.

Jake's grin returned once more. He thought he owed it a final outing for his old adversary. "You too, Mr Humpty. Avoid any high walls; you don't want a great fall or anything like that."

"Come on, mate," said Packard, nudging Jake toward the door. "I'd like to get you settled into your new home before nightfall."

Jake fell forward stubbornly. "Where are we going?"

"Oh, you'll love it," said Packard. "It's perfect for a lad like you."

'We'll see about that,' thought Jake, leaving Humpty's office. The familiar door clicked shut behind him for the last time. As he walked away Jake couldn't help imagining Humpty indulging in a dance of joy in his tiny office; a wobbly, sweaty jig accompanied by a child-like song, something along the lines of 'I've got rid of Highfield. I've got rid of Highfield'. The thought of Humpty being happy did not make Jake feel comfortable at all.

NOT SO GREAT ESCAPE

Right from the point when Packard had insisted on carrying Jake's packed holdall and placing it in the boot of the car, Jake had decided his new adversary was going to be an easy job. Even Humpty, who had gone way out of his way to be gracefully helpful and positive, was a tyrant compared to this ever-pleasant and calm fool. Packard filled every available moment with friendly banter in an obvious attempt to put his new charge at ease and win over his friendship.

After two hours of driving and mindless one-way chatter, Jake was reaching the end of his patience. He turned his head and stared at Packard. "Do you ever shut up?" he said coldly.

For a split second Jake thought he saw a break in Packard's smile. He was just about to congratulate himself on getting a chip in the man's armour of relentless cheerfulness when Packard interrupted his thoughts.

"Would you like me to stop talking, Jake? I can do if you want, it's your choice. I was just trying to break the ice so you and I can become friends as quickly as possible. Then we can work together from there." Packard smiled even more broadly in reply to Jake's stern gaze.

"I am not your friend," hissed Jake.

Packard focused his attention back on the motorway down which, Jake had noticed, with no surprise, he was travelling at a constant sixty-seven miles per hour. "Maybe not yet, Jake, but I have a feeling we're going to be."

Jake had had enough sugar-coated bull for one day and decided if he couldn't shut Packard up he could at least control the conversation. "Where is this new prison you're taking me to?"

"It's not a prison," chirped Packard. "I like to think of it as an institute of opportunity for troubled youngsters."

"Really," said Jake, showing his disinterest in the man's opinion by turning to look out of the passenger side window.

"It's called St. Margaret's," continued Packard, "though most of the students just call it the Academy. You'll love it. It's set in the most beautiful countryside and—"

"Academy," repeated Jake chewing off the tip of a finger nail and spitting it into the foot well. "Sounds a bit posh."

"I suppose it does," admitted Packard. "To tell you the truth, St. Margaret's used to be exactly that in a past life. It was a boarding school for the children of rich Victorian merchants. Those kids not quite good enough to mix with the aristocracy of the day."

Jake continued to watch the embankment of the motorway glide past his window. "Sounds familiar," he said quietly.

"But it's a fantastic place now. No hint of class or wealth privilege at all," said Packard enthusiastically. "A really modern-thinking establishment with bang up to date educational and training facilities and the accommodation is out of this—"

Jake turned his head to his chatty chauffeur. "Hold on, you mean I'll live *and* go to school at this place?" He felt his flippant comment about prison was coming back to haunt him.

"That's right," beamed Packard. "The Academy is a completely self-contained unit."

"Twenty-four hours a day?" said Jake, the obvious disgust written in his face. "Every day in the same place?"

"Well," said Packard slowly, "there are field trips and visits to places of interest and the like."

Jake fell into a silence as he mulled over this new turn his life had taken. The thought of being stuck in one place all the time did not appeal to him at all. At least in the last place there was always the opportunity between there and school to slope off and lead his own life, but this Academy thing sounded like prison; prison under a different name. Temporary accommodation overnight in a police cell before being picked up by Humpty was one thing. Being permanently banged up was another thing altogether.

Jake looked at the motorway sign that swept slowly past his window. It told him Birmingham was only eight miles on. 'The Midlands' he thought. 'Bang in the middle of the country; that'll do me. I'll take some finding when I've got every direction to choose from to run in.'

Jake let his face drop and half closed his eyelids.

"Are you alright, Jake?" asked Packard a few moments later when he saw the slack expression on his passenger's face.

Jake swallowed before answering, to add effect.

"I think I'm going to be sick," he mumbled, keeping his head bowed.

"Okay, okay," said Packard, straining his neck to help him read the approaching road sign. "There's a service station up ahead. We'll stop there and get some fresh air and maybe a cup of tea?"

Jake faked a retch.

"Maybe not tea then," said Packard, putting his foot down on the accelerator and speeding up to a breakneck seventy miles per hour. "Hold it in, Jake; we'll be there in a second; breathe deeply...or something?"

Jake glanced at the sign indicating it was half a mile to the services. Turning his face from Packard he allowed himself a grin that lasted until the car drove off the motorway and into the service station filter lane.

As Packard's car came to a stop, parked perfectly in the middle of the two white lines that marked out the bay, Jake slipped off his seatbelt and opened the passenger door. He leapt from the car and immediately sprinted away, leaving the passenger door wide open. He pounded his feet against the hard tarmac. He kept his eyes on his objective and within seconds he had reached the small wooden fence that separated the service station car park from the fields it bordered. He vaulted over it with a cursory glance over his shoulder. Packard had only just managed to cover a few yards from the car. Jake grinned. "See ya, old pal," he muttered and made his way to freedom.

After a few minutes Jake had settled into a steady jog. He made his way across the field, which wasn't easy due to the waist-high crop, and ploughed furrows in the hard soil. 'Not to worry,' he thought to himself confidently after many experiences in such situations, 'blokes in suits can't run for sh—' Something snagged at his ankle and Jake hit the ground hard. He instinctively threw his hands forward and tried to save his head from taking the full impact of the fall.

"Going somewhere, Highfield?" said a voice from above him. It sounded like Packard, but the tone was different.

Jake rolled over quickly and got to his feet. "That wasn't a very friendly thing to do," he said, in a defiant tone, trying to hide his surprise at being caught.

Packard grinned and it bore none of the gentleness of his previous smiling. "Perhaps not, but it certainly got your attention."

Jake was enraged. He looked at the man before him who was breathing only a little harder than he had been when he was driving and yet he'd managed to catch him with apparent ease. "How the—"

"Basic trigonometry and predictive psychology," interrupted Packard. "You'll learn all about it at the Academy."

"I'm not going to your crappy prison," hissed Jake, his hands clenching into fists.

"Oh, but you are, Highfield," replied Packard with a matter-of-fact tone. "I don't particularly care how you get there. But you are. To be honest with you, I was getting a little tired of the easy, gentle way myself. Not really my style."

Jake leapt forward. Both feet left the ground in an attempt to make up for the height disadvantage he was facing. Then he swung his fist with all his might at Packard's face.

The man swayed to the left, drove his knee into Jake's exposed stomach and then playfully cuffed the boy to the floor with an open hand. "You've got spirit, Highfield," he laughed. "Awful control, but plenty of spirit. Given time, St. Margaret's will really make something of you."

Jake stood up again, ignoring the pain in his stomach and the choking effect it was having on his breathing. His brown eyes were damp, forming tears made up of anger and pain in equal measure.

"And again?" said Packard, seeing Jake's obvious murderous intent. "Excellent, Highfield. Try to be less emotional this time; use your brain before you use your fists."

Jake snarled like a wild animal and swung out at the man with all he had. He thrashed his fists in huge arcs one after the other; left, right, left, right, each as ineffective at hitting its target as the last. As his arms quickly tired, he tried kicking out, but all his attacks were dodged or blocked by Packard who continued to grin throughout with delight.

"That's it, Highfield," said Packard, egging Jake on. "Let it all out."

Jake's head pounded with frustration and overheated blood. He ground his teeth one last time and feinting with his left hand threw his right fist. To his surprise it made contact with Packard's mouth. The man staggered back a pace at the blow, but Jake was too tired to follow up the attack. He stood still. All his remaining physical energy invested in dragging air into his lungs. He was just able to keep his fists ineffectually raised by the power of his will alone.

Packard placed the back of his hand to his lip and pulled it away stained with a smear of blood. "Nice shot, Highfield," he said, the grin still nailed to his damaged mouth. "You've got a solid attack, a bit wayward, but solid nonetheless. Let's see if your defence is up to anything. Ready?"

Jake discovered he was anything but ready. Open-hand slaps rained in on him from every angle and even though he knew the man was merely toying with him and not using his clenched fists, Jake had no energy left in his body to make any kind of attack in reply. All he could do was stay on his feet and curl from the waist, keeping his arms tight to his sides to protect his ribs and head. Eventually the slaps stopped, but the stinging from their accurate strikes did not.

"Well, that was fun. Wasn't it, Highfield?" said Packard, fixing his tie.

Jake straightened himself and looked Packard in the eye. "That was assault," he barked into the man's face.

Packard chuckled. "Don't be stupid, Highfield," he said, pulling on his shirt cuffs. "That was self-defence." The man's face suddenly relaxed from its joviality into a blank, emotionless state. "This is assault."

Jake didn't see the fist coming but he felt its impact alright. He'd once crashed a bike he'd stolen whilst trying to escape from the police and gone straight over the handlebars face-first into a brick wall. This, he decided, felt worse. He hit the hard ground for a third time with a bone-jarring thud.

"Are you going to lie there moaning for the rest of the day?" said Packard, after a few moments.

Jake looked up through tear-filled eyes and could just make out the outstretched hand. He didn't need to touch his face to find out whether Packard had also managed to draw blood in revenge for his injury; he could feel it running across his cheeks and hear it trickling into his ears.

"Well?" said Packard, thrusting his hand further forward insistently.

Jake grabbed the hand and allowed himself to be pulled to his feet. He didn't know what to say. He'd never been hit like that by an adult before. Even the coppers weren't allowed to touch him, no matter what he'd done.

"I think that makes us even," said Packard. "We've both tapped the claret."

"What?" said Jake, dabbing at his bloody nose with his sleeve.

Packard passed Jake his handkerchief. "Claret, Highfield. It's what old-time boxers used to say when they made their opponent bleed."

"Oh," said Jake absently, wiping the blood from his face and then forcing himself, despite the pain, to blow his nose clear. He looked at the crimson hanky. "You've broken my nose."

"No, I haven't," said Packard with a confidence that said 'I could have if I'd wanted to'. "It was just a knock; let you know the score, who's in charge here, that's all."

"But—"

"New life, new rules, Highfield," interrupted Packard sternly, before adding in a calm tone, "I'd happily tell you more but the Headmaster likes to welcome the new students personally and give them the full speech himself." Then suddenly he clapped his hands together and said, "Right, after that little work out I could do with a cup of tea; how about you?"

Jake felt like he had little choice but to nod his agreement; he had no wish to instigate another assault from the man. He fell into step alongside Packard and strode back through the long corn towards the service station.

'Little choice for now, anyway,' thought Jake, a scowl deepening on his face.

ST MARGARETS

It was early evening and the daylight was beginning to fade. Packard was driving down the winding B-road, slowing only for corners before gunning the car along the straighter sections. Boredom made Jake feel like they had been driving for hundreds of miles since leaving the motorway. An endless sea of countryside greenery had passed by his window, broken only by the occasional village or lonely church. Having never known anything but city life, Jake felt like an alien on a strange planet where the dominant life forms were grass and leaves.

Packard changed down two gears, spun the steering wheel hard to the left and heavily applied the brakes. The car stopped in front of an impressive high gate in a wall that Jake assumed must have run in either direction but was hidden from the road by a dense hedge. On the other side of the stone barrier, where this new road continued beyond the gate, was the forest that had kept the car in its cool shadow for some miles previously.

Jake noted the wrought iron gates, at least four metres high, were held in place by two thick, natural stone pillars. These were a further metre higher than the gates, weathered black by years of silent service. On top of the left-hand pillar, Jake noticed a security camera swing to point its suspicious gaze down in their direction.

Jake watched Packard slip his hand under the car's dashboard, obviously operating some kind of remote control. There was a loud buzz and slowly the heavy gates began to sweep inwards, with the odd complaining 'clank', to allow the car through.

The car laboured on the slightly inclined road beyond the gates as its wheels fell into and climbed out of the many dips in the uneven surface. It looked like someone had rolled out a length of tarmac carpet casually between the trees, paying no attention to finishing touches. The black uneven edges of the strip merged roughly with the dead brown sponge that was the forest floor. The trees were densely packed on either side of the car, leaving only a scar of sky amidst the all-consuming gloom to focus upon. Jake turned his head to the left to look into the mass of trees, his eyes finding it hard to send his brain a clear image as the speed of the travelling car blurred his view.

"It goes as far in the other direction as well," Packard said calmly, breaking the silence he'd kept since he had demonstrated to Jake who was in charge.

Jake didn't reply. He could see the trees were tightly packed and a tangle of other vegetation dominated the forest floor. He'd also noticed that they'd travelled a good distance since passing through the gate and there was still no end to the trees in sight. 'It's only a bunch of trees,' thought Jake, and although the wall and the gate were high, he knew from experience he could climb either in his sleep. Something flickered between two trees. Its lighter form threw a contrast with the darker tones of the bark, catching Jake's attention.

"I think I just saw something," said Jake, without thinking or meaning to say it out loud.

"Probably a deer," replied Packard. "Welcome to the Academy, Highfield," he added, with little sense of warmth to his voice.

The nose of the car dipped down as it broke free of the forest boundary. The rough road changed from incline to decline and they now ran between flat grassed grounds. Despite his determined mindset not to be moved or impressed by anything that Packard showed him, Jake found his eyes widening. The curtain of trees was drawn to reveal a building that dominated the landscape. It looked like all the power of nature around it bowed down, as if before a king. From this point of elevation on the road Jake could see that the forest surrounded the grounds in every direction. Its boundary formed a huge circle, in the centre of which St. Margaret's proudly stood. He got the feeling that the trees looked too frightened to approach any closer to this man-made structure.

The tarmac continued on, bringing the imposing building closer and bigger. It ended its casual run by spilling into a huge round patch of almost golden coloured gravel that crunched loudly under the wheels of Packard's car. Now he was up close to the building, Jake could see it was a mix of periods and ideas from different craftsmen.

The central piece of the architectural jigsaw was obviously older than the rest of the front aspect of the building. Extensions had been tagged on either side with some effort to mimic the plain yet sturdy original construction. Columns of windows three floors high ran the length of the building, broken only by the presence of a large arched entrance in the centre of the ground floor, over which a coat of arms had been carved into a sandstone block. A slate roof, high and steep, capped the building like a dark frown, unhappy with the show of unnecessary bright colour the bricks gave off.

Packard parked the car at the foot of a flight of steps that led up to a grand set of half-glazed double doors and switched the engine off. "Okay, out you get," he ordered.

Jake did as he was told. He looked up at the building. Its three stories seemed to roll forward and loom over him, giving him the weird feeling that St. Margaret's was trying to study him in return.

"Move it, Highfield," barked Packard as he jogged up the steps. "The Headmaster doesn't like to be kept waiting."

Jake slammed the car door shut, followed Packard up the steps and through the outer wooden doors. Inside, Jake discovered the building was even more of a hybrid than it was on the exterior. Down the corridor to his left he could see where the modern world had encroached on the once dominant wood and brass. Slim, white central heating radiators sat under thick dark rails of wood that ran horizontally along the plain walls, which rose up to join the ceiling at perfect angles. Modern high efficiency bulbs sat in ornately worked brass light fittings and the wooden floors were dotted with the tell-tale metal plates that covered power sources.

A voice piped up from his right and Jake turned to see a boy a little older than himself walking up the corridor. "Good evening, sir," said the well turned out pupil in Packard's direction.

Jake stared at the boy, making no effort to hide the sneer

that graced his face. 'Creep,' he thought to himself as the boy walked past him and continued on down the corridor. His feelings of distain were cut short by Packard.

"Move it, Highfield," he said and started up a highly polished wooden staircase, taking the steps three at a time.

Jake had to jog to keep up. 'This Headmaster must be one sod if he has this head-case on edge,' thought Jake, as he made his way up to the second floor.

Jake found Packard waiting for him outside a dark panelled door. "Right, Highfield, just two rules when you meet the Headmaster, shut up and stay shut up. Got it?"

Jake grinned. "Are all the other teachers this nervous around the Headmaster?"

"I'm not a teacher," said Packard, pausing slightly to find the right words before continuing. "I'm more of an ex-student who helps out. And take my advice, it will do you good if you are wary of the Headmaster. Believe me." Then he knocked on the door loudly.

"Enter." The command resonated from the other side of the door.

As soon as he put one foot in the Headmaster's office, Jake could tell that here was one place in St. Margaret's where the touch of modernity had little influence. The room wasn't dark, but the décor of wooden panelled walls seemed to be feeding on the light to leave a feeling of gloom in its place. Even the large desk that dominated the floor space looked darkly menacing, like a guard dog ready to pounce. Oil paintings of historic battle scenes adorned the walls and a torn flag hung limply from the ceiling. A huge fireplace that looked too clean to have been used for many years dominated one wall of the room.

Above this hung the largest of the bloody scenes of carnage: red-coated men fighting semi-naked African natives.

In the centre of this museum stood a man who looked perfectly at home. He stood tall and proud in his tweed suit behind the desk, tugging gently on his thick grey moustache that blended into his bushy sideburns. His hair too was the colour of polished steel and Jake guessed he had to be at least fifty years old, yet blue eyes shone from his pale skinned face with the energy of a much younger man.

"Sorry we're late, Headmaster," said Packard, pushing Jake in front of the desk and placing the file Mr Humphrey had given him onto the green leather inlay. "We had a little...delay in our journey."

Apart from the Headmaster, Packard and himself, Jake saw the room also held a well built man with tattooed arms. He was wearing a vest and a pair of camouflage pants that were tied tightly at the ankle above highly polished boots. The man's large, deeply tanned head was shaved smooth and shone like syrup under the ceiling light. A white scar that ran from his ear to his temple stood out like a streak of lightning. He stood as stiff as a statue with his hands clasped behind his back.

In front of him, barely reaching up to the bald man's chest, was a girl who Jake figured was about the same age as himself. She was thin and pale, but the first thing he noticed about her was her long, thick, untidy dark hair, a fistful of which she was chewing on nervously with the side of her mouth. With her head hung low, the curtain of hair hid most of her face from view.

The Headmaster looked at Packard and then at Jake. He seemed satisfied with the word 'delay' as an explanation and sat down into the high-backed leather chair behind his desk. He reached for the file Packard had placed before him and opened it.

"Mr Highfield," he said slowly after a few moments flicking through the loose leaves of paper, "I am the Headmaster of St. Margaret's. You will refer to me as such or you will refer to me as 'sir', whichever you feel more comfortable with." He lifted his face from the file and without a hint of humour added, "To my face at least."

Jake grinned but the Headmaster's face did not lose its stern expression. He returned his attention to the file before him. "Jake Highfield," he read out loud. "Abandoned at birth and found outside a café called 'Jake's Butty Bar' on Highfield Road...and imaginatively named by the nurses that first cared for you."

"It could have been worse," said Jake, "I might have been found outside Hugh's Butty Bar on Jarse Lane."

The Headmaster looked up from his reading. "I shall assume for this one instance that the expression 'A child should be seen and not heard,' is new to you," he said coldly.

'Really?' thought Jake, 'I'll make you hear me, you old dinosaur.' But he only got as far as opening his mouth before Packard's hand fell on his shoulder in a firm warning of silence. Jake closed his mouth.

The Headmaster continued to flick through the pages of the dossier. "Quite an impressive record of mischief for such a young man," he said. "Burglary, joy riding, shoplifting, vandalism, arson..."

"I never started that fire," said Jake calmly.

The Headmaster paused his page flicking. "Of course not, Mr Highfield. The world is full of jails filled with innocent people," he said, his tone laced with disbelief. Jake decided not to push his point; he knew he'd done all the other things in his file. He got the feeling the Headmaster didn't care if he was guilty of one or all of them.

The Headmaster hurried through the last few pages, obviously having seen enough to reach a conclusion. "Well, Mr Highfield, I am sure there are several agencies, not least the police, who will have to cut their overtime now that you are with us."

"I do my best," began Jake before wincing in pain at the grip Packard applied to his shoulder. He couldn't help but notice that the Headmaster and the man in the vest did not even flinch, let alone condemn, the undue use of pain as a control method. As soon as he could, Jake decided, he was getting out of this asylum.

The Headmaster closed the file, got out of his chair and walked over to the single lead-light window in the room. He removed a handkerchief from his pocket and rubbed gently at a smear on the glass. The window dominated the wall behind the desk. The centre of this glazier's masterpiece of bright stained glass depicted St. Margaret standing on the back of a slain dragon, her face an expression of serene tranquility. The fallen dragon, even with its heart pierced by a lance, looked as if he slept peacefully, his soul purged of evil by the blessed female. Around the edge of the expertly cut delicate shapes that formed the scene were clear, diamond-shaped panes of glass which scattered out to fill the remainder of the frame.

"We here at St. Margaret's do not bear grudges about a young man's..." he glanced fleetingly toward the girl in the room before returning to his study of the glass before him, "…or young woman's past. Nor do we pass judgement on them." For a second Jake thought he saw a dream-like serenity fall over the Headmaster's face. "The world's great empires would never have risen had their builders been judged too early in their lives." He paused letting these thoughts sink in before turning again to address Jake and the girl. "Future digression, however, will not be tolerated in the slightest. In its long and proud history, St. Margaret's, in its different forms, has prepared and moulded the young blood of this nation. Taught and nurtured them before sending them out into society proud and ready to make a difference to the world. You have been given to St. Margaret's so you can follow in their footsteps and there can be no deviation from that path." The Headmaster paused again, his face set like stone. "Be assured the rest of society has washed its hands of you. We, and St. Margaret's, are your last hope."

"I…" whispered the girl almost silently.

"Quiet!" barked the man in the vest, making the girl jump at his voice.

Jake assumed this loud bully was her equivalent to his 'pal' Packard.

"While you are here," continued the Headmaster, regaining the seat behind his desk, "you will do as you are told, when you are told. Without exception. St. Margaret's is not a normal academy and so it follows that you are not normal students. Your actions to date have relieved you of the right to normality and so you are bound to St. Margaret's and all of her rules. You will work for your board, lodging, education and training. There are no free rides at the Academy."

"A boot camp," sneered Jake, earning himself another dose of pain from Packard's grip.

"You will also be expected to take part in certain extra curricular activities," continued the Headmaster, ignoring Jake's comment. "As a form of repayment towards the debt you owe to society, shall we say. But you will learn more about that aspect of your new life as you progress with us at St. Margaret's."

Before Jake could even start to imagine what the Headmaster's last comment meant, he was stopped by the girl at his side.

"I can't stay here!" she screamed, her shaking hands covering her face. "I can't!"

"Quiet!" bellowed the man in the vest again, this time punctuating his demand by hitting the girl so hard with the back of his hand that she was knocked to the floor. There the girl lay, curled up in a ball, her face buried into the carpet, sobbing. The man in the vest clenched his fist and raised it above his head, ready to strike down at his helpless victim.

Jake didn't think; he just reacted. He pulled himself free of Packard's grip and jumped up, sinking his teeth into the raised muscular forearm, dragging it down under his body weight.

The man let out a gasp of pain as Jake bit down as hard as he could.

A split second later Jake felt Packard's hand grasp him round the back of the neck and squeeze tightly. His automatic response was to scream, thus releasing his grip on the arm between his teeth. His eyes half closed with pain, Jake could just make out the man in the vest turn on him, ready to have his revenge.

"That'll be the last time you use your teeth on me, Boy!" the man growled, pulling his fist back ready to practice some very basic dentistry. Jake could see from the man's sparsely toothed snarl that he was already way ahead of him in those stakes.

"Mr Routledge," said the Headmaster sternly without making the effort to shout. "This is not a barrack room and I will not have undisciplined brawling in it. Do you understand?"

"But Sah—" protested Routledge, his fist still poised and aimed at Jake's screwed-up face.

"Do you understand, Mr Routledge?"

Jake had raised his arms as best he could in an effort to try and block anything that was coming his way.

Routledge kept his eyes on Jake but his body relaxed. "Yes, Sah, I understand, Sah."

"Good," said the Headmaster. "I am sure you and Mr Highfield will get off to a better start once he is on the assault course, Mr Routledge."

Jake saw Routledge's grin grow, revealing only a few teeth. "Yes Sah, I'm sure you're right, Sah!"

The grip on Jake's neck relaxed and he snatched himself free from Packard; daring to allow himself a sneer in the man's direction. 'Great,' he thought, straightening his clothes. 'This loony bin has got an assault course run by a psycho too. Can it get any better?'

"Right, I think we have finished for now," said the Headmaster, rising from his desk and looking out of the decorative window once more. "Get Mr Highfield and Miss Dunne settled into their new accommodation and make sure they have all the required timetables for their new beginnings."

"Yes, Headmaster," said Packard, pulling Jake by the arm towards the door.

"Get up, Girlie," barked Routledge as he bent down and hauled the girl up off the floor.

The girl had her head lowered and her face was completely hidden by her hair. She was pushed by Routledge out of the Headmaster's office back toward the stairs. Jake could still hear her sobbing and her situation only served to strengthen his own desire to escape as soon as possible.

"Mr Highfield," said the Headmaster as he and Packard reached the door.

"Yes?" replied Jake.

Packard prodded him in the ribs.

"Yes, Headmaster," corrected Jake with as little respect as he could muster.

"I would never have had you down as one for chivalry. There is obviously much more to you than a file full of foolish errors."

"What?" said Jake, confused by the man's statement.

"Saving the damsel in distress," said the Headmaster, retrieving a pipe from his jacket pocket. "We will make a knight of the realm out of you yet, Mr Highfield."

'What are you talking about, you nutter?' Jake thought to himself, but out loud he said, "Yes, Headmaster." At this moment, when his world had been turned upside down and inside out, it was all he could think of to say in reply.

Packard pulled him out of the room and closed the door.

FIRST NIGHT NERVES

"There you go, Highfield," said Packard, opening one of the many doors along the first floor corridor. "Home sweet home." He flicked on the light.

Jake stepped into the room and took a quick look around. It was small but clean and in good repair. 'I've stayed in worse places,' he thought.

"And look," said Packard pointing. "No bars on the window."

Jake gave a small nod in admission to that fact.

"Well, I'd love to stay and chat," said Packard sarcastically, "but duty calls and all that." He paused and Jake could tell he was thinking carefully how to say what he wanted to next. "You should give St. Margaret's a chance you know, Jake, it could be the best thing that ever happened to you."

Jake raised one side of his mouth in a half smile to show he highly doubted the man's optimism.

"Good night, Highfield," said Packard, and he closed the door. Jake half expected to hear the sound of a key being turned in a lock but it never came.

Jake took in some more details of the room. The single bed, the small wardrobe and three-drawer desk, the low, square bedside cabinet. All were made of clean pine wood and perfectly arranged to allow a small pathway of clear floor space between them all. To the right of the desk, a door claimed the rest of the wall. Jake opened it and walked into a small en suite shower room. Basin, toilet and shower cubicle were arranged in a similar space-efficient manner as the furniture in the bedroom.

'You could swing a cat in here,' thought Jake, 'though it would be a bit shorter by the time you'd finished.'

Returning to the bedroom, he went to the window and found it looked out over a quadrant of grass, around the edge of which ran a narrow shale path. In the fading light, it was hard to make out details. It appeared each corner was decorated with a statue of some sort. Releasing the catch, Jake pulled up the single glazed sash window and was surprised it slipped open so easily given the age of its construction. He stuck his head out into the rapidly cooling night air.

All around the quadrant, the old building was dotted with windows exactly the same as the one he was leaning out of. Whether they were all rooms like his he didn't know. Some, noticeably those on the ground floor, were in darkness showing no signs of life from within. Others shone out and Jake could see the other 'residents' of the Academy moving around their rooms or sitting at their desks, heads lowered in study.

The structure opposite him was an exact mirror of his. It was three storeys high with a double door allowing access into the building. To his left, a large archway had been built into the structure. It rose from the ground and looked as if a subterranean beast had risen and taken a huge bite out of the building, just missing the windows on the second floor that ran across the top of the arch. Even when he leaned out further, Jake could not see what lay beyond the arch. He could only assume it led to things like the assault course and the date he'd been promised there with Routledge. In the centre of the steep sloped roof above the archway, a small clock tower, only three metres in height at most, Jake guessed, pushed into the night sky. In the dim natural light he found it hard to make out if the hands showed the correct time or not.

The window to the right was almost as striking as the arch it looked over at. Light from the Headmaster's room filtered through the lead-light window. Dots of blue, red, green and yellow displayed the vivid image of St. Margaret standing on the fallen dragon. A shadow flickered across the scene, dulling a part of the light show. It stayed frozen in place. Jake could almost feel the Headmaster's gaze meeting his. He pulled his head back inside and flopped down onto the bed.

He stared up at the ceiling and let his thoughts wander. The digs weren't bad, he had to admit. They were more comfortable than a police cell and at least lacked the trendy band posters and cuddly toys he'd encountered at some of his foster homes.

Jake let his eyes move to the bright bulb in the light fitting, holding them there despite the discomfort. 'It's still a prison though,' he told himself coldly. "And one run by loonies by the looks of it," he said out loud, thinking over the physical violence he'd been victim and witness to over the last day.

"Face it, Jake," he told himself. "Your arse is out of here tonight."

Without warning the light in his room went out.

Jake swung off his bed and tried the light switch. Nothing. Being as quiet as he could, he opened the door and put his head out into the corridor. The bright light had been replaced with a lower, dimmer lighting. The natural light coming in through the windows twisted their shadows into skewed crisscross rectangles on the floor. Closing the door, he vaulted back over his bed and looked out of the window into the quad. Every light had been extinguished in every room, all except one, the Headmaster's. In the darkness, a pale, watery image of St. Margaret, triumphant over the dragon, stretched across the grass below.

The clock on the bedside cabinet, which he had not noticed until the enforced gloom, told him in day-glo green digits that it was ten o'clock. Jake smiled. "Not a prison hey, Packard?" he said, as if the man himself was there. "Why lights out then?"

Jake had a decision to make and he had to make it quickly. He had no idea what kind of security systems the place had, if any, but the longer he waited the more chance they had of being armed.

'Sod it,' he thought. 'Being impulsive never got me into trouble before…much.'

He opened the window fully and curled his body through it until he was standing up on the ledge outside. He wasn't worried by the drop; he'd jumped from this height on numerous occasions and survived injury and capture. The only trouble was he knew he had to jump far enough out to clear the shingle path to avoid being heard.

With a quick glance up at the stained glass window for any tell-tale signs of a shadow, he launched himself off the ledge. Jake just cleared the path, but he hit the grass hard.

Stumbling forward, he let out a grunt of air as he felt the shock of the impact judder through his feet into his knees. Unhurt, he quickly found his balance and began sprinting towards the relative safety of the arch. For an instant he thought he saw someone watching him from the corner of the square but it was only one of the statues he'd seen earlier playing tricks on his racing mind.

Once under the arch Jake stopped running and slowly made his way with his back pressed tight against the brickwork. At the end, he crouched and tried to make out what he could from the dark landseape before him.

There was a lot of open space to cross before he could reach the cover of the trees – if he made it that far. Jake made to move, but then hesitated. From here, the trees looked like a thin black line against the horizon but he knew how far back they reached. He didn't have a clue what lay beyond the wall that halted their march. Any direction he took could mean escape, but it could also lead to a whole lot more trouble. As far as he knew he could end up running headlong into another part of the Academy.

"You haven't got time for this," he said to himself. "Just head for the trees on the right." Jake clenched his jaw and ground his teeth together trying to build up his wavering nerve. "You could always go back," he whispered to himself full of spite. "Say 'Oh, I'm so sorry, I don't know what happened, I just fell out of my window'." Jake felt disgust with himself welling in his stomach. "Come on chicken, two hundred metres at most and you're in the trees, you can do it."

Jake sprang from the arch and ran. He pumped his arms as fast as he could; stretched his legs as far as he could. Head down, eyes fixed on the approaching tree line. He knew he was exposed, easily spotted by anyone who might just glance at the open ground but he kept going, kept pushing until with one final effort he hurled himself into the fern and bracken that curled at the feet of the tall trees.

Staying low and turning to face the open ground he had just covered, Jake fought hard to keep his gasping breath quiet and slow his hammering heart, which thundered in his ears. After a few minutes nervously scanning the grounds, he was happy that no one had noticed his flight or was following him, but he was still far from safe.

From this vantage point, he could also see that the buildings of St. Margaret's were much more extensive than he had first thought. Newer, more modern annexes were tagged on to the rear of the main structure, linked with arched plastic tunnels, obviously there to protect the users from the elements as they moved between the structures.

'This is not the time to get a sudden appreciation for architecture,' his otherwise occupied mind told him. Staying low, he backed himself some way into the forest before getting his feet. "See ya, St. Margaret's," he whispered, adding a wink, and he turned his back on the sleeping Academy.

STRANGERS IN THE NIGHT

Within ten minutes of walking into the dense wood Jake was out of his depth. It had been an uneasy feeling for him, a city dweller all his life, to see the openness of the countryside in the daylight but in the pitch dark of night, within a dense forest; his senses had been completely hijacked.

Shadows and solid reality merged into one. Even when his eyes adjusted to the darkness, he stumbled and tripped on roots and plant life snagged his feet as effectively as any snare. Eventually he took to walking like the living dead he had seen in movies, arms outstretched in front of him, trying to feel his way forward.

But what shook Jake most were the sounds. In the city, he was used to the sound of passing cars hissing along roads in the early hours of the morning; raised voices, full of anger echoing about back alley walls threatening the onset of a drunken brawl; police sirens; barking dogs and even the cry of cats wailing out like abandoned babies. Here, within the trees and grasping bracken, the sounds were strange to him. It was a completely new audio track for which his memory had no files to recognise. Things crunched along the forest floor or rattled the branches of the trees. Everything he heard defied being static, as if one sound could come from each and every direction at the same time.

'It's the countryside,' he told himself. 'Animals live in the countryside.' Another branch snapped to his left. Or was it his right? Or straight ahead? 'They're more frightened of you than you are of them,' he forced himself to think. Something high in the trees let out a screech that echoed in every direction. 'They must be absolutely crapping themselves then,' thought Jake, trying to raise his own spirits.

Despite what he was telling himself, his mind had made the decision for him. This place was dangerous…evil…and definitely knee-deep in chainsaw-wielding psychopaths escaped from the local mental institution. Jake could not help but smile to himself and think of St. Margaret's and how that might not be too far from the truth, judging by what he'd seen already.

Jake picked up his pace and raised his legs high in a bouncing jog to try and avoid nature's obstacle course. 'I'm getting out of this weird, haunted place and I don't care how much noise I make doing it.'

The blow to his shin was sharp, causing him to cry out instinctively with pain. The next blow hit him across the forehead and knocked him on his back and before he could react in any way, the weight of someone, or something, was on his chest.

Stinging slaps shocked against his face, fingernails grazing the skin, each one accompanied by a shrill cry.

The surprise and the darkness combined to rob him of a clear visual input but whoever, whatever it was that was pinning him down, he was going to get it off. With all the strength he could muster, Jake pushed up with both arms and slammed his open hands into the attacker. To his surprise he met little resistance and easily rolled over, reversing the situation. The form under him wailed with even more panic, thrashing to be free. As Jake raised his fist, his only thought to pound whatever it was into pulp, his eyes were finally fed enough light to form an image to send to his brain and he recognised what he was about to strike.

"You!" Jake said, with a gasp.

The girl continued to struggle, trying with all her might to dislodge the bigger, heavier form of Jake. "I won't go back!" she screamed. "You can't make me! I'll…I'll kill you!"

Jake lowered his fist, but, as he relaxed, a hand reached up and slapped him across the face again. He let out a grunt and pinned the girl's arms to the forest floor. "Take it easy will you, that bloody hurts!"

"You're not taking me back!"

"That's right, I'm not," agreed Jake. "And as soon as you stop slapping me about, you can go wherever you like."

The tension left the girl's body and Jake's eyes grabbed enough light from the gloom to see the shock on her face that was backed up by the tone in her voice. "You don't want to take me back?"

"No," confirmed Jake. "Taking you back would mean me going back and I assure you I'm not doing that."

"Then why were you following me?"

"Following you?" said Jake, releasing his grip. "I can barely follow my own nose in this place. I didn't even know you were out here. I thought I was on my own, apart from the—" Jake stopped, deciding it was better to leave out the chainsaw psychos of his imagination.

"Oh," said the girl slowly, as she realised she had been wrong. "Well, in that case would you mind getting off me?"

"What? Oh, sorry." Jake stood up and offered his hand to help, which the girl made an obvious and defiant refusal to take so he let it fall back to his side. "So you decided the many pleasures on offer from St. Margaret's weren't for you either then?"

The girl got to her feet awkwardly and brushed at her jacket, staring at Jake as she did so. "You're the boy from the office," she said.

"That's right, I'm Ja—"

"Jake Highfield. I know. I was there when they laid out your past life, remember?"

"Yeah, they'll make a film out of it one day," replied Jake with a smile. "And your name's Deal…Dale…?"

"Dunne," corrected the girl. "Angel Dunne."

"Angel?" said Jake, unable to hide his surprise. "In a place like this?"

"I had a mother who had no idea how ironic that would be, okay?" said Angel. "At least I wasn't named after some fat, greasy bloke who served bacon on toast for a living."

Jake chuckled quietly. His fear of the forest was being pushed to the back of his mind as he focused on the company he found himself in. "Fair enough, Angel, you win the name game." There was a pause. "What are you going to do now? Try to get back to your mum?"

"I said 'had a mother', if you'd been paying attention," snapped Angel.

Jake opened his mouth. For some reason he thought 'I'm sorry' suited the situation but before he could speak,

Angel cut him down.

"Before you get all sympathetic on me, she had problems...problems she loved more than me. It was only a couple of months ago, and I nearly had all the money we would have needed to get her help but she..." Angel sniffed. When she spoke again the anger she felt towards herself for opening up to this stranger was evident in her voice. "Why am I telling you this, it's not like a loser like you can do anything about it!"

"I'm a loser?!" snapped Jake. "You're not exactly collecting the gold medal yourself at the moment! Otherwise what would you be doing in a place like this, with a loser like me?"

"I'm not like you," spat Angel. "A petty criminal; an out-of-control thug."

"Oh really? I suppose they invited you here for your winning personality and charm?"

"I only took the money to save my mum. She was all I had left," blurted Angel before calming down a little. "Besides, banks have lots of money and no one got hurt."

Jake grinned as he caught on. "You don't look the type to go in the front door guns blazing, so I assume you're a hacker?"

"I hate that word," hissed Angel. "Makes it sound so easy; besides, I only did it..." Her voice trailed off.

Jake felt a quick change of subject was needed. He could see why he'd been dumped at St. Margaret's. He was documented as a hopeless case, but this girl just seemed to be on the wrong end of a trail of bad luck. Besides, this pointless argument was wasting valuable escape time. "What are you going to do now?" he asked.

"Same as you're trying to do," said Angel, pointing

over her shoulder with her thumb. "Get as far away from that place as possible."

Jake nodded. "Good luck then."

"You too."

A silence fell and Jake could sense the lack of willingness they both felt for being alone in the forest again.

"Thanks by the way," said Angel.

"What for?"

"Helping me out, when that idiot was about to hit me," explained Angel.

Jake smirked. "I don't know where that came from, to be honest."

"Well, thanks anyway."

"No problem. Tell you what," said Jake putting a deliberate cheerfulness in his voice. "Why don't we get out of this place together and then go our separate ways? Those nut-jobs could have sent someone out looking for us. We've got more chance of spotting them before they spot us if we're both looking out."

Jake could hear the relief in Angel's voice, even though she was doing her best to mask it with indifference. "Sounds sensible to...what was that?" Angel's voice dropped into an almost inaudible, panicked whisper and her head had snapped round to stare into the trees behind her.

Jake swallowed. He hadn't heard anything but he still had to fight against the fear rising in his stomach. He too dropped his voice to a whisper as he remembered the flicker of movement he'd seen in the trees from Packard's car earlier on. "Could have been a fox...or a cow or something?"

"A cow! In a forest?"

"Alright," snapped Jake. "I'm not exactly David bleedin'

Attenborough, you know; all this nature stuff is new to me."

"There it is again," said Angel and this time Jake heard it too. It sounded like a foot being carefully placed with a stalking, determined pace that knew where it wanted to be.

"What are we going to do?"

"Screw this," hissed Jake. "Run!"

Jake took off. He didn't have a clue where they were, so the obvious direction to take was away from the noise they'd heard. Behind him he could hear Angel's feet crashing through the foliage, keeping pace behind him. But beyond that noise he could hear another noise, something more menacing, quickening its own pace to keep up.

Branches smacked against his body, his legs, his arms, threatening to tear the eyes from his face but still Jake ran, his legs trying to keep up with the beat of his racing heart. He heard a thud and scream as Angel fell behind him. Despite his instincts telling him otherwise, he stopped and reached back, offering his hand. "C'mon, we've got to keep going!"

Now the sound of pursuit was coming from his right. "This way!" he ordered as Angel took his hand and he hoisted her back to her feet, dragging her forward.

Pulling the girl behind him, Jake was struggling. He could taste blood in his mouth and his breath burned the back of his throat. His foot caught on a tree root and he tumbled face first, dragging Angel down with him. She screamed out with the impact.

Jake lay still for a second, his hand tightly gripped around Angel's fingers.

"You're hurting me."

"Shh," hissed Jake as he tried to make his ears hear anything but the pounding pulse in his head. "Can you hear anything?"

Angel was sobbing. "No, I…" she paused. "To our left I think."

"That's what I thought, I can hear something on the other side as well, there must be two of them."

"Two of what?" sniffed Angel.

They both heard the low, rumbling growl.

"Dogs, I think," answered Jake, getting to his feet, his firm grip demanding the same of Angel. "Big ones. Let's go."

Jake ran again, hauling Angel with him, who seemed even less willing to flee this time. It felt like he was dragging a trailer behind him, a trailer with flat tyres.

"Keep going!" he urged. "I think the forest is thinning out up ahead. I can see more light. We're going to make it out of here! We're going to make it!"

Jake cleared the edge of the trees and kept up his frantic flight but the sight that greeted him robbed his legs of their last will to keep going and Angel slammed into him as he juddered to a halt. Before them, standing out like a smug grin on the flat ground, was St. Margaret's.

"Great," groaned Jake. At his side, having also seen the pointlessness of her failed escape, Angel fell to her knees and began to sob.

Behind them, the sound of parting vegetation caught their attention. They turned to see a lean, muscular Doberman. Its ears were pulled back flat to its head. It broke free of the forest, quickly followed by a heavy-set Rotweiller. 'Some deer,' Jake thought, swallowing and remembering Packard's dismissive comment in the car. Both dogs, teeth bared under curled-back muzzles dripping with saliva, slowed their charge and walked menacingly towards their prey. Then they stopped before Jake, so close that he could feel their breath on his shaking hands.

"Jake, I'm scared," stuttered Angel, slowly getting to her feet. The hand not gripping his was held up to her throat to protect it from the slavering jaws.

"Get behind me," said Jake, guiding her so he was between her and the dogs, wondering himself where this macho stupidity was coming from. "It'll be alright. I don't think they're going to attack us." Angel merely sobbed in reply.

Jake and Angel slowly made their way backwards towards the Academy. The dogs kept pace, all the time flashing their teeth as if eager to punish one foolish change of direction. "Now I know how sheep feel," said Jake, his eyes fixed on the dogs, looking for the slightest sign of attack, although completely at a loss as to what to do if they did.

Suddenly, the dogs stopped and sat on their haunches and an abrupt voice called out. "Away!" The two dogs turned and made their way back to the woods. Jake and Angel watched the vicious looking animals get a good distance from them before daring to turn their attention away. When they did they were greeted by the Headmaster. Next to him was Routledge, his white vest shining out brilliantly against the night.

"This is a surprise," said the Headmaster, removing the pipe from his mouth. "As far as you are concerned anyway, Miss Dunne. As for you, Mr Highfield, I expected nothing less."

Jake was still shaking with fear but now anger was welling up to add to the cocktail of emotions. "Those dogs could have ripped us to pieces!"

Routledge made a move, obviously eager to instil some instant discipline and respect into Jake one way or another, but the Headmaster raised his hand. The bald man, though obviously disappointed, stood his ground. "On the contrary, Mr Highfield," said the Headmaster calmly. "Satan and Lucifer, amongst others, are merely here to help the strays back to the flock." The Headmaster sucked at his pipe but it had gone out. "Had you, on the other hand, insisted in going the wrong way, then they may have got a little over zealous, but never anything serious…not yet, anyway."

Jake still had tight hold of Angel's hand as much for his own comfort as hers. "You can't keep us here."

The Headmaster carried on smiling. "I think you have just had a demonstration to the contrary. Did you know the Ancient Romans used dogs as weapons of war? Very effective they were too."

'Just what I need,' thought Jake, 'a history lesson with a practical exam.'

The Headmaster poked at the air between himself and Jake with his smokeless pipe. "I have a good feeling about you, Mr Highfield; you too, Miss Dunne," he said as if he was thinking aloud. "With the right training you both have the potential to be among the best that have ever come out of St. Margaret's; a real credit to the Academy and your country in the years to come." With no more explanation he turned to address Routledge.

"I think that is quite enough excitement for one night, Mr Routledge."

"Yes, Sah," replied Routledge and he and the Headmaster turned round and made their way back through the arch.

Jake and Angel remained where they stood, watching the men fade into the gloom of the tunnel.

"What now?"

Jake looked over his shoulder at the line of trees. The dogs were nowhere to be seen; obviously they had gone back to their patrolling. "I don't know, but this place is like nothing I've ever seen and I've seen a few."

"Why did they just leave us here?" asked Angel, finally feeling safe enough to let her hand slip from Jake's. "Don't they think we'll run away again?"

"Do you really want to try?" said Jake, nodding his head toward the trees. "They know we're going to go back to our rooms like the good little prisoners we are, because we haven't got any other choice."

Angel shook her head. "What do you think he meant by 'training'?"

Jake shrugged. "I have no idea but I have a nasty feeling we're going to find out." He looked at Angel and grinned. "By the way, your hair's a right mess."

"Is that all you can say after what we've just been through?" Angel exclaimed in disbelief, but she couldn't help feeling the joy of the relief just to be alive. "I have an IQ of over a hundred and fifty; you can't expect massive brain activity like that not to have any side effects."

"Well, I hope your massive brain can think up an idea to get us out of this place one day," said Jake. "And the sooner the better, hey?"

Present Day

TODAY'S LESSON IS...

Jake was awoken as usual at seven a.m. by the light in his room flicking on and off repeatedly until he got out of his bed to hit the wall switch and override the Academy's early morning alarm call system. He yawned loudly and stretched his body, the odd bone joint clicking as his muscles put pressure on them. He shuffled wearily to his shower room.

St. Margaret's alarm call didn't distinguish, or care, if you'd gone to bed at five p.m. or five a.m., as in Jake's case. Every student was expected to be out of bed by seven, six days a week. He moaned a little and talked to his reflection in the mirror over the sink. "Just once, a lie-in wouldn't be so bad, surely?" He moved his head to the left and right and noted the splatters of mud that decorated his face. "Especially since I was out doing my bit for Queen and country most of the night. No sense of appreciation, that's Margaret's problem, and she calls herself a saint."

Jake turned the cold tap on and caught handfuls of the icy water, throwing them onto his face, neck and shoulders. He couldn't help thinking that this old American-Indian trick of shocking his system into a state of alertness was not as beneficial as another few hours of sleep would be.

Looking up again into the mirror, Jake studied the map-like pattern of tiny red veins in his tired eyes. His mind ran back over the disastrous mission of the night before. The guard should have been out of the way for much longer than he was; the drug in the dart was formulated to last eight hours minimum and in his experience that had always been the case in the past.

Jake breathed out loudly. "Bloody dodgy equipment," he mumbled. "At least I got the job done; in, out and safely away," he said to his reflection, which looked a little less convinced than he had hoped it would. "Ah, what do you know, anyway?" Jake snarled, and turned from the sink.

By seven thirty Jake was showered and dressed in the uniform of St. Margaret's: white shirt, black trousers, blue blazer with gold trim and a blue and gold striped tie. Leaving his room, he walked up the corridor. The Academy, as usual even at this early hour, was going efficiently about its business. Students were making their way to classes or breakfast; some in uniform, others in PE kit or laboratory coats depending on what their timetable dictated. Jake nodded and smiled his morning greetings to students he knew, which were returned in a similar fashion with the occasional friendly insult thrown in for good measure.

As he drew level with the last door on the corridor, it opened and a short pale-looking boy stepped into view.

"Morning, Pete," said Jake cheerfully.

Peter Philips was one of the newest recruits at St. Margaret's and was having a tough time fitting in with the strict regime of the Academy. Jake had heard crying one night in the quad and lowered himself out of his window to find Pete hiding behind one of the statues. He'd been trying to build up the nerve to make a run for it. A quick recounting of his own experience of trying to escape soon had the new boy back in his room. From that point on, Jake felt he owed it to Pete to look out for him.

"Hi, Jake," replied Pete.

"Jesus, you look rough," said Jake, instantly regretting his choice of less than sympathetic words as he noticed the black rings under the boy's eyes.

"I didn't sleep much last night," explained Pete. "Kept hearing weird noises. I think they were..." His voice trailed off.

"Ghosts?" finished Jake, helpfully.

Pete lowered his eyes and nodded.

Jake laughed. "If all the stories about ghosts in this place were true, they'd have to queue up twice round the quad to get a go at rattling the chains. My favourite is the legless and armless butler who fell into the toilet and drowned. Bob I think his name is. I've been waiting for ages to meet him."

Pete looked up at Jake and a quiver ran along his lips before he spoke. "But I really did hear noises."

"I'm sure you did," agreed Jake. "But this place is full of jokers, Pete, you know that. Why else would we both be here?"

Pete's face broke into a weak smile.

"I bet you anything you like that the ghost you heard is as flesh and blood as us, Pete," reassured Jake. "Nothing that a swift kick in the goolies couldn't deal with, okay?" Jake grabbed Pete by the shoulders. "Who you gonna call? Nuts Busters!"

Pete nodded, reassured by the older student. "Thanks, Jake."

"Will you stop saying that! I'm your mate, that's what

I'm here for. Now wash your face and get your tie on or you'll have the ghost of Routledge chasing you round the assault course."

"Thank—"

"Ah. Remember, mates," interrupted Jake. Pete held up his hands in silent apology, stepped back into his room and closed the door.

Jake looked at the blank wooden panel for a moment, wearing a frown and remembering how tough he had found St. Margaret's at the start, but he pulled his eyes away and jogged down the stairs.

Jake made the ground floor and half way down the north corridor walked through the double doors out into the cool fresh air of the quad. He took in a deep breath and smiled at the warmth the low sun gave his face, noticing how it shimmered over the clock tower. He caught a glimpse of one of the hideous stone gargoyles that watched over the quad from each corner. It seemed to Jake to be looking at him even more suspiciously than usual.

Jake made his way under the arch that sat opposite and under the gaze of the Headmaster's office. As he entered its dim confines he began to smell the tempting aromas wafting from the canteen's extractor fans. He breathed deeply. His empty stomach grumbled in reaction to the smell.

"Jake!" gasped a tall and very thin, red-haired boy running awkwardly towards him. The glasses he wore were steamed up and his uniform hung limply from his fragile frame as if he was made of bamboo canes.

"Alright, Danny? Been jogging—"

Danny gasped for air. "It's Angel…Clarkson…she…"

"I get it, Danny," pushed Jake impatiently. "Where is she?"

"Boiler…house."

Jake left the wheezing Danny doubled over with his hands on his knees and ran, all thoughts of food gone from his mind.

As he drew level with the boiler house, a building the Victorian builders had taken just as much architectural care over as the rest of St. Margaret's, a familiar voice called out in protest.

"Get off me!"

Jake frowned. Of all the voices he had grown to recognise, Angel's was the most distinctive. 'Alluring' she would claim; 'nasal' he would counter. Weaving between the numerous wheelie bins he found the source of, and reason for, the outburst.

"Morning, Angel," Jake said, ignoring the large boy who had her trapped between his outstretched arms; one large hand placed either side of her head, flat against the boiler house wall. "Funny place to get breakfast."

"Beat it, Highfield," sneered the boy, not even bothering to look at Jake. "My friend is helping me out with my anatomy homework."

"Oh hello, Clarkson," beamed Jake, as if he had just noticed him. "I didn't see you there amongst all this other crap." If there was a complete opposite to the stick-like Danny, then Clarkson was it. There was no chance of his blazer rattling against his bones in a breeze. He was built as solidly as a bridge.

Clarkson slowly turned his head, his face screwed up with rage, a facial expression that was nearly always present beneath his round, tightly cropped head.

"Tell you what, Angel," grinned Jake, "maybe you should help him out. It's a well known fact that

Lard Boy hasn't got the brains to find his own arse with both hands…which is amazing considering the size of it."

Clarkson was not known for his intelligence or subtlety. In fact, most students at St. Margaret's suspected he couldn't spell the words, let alone display the attributes and so his next move was not a surprise to Jake.

As Clarkson hurtled towards him, Jake took a deep breath and relaxed his body as he'd been taught to do in his unarmed combat training. He knew tension in a physical situation was no good; it had to be released before any move could be made. Besides, from past experience, Jake had no need to be frightened of Clarkson.

A substantially sized fist came cannoning from as far back as Clarkson could send it. It was so predictable, Jake wondered why Clarkson hadn't bothered to send him a text message warning him of its arrival.

Jake calmly turned his shoulders and the blow breezed past his nose to collide with the hard red Victorian brick. Clarkson yelped in pain and rage, then turned to face Jake and lunged forward again. But Jake was shuffling on his toes like a professional boxer and he stepped to the side, sweeping Clarkson's leading leg out before it could find its balance. With a gentle push on his back, Jake sent him headlong into an innocent gathering of wheelie bins.

"Do you know what, Clarkson? I think I was wrong. If you put this kind of dedication into your anatomy studies, I reckon you would be able to find your own arse after all," Jake smiled. "Eventually."

Clarkson leapt to his feet. He was swearing so hard that pockets of foam gathered at the corners of his mouth. "You're dead, Highfield! Dead!"

Jake prepared himself for the onslaught.

"Highfield! Clarkson! Dunne! What's going on here?" demanded Routledge. The Academy's physical training instructor stood impeccably dressed in his usual white vest and combat trousers, at the corner of the boiler house.

Jake and Clarkson didn't answer. Their eyes were locked on each other. Neither was prepared to give the slightest advantage by breaking their concentration.

Angel spoke up quickly. "They're practising some of the new moves they've been taught, sir."

Routledge looked at Angel for a moment and, though obviously not believing the lie, took it as a good enough excuse to put an end to the situation. "If you two clowns have got that much energy, I could always arrange some extra training," he barked.

The teacher noticed the bleeding knuckles on Clarkson's scuffed right hand. "Get that seen to at once, Clarkson. You know the rules. One hundred per cent fit at all times. Get to the medical centre."

"Yes, sir," hissed the bully, reluctantly lowering his fists. Then he shoulder-barged his way past Jake and gave him an unmistakable 'we'll finish this later' look before disappearing around the corner of the building.

"And you; get moving too," ordered Routledge.

Jake and Angel began to walk.

"Not you, Highfield," he added, grabbing Jake's shoulder. "The Headmaster wants to see you in his office."

"But sir, I haven't even had breakfast yet," pleaded Jake with genuine concern on behalf of his empty and protesting stomach.

"You should have thought of that before you starting practising your moves," said Routledge, pulling a three-toothed, sarcastic grin. With a quick about-turn, Routledge marched off.

Jake's shoulders dropped. This could only be about one thing. Even the Headmaster couldn't have got wind of the scrap with Clarkson this quickly.

"Fine, thanks," said Angel pulling her blazer straight.

"What? Oh, sorry, you okay?"

"Great," said Angel. "I love to start my day off with a quick encounter with halitosis."

Jake grinned. "You sound okay to me. Besides, you're not the one with the royal summons."

"Probably just wants to give his favourite pet a little tickle under the chin," mocked Angel.

"I'm his pet? What about the 'gifted Miss Dunne', 'queen of the Tech section', we're all tortured with at assembly every time you do something geeky?" argued Jake with deliberate sarcasm. "I hear you're the one giving the lessons now."

Angel frowned. "I help out occasionally, that's all. Besides, it wasn't me who fell into line within a week of being here. 'It's not so bad, Angel', 'There's worse places to be, Angel', 'I could get into this, Angel'."

"I didn't hear you complain once they took you off the assault course and out of the gym and shoved you and your weird brain behind a computer," replied Jake with a smile. "Anyway it wasn't a week…it was ten days at least."

Angel changed the subject as they rounded the corner of the boiler house. "How did last night go?"

"Okay," shrugged Jake, not wanting to share his as-yet unfounded concerns. "Not perfect, but I got the job done."

"Not perfect," repeated Angel, sucking in a sharp breath

of air loudly to signify her unease. "That's not what the Headmaster likes to hear."

"I know; I just hope I'm not going to miss breakfast and suffer one of his famous long-winded lectures," sighed Jake. "Still, if he keeps it short, I could still make last sitting. What you up to now?"

"Advanced internet surveillance techniques."

"Wow. That sounds really interesting," grinned Jake.

"It will be," said Angel, walking away from Jake. "I'm taking the class."

IT COULD HAVE GONE BETTER

Jake took a quiet, deep breath and raised his fist to knock on the Headmaster's door. His hand was shaking. "Get a grip, Jake," he muttered to himself and rapped boldly on the dark wood before his nerves had time to fail him completely.

"Enter," commanded the Headmaster from within his office. Jake grasped the brass handle, polished over the years by many sweating, nervous hands just like his, and opened the door.

Jake entered the room, closed the door, took a couple of paces forward and then stood tensely near the centre before the heavy desk. In the corner, a grandfather clock ground noisily before striking the quarter hour. "You wanted to see me, sir?"

The Headmaster raised his hand but did not move his eyes from the text in front of him, in a call for silent patience.

Jake complied and looked about him to take his mind off the butterflies in his stomach. The Headmaster's office was one of those rooms that seemed to reveal more details to Jake every time he found himself in it. This time his eyes wandered over to a stuffed owl that was so lifelike, it seemed to be staring him out, daring him to move so it could swoop down and attack. Why he'd never noticed such a striking object before, he didn't know. It must have always been there; everything in the Headmaster's office had the feeling of having always been there. Even the Japanese dagger resting upon its cradle at the front of the desk, though displaced through hundreds of years and thousands of miles looked 'right' in this setting. Jake moved his gaze down and looked at the carpet. There was a green and brown leaf pattern weaved into its structure that tricked the eyes with such a perception of depth that staring at it for too long led to a slight feeling of vertigo. Jake suddenly noticed his shoes; his heart sank. His run-in with Clarkson had left his shoes scuffed with a smear of something unknown from the bins. Dirty shoes were one of the Headmaster's many pet hang-ups and if he saw them…

"Mr Highfield," said the Headmaster, eventually breaking the silence.

Jake's head shot up and he straightened his back, almost standing to attention.

The Headmaster retrieved a bookmark from his desk, slid it carefully on the page and delicately closed the book before speaking again. "Are you familiar with Sun Tzu, Mr Highfield?" said the Headmaster, letting his gaze fall onto Jake.

"He wrote 'The Art of War', sir," replied Jake.

"He did indeed, Mr Highfield. A fine book of instruction it is, too. Maybe you should read it sometime?"

Jake was going to lie about having read it already, as it was a set text for his year, but he knew this would only lead to a line of in-depth questioning that would find him out. "Yes, sir, I will."

"Good," smiled the Headmaster, rising from his chair. "Good. Tell me, Mr Highfield. How did your extra-curricular activity go last night?"

Jake swallowed nervously. "Fine, sir. I achieved all my objectives and the information gathered was delivered safely early this morning."

"I see," said the Headmaster, turning to look out of the window. "And the small matters of a violent physical encounter, weapons fire, alerting everyone in a three-mile radius of your presence and being the instigator of a widespread manhunt in the process is all part of your 'fine' assessment is it?"

"I…"

"I!" repeated the Headmaster sternly. "I is the crux of the problem here. This is not just about you, Mr Highfield! You were seen! And when you have given a man a permanent limp for life, you can be sure he is going to remember your face."

"It was dark, sir," spluttered Jake. "I reacted too quickly for him to get a good look at me, I was out of—"

"You were out of control, Mr Highfield. Had you bothered to read Sun Tzu, you would be familiar with the importance of his doctrine, 'Know the enemy'! You could have done only a little more damage had you given the guard your phone number and an invitation to your birthday party!"

Jake cast his eyes to the floor. His mouth was dry, his stomach was tensing into knots and the added optical illusion of the carpet was not helping his sense of balance.

"Have you seen the papers today, Mr Highfield?"

"No, sir."

"Well, if you spent less time feeding your ego by squaring up to Clarkson and more time concentrating on your duties, maybe you would be better informed," said the Headmaster. Jake knew he was only mentioning Clarkson to prove he knew what was what at the Academy and who was in charge. At all times.

The Headmaster picked up a handful of daily newspapers from his desk and dropping each back down in turn he read out the headlines. "'Animal Rights Activists Suspected of Break In', 'KTI Infiltrate Labs', 'Unarmed Security Guard Feels "Furry" of Animal Loonies'."

Jake could not help but smirk at the terrible pun.

The Headmaster stared at him hard. "Do you find this funny, Mr Highfield? Because I do not."

Jake gave a little cough to clear his throat and knock the grin off his face. "No, sir. Sorry, sir." The Headmaster turned away from Jake to look silently out of the window that bore the gaudy image of St. Margaret. "But at least the papers have bought the animal rights angle, sir. That puts me, I mean the Academy, in the clear."

The Headmaster shook his head. "There you go again, Mr Highfield, misusing the brain God gave you, in a spectacular way. The papers do not know their backsides from their elbows; they will print whatever is fed to them, by whoever. It is fortunate for us that we have a tight grip on their feeding spoon." He rubbed at a small mark on the window before him with his finger until he was satisfied the glass was flawless. "However, there are those who do not read the papers. Those who like to get their information a little closer to the source."

"I was very careful not to leave a trail, sir," said Jake quietly.

"Let us evaluate last night's fiasco, Mr Highfield, and see if I agree with your expert debriefing." The Headmaster began to pace. "Point one, as I said before, we have a crippled man who could very possibly identify his assailant. This crippled man is sure, though the papers do not print this detail, his assailant was a youth no older than fifteen. Point two, no animals were liberated nor cages tampered with during the break-in, a suspicious change of tactics for an animal rights organisation, do you not think? Point three, the only area apparently disturbed was the office of one Dr Watkinson, Head of Micro-Biology at the site. And point four …" The Headmaster stopped his pacing to stand directly in front of Jake. "You will like point four, Mr Highfield." The Headmaster had the smug look of a vulture that had just landed on a fresh carcass as he placed his face close to Jake's, so close that he could smell the pipe tobacco on the Headmaster's breath as their noses almost touched. "Point four, half of the facility's hi-tech security system had been scrambled with top-secret military-grade technology."

Jake's face dropped.

"And do you know how they know this, Mr Highfield?" continued the Headmaster, a menacing hiss evident in his voice.

Unfortunately, Jake did know and he could feel the pit of his stomach lurch at the realisation of his mistake.

"Because, Mr Jake Highfield, codename Chaos, decided it would be better fun to have a game of hide and seek with the enemy than to release the security system off lockdown before he left the area of operation!" The Headmaster's face was purple with rage and the contrast this made with his silver facial hair made him look like he was wearing a tribal war mask.

"I…"

"I, nothing, Mr Highfield," spat the enraged Headmaster, maintaining his close proximity. "You have got the enemy somersaulting for joy. They know we are watching them now." He flung a pointed finger towards the window, "They are out there digging themselves in deeper. More careful, more alert. They might not know who is watching them but they will try to find out. They will be trying to pick up your trail and believe me, they really want to find it. And when, not if, Mr Highfield, when they find it, they will come right here, right here to St. Margaret's and then there will be the devil to pay. And not just for you, Mr Highfield, for all of us. How is that for a more accurate debriefing?"

Jake was stunned, shaken. This verbal onslaught had been much more than he expected. To his mind, up until this point, his mission had been a relative success. A few things beyond his control had happened, that was true. But considering the faulty dart and an unexpectedly conscious guard, he'd done well. He'd got back with the information as required, without capture or injury.

"Sir, I…"

"Mr Highfield, the powers that be are leaning on me heavily, very heavily." The Headmaster interrupted, walking over to the window. "St. Margaret's is crucial to national security and they take a dim view when its position is compromised. They want answers."

"It was the dart, sir," he blurted out.

"What?" barked the Headmaster, his temper high, and still rising.

"The dart from the wrist gun," expanded Jake. "The one I took the guard out with. It was faulty. It didn't last the full eight hours."

The Headmaster's breathing was deep and long. It looked as though he was trying to blow fire from his nostrils to illustrate the burning rage he was feeling inside. "Are you trying to suggest that this mess was not your fault, Mr Highfield?" he said, with deliberate slowness.

"No...yes...I..." stammered Jake.

The Headmaster ignored Jake's verbal stumbling. "Let me see if I have got this right. You are putting forward the argument that faulty equipment is to blame. That you are innocent of this matter in all respects?"

Jake opened his mouth but his brain could not supply any words.

"It was, in fact," continued the Headmaster calmly as he reined in his emotions, "the faulty dart that broke the man's leg? It was the dart that forgot to cover its tracks? And in the final analysis, it was the dart that has caused all the mayhem that will follow?"

"No, but..."

"Then maybe, Mr Highfield, you are suggesting something more sinister? Something far more sinister indeed?"

"I..."

"A traitor, perhaps?" said the Headmaster helpfully. "Someone who is out to get you and through you bring St. Margaret's tumbling down?" The Headmaster paused, letting the idea grow and mature. "Is that what you are thinking, Mr Highfield? Do you consider yourself so special that you have been singled out as the crucial part of an evil plan?" The Headmaster laced the words 'special' and 'evil' with a heavy dose of sarcasm.

"No, sir. I don't think—"

"Exactly, Mr Highfield," interrupted the Headmaster.

"You do not think. And the fact that a piece of equipment may or may not have been faulty is neither here nor there. It is an operative's job to succeed at all times, whatever the circumstances. Excuses are for the weak and those that have failed." The Headmaster's unwavering gaze told Jake that the matter of the faulty dart was closed for good.

Jake swallowed hard; he didn't know if he could speak without his legs buckling under him. "Sir," he said shakily. "Sir, maybe I could go back into the field? Retrace my steps and see if anyone is getting close to me. And if they are I could lead them away from St. Margaret's? Set a false trail?"

The Headmaster didn't reply.

"Sir, I said—"

"I heard what you said, Mr Highfield. The answer is no. We have already got other operatives in the field doing what is required, operatives who do not think their training is unnecessary. If disaster is to be avoided, they are the ones to do it." There was a pause that seemed to last for several minutes before the Headmaster spoke again. "We do have one problem that you may be able to help with though."

"Anything, sir," said Jake earnestly. "If I can help in any way."

The Headmaster's face was emotionless. "We seem to have an operative who has...fallen out of favour with the Academy somewhat. Any suggestions as to what should be done with him, Mr Highfield?"

Jake's body stiffened with tension. He felt as if someone had reached into his guts and was shaking his internal organs around. He knew the operative the Headmaster was asking about was him, but how he was supposed to answer this question he did not know. Nor was he sure he was supposed to.

A single rap on the office door was immediately followed by it being flung open. "We've got a problem, Headmaster, another operative has van—" The middle-aged woman standing in the doorway stopped speaking as she first saw the scowl on the Headmaster's face and then noticed Jake.

Mrs Dawson, Jake's maths teacher, looked unusually stressed. Her short hair as usual was tidily cropped and bleached and she was wearing a smart two-piece trouser suit, but she was sweating and had a panicked look in her eyes. In addition to arithmetic Dawson was also the Academy's Advanced Vehicle Manipulation instructor. It was common knowledge in the Academy that there wasn't a machine with an engine which drove, flew or floated that she couldn't handle in an expert manner with nerves of steel.

"I'm sorry, Headmaster, I didn't know you had company," apologised Mrs Dawson, quietly.

"Quite," noted the Headmaster. "Which is why it is normal to knock and then wait to be invited to enter."

"Yes, Headmaster," whispered Mrs Dawson, flushing with embarrassment. "Sorry, Headmaster."

"You are excused, Mr Highfield," said the Headmaster, turning his attention to Jake. "We will continue the conversation about this matter at a later date."

"Yes, sir," said Jake, almost collapsing with relief on the gaudy carpet.

As Mrs Dawson moved aside from the open door to let Jake pass, the Headmaster added, "And Mr Highfield, should you have any suggestions that will help our little problem, do let me know."

"Yes, sir. I will, sir."

"And polish your shoes."

"Sir," said Jake, before closing the door and making his way down the stairs to get his lungs full of some clean, fresh air as quickly as possible.

DETENTION IS FOR LOSERS

The canteen at St. Margaret's was not the warmest place in the Academy. High ceilings and the lack of proper heating meant that most of the students spent as little time in there as possible. Get in, eat and get out was the usual way of things.

Jake sat alone at a table, slowly ploughing his fork back and forth through an unappetising fish-based pasta dish, covered in a sauce that he could only assume was made from tomatoes. It was lunch time and his mind was still too occupied from his visit to the Headmaster's office to worry about the discomfort of the cold air around him or the need for food, even though he had missed breakfast.

The rattle of Angel's food tray on the table and the screech of her dragging the chair closer across the old wooden floor preceded her enquiry. "Things didn't go too well with the Headmaster, did they?"

Jake narrowed his eyes. "What? How do you know?"

Angel shifted nervously in her chair. "Well…judging by the happy smile on your face." she said, with a flicker of a grin.

"Let's say he didn't pin any medals on me. To be honest, he wasn't wrong," said Jake sullenly, stirring his food once more. "Do you think they'll ever let us have chips?"

"Not likely. Healthy mind, healthy body; you know how they think," answered Angel.

An awkward silence hung between the two. Jake could tell his friend was dying to say something and he knew if he left it long enough she would come out with it.

After a few mouthfuls of food, Angel broke the silence. "What do you reckon Skidmarks was going to say?" she blurted out, unable to hold her curiosity in any longer.

Jake tilted his head with suspicion. Skidmarks was the students' nickname for Mrs Dawson on account of the speed she drove at and the fear it instilled in her passengers. He kept his eyes on Angel, who was biting her bottom lip with her head lowered, staring intently at her dinner, and put his hand into his blazer pocket. He pulled out a packet of chewing gum. "This is new," said Jake, turning the packet over in his hands, "I wonder how this got there? Haven't been bugging me again by any chance have you, Angel?"

Angel dropped her cutlery with a clatter onto her plate. "Well, of all the things to suggest," she gasped. "How could you think I would do such a thing?"

Jake turned the packet over in his hands. "Oh I don't know, probably because you've done it before."

Angel chewed at her lip for a few seconds more. Jake could tell she was toying with the idea of trying to keep the pretence up, but as usual she cracked under her own pressure. "Okay, I wanted to test out a new low frequency device and it just seemed like the perfect opportunity. It worked a treat. And it should be almost impossible to detect."

"I'm happy for you," said Jake, sliding the disguised device across the table.

"Slipped it into my pocket after our meeting with Clarkson, I assume? You want to be careful; you may hear something you don't want to."

Angel smiled. "Maybe you're right; I'll ask your permission next time."

"Of course you will," said Jake, not believing a word of it.

"So, what do you think Skidmarks was going to say?" pushed Angel excitedly. "Do you think it has anything to do with the vanishings?"

"The what?"

"The vanishings; it's what they're calling the disappearance of operatives who have gone missing in the field without a trace."

"What the hell are you talking about, Angel?" said Jake, genuinely confused.

Angel leant forward over the table to get closer to Jake and talked in a hushed whisper. "Rumour has it that four operatives have vanished and no one knows where they are."

Jake shook his head. "Rumours have it? And where did you hear these rumours?"

"Danny told me."

"And Danny is the source of all knowledge now, is he?"

"Some of them have been missing for over a month," argued Angel, pressing her case earnestly.

"So? You can be in the field for that length of time. It depends how deep your cover is."

"Not without contact, you can't."

Jake sighed. "Angel, they're rumours. This place is alive with rumours and secrets and lies, it's how the Academy operates. Very little is what it appears to be." Jake could see he wasn't convincing Angel at all. "These *Vanishings* are no more real than the ghosts that supposedly haunt this place."

Angel leant back in her seat. "So what was Skidmarks so stressed about then?"

"She didn't seem that stressed to me. She doesn't relax unless she's doing over a hundred miles an hour, anyway."

"Well, according to the equipment I was using to receive the bugging device, her voice stress-level was off the chart. How do you explain that?"

"Maybe the equipment was faulty," suggested Jake.

Angel's face flushed with anger and Jake could see she was doing her best to keep her voice under control when she spoke. "The equipment is not faulty," she hissed. "I designed it."

"Okay, okay. But she could have been strung out about anything. You can't suddenly jump to conclusions like this based on a rumour. Maybe someone had wrecked her favourite car?" said Jake, unable to hold back a grin.

Angel's eyes narrowed into slits. "You can think this is funny if you like but I think something is going on and I'm going to find out what."

"Whatever," said Jake, dismissively.

A silence fell between them for a few moments before Angel spoke again. "Thanks for helping out before with Clarkson by the way. He's really giving me a hard time lately."

"No problem; I enjoyed it," replied Jake, thankful that

the subject had been changed before it got too heated. "I could always teach you some moves so you could defend yourself against Clarkson."

"What, get into a fight and risk ending up brain damaged like you?"

Jake smiled. He grasped his tray of untouched food and rose from his seat. "I've got to get off. Got a date with the assault course this afternoon."

"Lucky you," replied Angel, before a seriousness crossed her face and she added, "if there's anything I can help with, Jake, you know…with the Headmaster?"

"Unless you've invented a pack of chewing gum that can turn back time, I don't think you can help, to be honest."

"I'll get on it right after lunch," said Angel, smiling broadly. "I'll just need to know how far back you want to go."

Jake rose from his chair and lifted his tray. "I'll get back to you on that one, Angel," he said. "At times like this, about twenty-five years sounds good."

*

"Highfield!" barked Routledge as Jake walked toward him. "You're late!"

Jake knew if anything he was early but he only got as far as opening his mouth in protest.

"Twenty times round the quad, you 'orrible little toad!" barked Routledge. "Be quick about it and don't forget to pat each one of your mother's better lookin' sisters on the head every time you pass 'em!"

Jake saved his scowl until he had turned to start his run

around the quad. It wouldn't do to give the ex-military sadist an opportunity to do what he liked best. The number of pupils Routledge hadn't reduced to tears was only a handful and Jake was proud to be in that minority.

For half an hour, Jake pounded his way around the three hundred and fifty metre perimeter of the quad. There was a hideous stone gargoyle at each corner and he pointedly slapped each as he passed it. With his punishment complete, Jake jogged back to the assault course, doused in sweat.

"Highfield! What are you doin' back 'ere? I said twenty laps, not nineteen! Back you go," grinned Routledge, proudly displaying the few teeth he had left in his mouth. "And do the full twenty this time."

An argument was pointless so Jake turned around and jogged back to the quad for another twenty laps, determined that he would not be goaded by Routledge. Arguing with a teacher would just bring him a whole lot more trouble than he was already in.

As he entered the quad, Jake looked up at the open window of St. Margaret in the Headmaster's office to see the familiar figure dressed in tweed looking down on him. Their eyes met but the Headmaster didn't show the slightest flicker of acknowledgement before slowly turning away to sink back into the timelessness of his museum-like office.

'So, this is it?' thought Jake, as he gave the first gargoyle another slap. 'The punishment starts.' Jake knew he had made a mess at the research lab. Even if the dart had been faulty, he still should have known better than to leave without covering his tracks. He probably deserved all he was getting and, no doubt, going to get. But he'd show them, Routledge, the Headmaster, all of them, that

Jake Highfield was not a wimp who cracked easily under a little pressure. He'd show them he was better than they thought he was.

Jake pounded away at the distance, slapping the gargoyles and trying to let his mind think of more pleasant things than the pain in his legs and the stitch in his side. He was soon snapped out of his attempt at mental calm by an unwelcome voice.

"Lovely day for a run," said Clarkson, who must have come out of one of the doors that led on to the quad and was now jogging alongside Jake. "They reckon it's going to rain later though."

Jake lifted his head and blew a drop of sweat off the tip of his nose. "What do you want?" he hissed through clenched teeth. It was no secret that Routledge considered Clarkson his star pupil at the Academy and it would not be beyond the sadist's mind to send his pet along to make the punishment all the more uncomfortable.

"Now, now; don't be like that," mocked Clarkson, who, fresher than Jake, was easily keeping pace with him. "I just thought I'd keep you company for a while; wouldn't want you to feel lonely out here to add to your misery of falling out with the Headmaster."

'I haven't stopped myself being wound up by Routledge just so this idiot can get the better of me,' thought Jake. "How's the hand?" he asked with a forced smile, deliberately changing the subject and nodding at Clarkson's scabbing knuckles.

Clarkson's face dropped for a second, betraying the anger that boiled beneath the surface of his pleasantries, but he regained his composure quickly. "Fine, thanks," he said, curling the injured appendage into a tight fist.

"Actually, better than fine. I'm back in the field tonight. Something you won't be doing for a while…so I hear. And the really funny thing is, it's a mission you were marked to do. Until you screwed up."

At the sound of this news, Jake nearly tripped face-first into the gargoyle he was about to touch. "Really?" said Jake, fighting hard to keep his smile.

"Yeah," laughed Clarkson. "Still, I suppose they want the job doing right this time, High-*failed*."

"Well, don't let me keep you, Clarkson."

"Don't worry, I won't," Clarkson grinned, slowing his jog to leave Jake to carry on his solitary run.

With a wave of his hand, Jake shouted, "Have fun," over his shoulder. "I'll see you when you get back and you can tell me all about it."

Clarkson had come to a stop. "No problem, I guarantee I'll see you," he shouted back, touching his damaged knuckles. "We've got a lot to talk about."

'The only thing I want to discuss with you, Clarkson, is how far I can get my fist down your throat,' thought Jake, sickened by the unfairness of the situation. 'I'm wasting my time here, while you're out in the field stealing my glory. And I thought today couldn't get any worse.'

By the time he had finished his fortieth lap of the quad, Jake's lungs felt like they were full of coal embers and his grey t-shirt was blackened with sweat. Routledge looked at the stopwatch that hung round his neck on a lace, next to the obligatory PTI's whistle. "Where've you been lad? You're over an hour late; the rest of your class is way ahead of you."

Jake was panting hard. "Yes, sir. Sorry, sir," he managed to gasp.

"Well, what are you waiting for?" barked Routledge. "You'd better catch them up, hadn't you?" Jake stared into the eyes of the stern figure holding the stopwatch in his huge fist. "Somethin' to say, lad?" dared Routledge.

Jake managed to pull a lopsided grin from somewhere deep inside, "No, sir. Nothing at all." He set off at a sprint, ignoring the pain that erupted all over his body.

Jake spent the next two hours struggling through concrete pipes half submerged in water, clambering over mercilessly high walls and crawling under heavy cargo nets with his face pressed down in the dirt. All this set against the idyllic backdrop of miles of sodden marsh, rancid ditches and dense, nettle-ridden forest. Once completed, Jake found himself lucky enough to be told to do it again as Routledge, out of the kindness of his black heart, decided he could improve his time on a second run. This second attempt would be, in the bellowed words of instruction, 'character building'.

Just as Clarkson had predicted, the rain came and started to fall halfway through Jake's second 'character building' run of the assault course. With this new discomfort, and the quickly fading light, the thought of cutting a few corners and avoiding the odd obstacle or two crossed Jake's mind. Routledge and the other students wouldn't be hanging around watching or waiting for him to come back at this time of night, especially in this weather. If he did cheat a little just to make things easier, no one would know. Jake chased the negative thoughts from his mind; he was out to prove a point. Not just to Routledge or the Headmaster or even to St. Margaret's, he was out to prove it to himself. Prove he had what it took to push on, whatever the odds. Prove without doubt that nothing could stop him and no one could break him.

The clock tower was striking ten as he staggered back across the quad towards his room. The lights from the rooms overlooking him died on the final stroke. The rain was falling harder than it had for Noah and every piece of Jake's clothing clung to him and hung like a loose, uncomfortably heavy, second skin. He knew he should ache from head to toe. He was covered with cuts and bruises and stinging from the nettles that had raked at his limbs, but his exhausted body was beyond feeling such minor discomforts. He was in a state of numb automation. If he allowed his legs to stop now, he would end up sleeping where he fell in the torrential rain.

At last Jake feebly pushed down on the handle and leaned heavily against the door to his room. He could almost feel the inviting warmth reaching out from his bed towards his weary body.

As he collapsed face down across the mattress, careless of his sodden clothes, he heard the crunch of paper. With his eyes already shutting for sleep, he fumbled under his belly and retrieved an envelope with his name scrawled across the front of it. For a second or two he held it in front of his bleary eyes, toying with the idea of opening it, but the way his day had been going he decided it could only be more bad news.

"Sod it," he muttered to himself and let the arm holding the letter go limp and hang over the edge of his bed. Just before he drifted off to sleep, Jake felt the warmth of a solitary tear collect on the bridge of his nose and he half-smiled, happy in the knowledge Routledge was not there to get a kick from it.

MARKED FOR SPECIAL TREATMENT

Jake lay watching the lights in his room flash on and off. His whole body felt like it had taken a pounding inside a washing machine. Every muscle in his body ached and the desire to lie in bed, to hell with the consequences, was top of Jake's agenda. He turned his head and groaned at the twinge in his neck. The clock spelt out 0800 in bright digits. "Must be Sunday," Jake muttered to himself, blearily.

The last two days had been such a physical strain for Jake that they had seemed to bleed into one long PT lesson from hell. Both mornings he had been granted the pleasure of having Routledge burst into his room at five and 'encourage' him around the assault course before normal lessons began. To add to his fun, the ex-army bully-boy had been there to help him round the course again at the end of the day. His dinner times, under the watchful gaze of the Headmaster's leaded window, were spent completing circuits of the quad.

As he lay there, his body numb with exhaustion, Jake listened to the hypnotic drumming of the rain against his window and he wasn't sure he could face another day of physical punishment. He couldn't help feeling today could be the proverbial back-breaking straw. He'd taken everything so far without complaint, even finding the strength to raise a defiant smile occasionally, but if it were going to happen all over again today...

Jake caught his negativity. "Snap out of it, Highfield," he hissed at himself. "It's eight o'clock; if Routledge was coming he'd have been here by now." He threw his covers off and jumped, with a wince, out of bed. "You've got to prove your worth to the sods. And besides that, you've had a three-hour lie in, you wimp, so if they want to come and get you, let them."

Jake showered and dressed. Sunday morning meant chapel and chapel meant full school turnout, no excuses. Everyone had to make their appearance before God or at least the Headmaster's twist on Him. Jake seriously doubted that God would be bothered to get up for eight on a Sunday just to hear the Headmaster of St. Margaret's prattle on about some half-baked theological theories on His existence. This Sunday though, Jake had a good reason to be going to chapel. Before leaving his room, he pocketed the note from Angel he had found on his bed on Thursday night, the day his torment had begun, telling him to be sure to sit next to her.

It took some jostling, but Jake forced his way into the school hall and managed to grab a seat next to Angel. They exchanged a silent smile of acknowledgment and then turned to face the front where the Headmaster stood behind a lectern, waiting for the whole Academy to be seated and silent before starting.

"The weak often turn to God in search of strength..." boomed the Headmaster, looking over the heads of the students seated before him in neat rows.

"I got your note," whispered Jake.

Angel swallowed and looked around nervously with twitching head movements. "I gathered that," she whispered, so quietly even Jake had trouble hearing her. She looked round again, giving the impression of a meerkat strung out on coffee, before continuing. "I need to show you something."

"Okay," whispered Jake, finding his friend's paranoia disturbingly contagious.

There was a long pause in which Angel stayed silent, looking directly at the Headmaster.

"It is the strong that move the universe, not the weak."

"Well?" insisted Jake eventually.

"Not here," whispered Angel. "Meet me tonight in the Tech Department."

"Er, okay," agreed Jake. "What time?"

"Forgiveness is for the valiant to distribute, the vanquished can only accept what they are given."

After another long pause, Angel finally plucked up enough courage to speak again. "Midnight."

Jake grinned. "Of course, I should have known," he said, a little too loudly.

Angel smiled weakly at the pupils who half-turned to face them from the seats in front.

"God only answers those who shout loud and defiant in the face of what he sends."

Angel eventually spoke again. "I'm serious," she hissed. "It's very important."

Jake nodded, realising the stunted and drawn out conversation was over, which was just as well as he wasn't sure Angel could take the stress of it much longer. He turned his concentration to the still preaching Headmaster.

"Those who swim in the sea of failure shall drown there also, for that is their will, not the Lord's." With these final words of pseudo-religious babble, the Headmaster let his gaze lower to rest on Jake for a second before saying. "Now we will sing hymn number twenty-six, 'All Things Bright and Beautiful'. Everyone please stand."

*

After the last few days of exertion, Jake found himself fighting to stay awake but eventually the bright figures on his clock showed four zeroes. 'I hope the geek knows what she's doing,' thought Jake, tying the laces of his trainers. 'I'm in enough trouble without getting this dumped on me too.'

St. Margaret's had a strict 'no movement after lights-out' policy and anyone found wandering the grounds or buildings without permission or good excuse, which usually meant permission, was for it big time. Not that this rule was never broken by students, as the so-called ghosts haunting Pete proved, but the risk of punishment for getting caught kept instances to a minimum.

Jake stuffed two rolled towels under his bedclothes to fake him being tucked up for a good night's sleep. It was a bit of a 'Dennis the Menace' move, but it would fool a casual observer from the doorway. Hopefully that would be enough.

Padding softly to the door he leant his weight against it to avoid any clicking caused by the slack fitting mechanism. He gripped the handle tightly and slowly pushed it down. Looking through the crack he had created he could see the corridor to the left was clear. As far as the right of the door was concerned, a leap of faith was needed. He slipped into the corridor, armed only with a weak excuse of nausea for protection. His luck held and when he found the corridor was clear in both directions, he let out his breath and dropped his 'sick' expression.

The Tech Department was on the ground floor in one of the attached annexes and Jake was running a big risk of being seen as he was going to be exposed at all times en route. Once inside the department he had enough faith in Angel to know they would be relatively safe or at least less easily detectable. Walking quickly, but placing his feet carefully to minimise noise, Jake began to make his way to the rendezvous point.

He scurried down dimly-lit corridors like a furtive sewer rat suddenly finding himself on a city street. The fifteen-watt night-lights left gloom hanging in the air, but did not leave enough shadow to hide in at any point. The long featureless corridors and the many windows left Jake utterly visible from many different angles. Jake felt like he was playing a part in a burglar's nightmare made real. His progress was quick and within a minute he had reached the ground floor. He crossed in front of the main entrance and was at the top of the corridor that led down to the double doors and the annexe beyond. He leant his back to the wall and stuck his head round the corner. He snapped it back. A familiar figure was patrolling the building.

'Why him?' Jake cursed inwardly. 'Doesn't he ever sleep or need to wash his vest or something?'

Routledge was pacing quietly down the corridor, his back to Jake. He could feel disaster with a capital 'D' looming in the tension. 'If he turns round,' thought Jake, 'I'll have to leg it back to my room.'

Jake chanced another glance and again caught a glimpse of the back of Routledge's vest. 'Turn left you sadistic sod', thought Jake, willing the man on his way. 'Turn left'.

On the third glance the corridor was empty, which left Jake with a further dilemma. 'He could have gone into one of the classrooms,' he reasoned. 'And so could come back out into the corridor at any moment; or turned left to patrol the shorter corridor that comes to a dead end against the inner wall of the arch; or worse still he could have gone straight on through the double doors.' Jake hoped it wasn't the latter. That was the way he was going and if Routledge was in the Perspex tunnel he would be trapped and completely exposed.

Jake bit his lip and decided to chance it. He sprinted down the corridor, praying he wasn't making too much noise and reached the end of the wall without incident, before it turned left. He looked down the corridor quickly to see Routledge continuing his calm, measured pace. Jake readied himself for a second with a deep breath then moved forward to the double doors. If he made any sound, Routledge would turn and see him without a doubt and Jake didn't dare to think what extra trouble that would bring upon him.

Much to Jake's relief, the well-oiled hinges of the door worked without the slightest of groaning creaks and once through, he gently closed the door and crouched down in the tunnel beyond. The Perspex tunnel was arched in shape and rested on solid walls that rose up a metre to meet it and take the weight. Jake lay on the floor and slithered like a snake along the final corridor to the door of the Tech Department. He stood up, pressed himself flat against the door and pulled down on the handle. It was locked.

His mind raced. What now? What if Angel wasn't here? What if she'd been caught already? What if…

The door clicked and swung open. Jake, who had had his weight leaning on it, rolled into the room in an untidy heap.

"You alright?" whispered Angel. "You look like you've seen a ghost."

Jake was breathing hard. "Not exactly a ghost, but he was wearing white."

"You mean Routledge," said Angel, calmly shutting and locking the door again before walking toward a computer station. "Don't panic, he went down corridor E7."

Jake stood up and ran a hand through his hair. "E7? Have you gone so weird that you've started naming corridors for a hobby?"

"Witt-ee," mocked Angel. "Actually, I thought a bit of surveillance might come in handy, so I rigged up a few new fire alarms earlier today that just happen to be cameras. You can't be too careful, you know."

"Tell me about it," sighed Jake, looking about the Tech Department's windowless confines. He didn't like the room much. No fresh air, no natural light, but on the plus side even the ever-vigilant Routledge couldn't see through walls.

"This had better be worth disturbing a good night's sleep for, Angel, or I'll feed you to Clarkson myself when he gets back."

"It is," said Angel. "Though I can't guarantee it will bring a smile to your face." She took a seat in front of a computer and started to tap away at the keyboard.

"Don't they monitor who's using these things?" asked Jake, stabbing a finger in the direction of the screen.

"They do," Angel confirmed whilst continuing to type. "But you can get round it if you know how."

Jake looked at the flat screen. One quarter of it was flicking up images of the immediate corridors around the Academy; Angel's unauthorised surveillance net. The rest of the screen gave Jake the impression of watching a firework display made up entirely of opening and closing windows, each overlapping, shrinking and expanding, causing him to squint as he tried to follow the mayhem.

"And this makes sense to you, does it?" Jake said, looking at Angel to give his eyes a rest from the uncomfortable flickering on the screen.

"Mmm," replied Angel, vaguely, engrossed in her work. She made one final heavy tap on the keyboard. "Here we go; the St. Margaret's Academy file on Jake Highfield: codename Chaos."

Jake took a renewed interest in the now altogether more stable screen. "That's really my file?"

"Yes," beamed Angel. "Go on, you can admit it. You're impressed."

"I am," said Jake. "So this has all the information about my time at St. Margaret's? Details of missions, things like that?"

"It has, and about your life before, but it's so deeply buried in the system you need a six gigabyte spade to get at it."

"Is there anything in there about how good they think I am? Some kind of assessment of my training so far?" said Jake, staring intently at the screen.

Angel frowned. "Yes, but we don't have time tonight to see how marvellous the Headmaster thinks Chaos is," she said sternly. "It's worrying me enough just being here now, but there's something much more worrying."

Jake smiled, knowing that was true. It must be something really big to get Angel to take a risk like this. Just leaving her room after lights out was the equivalent of shoving her face into a tank full of scorpions.

"What is it? Something on my file?"

"Not any more," said Angel cryptically, "but it did leave the smallest trace of having been there."

"Well, that helps," said Jake, feeling none the wiser. "What left a trace?"

"A program that recently accessed your file."

"So? I bet a load of programs use my file."

"Not like this one," explained Angel. "The source was impossible to track. I can't even tell if it was generated within the Academy or if it was sent in from outside the system. It's extremely complicated coding."

"But it left a trace?" pushed Jake.

"Yes, but it's not just your file either, Jake," said Angel, opening several other windows on the screen. "It's been into these files, too."

"At the risk of repeating myself and sounding stupid," said Jake, still confused, "so?"

"These," said Angel, sitting back in her chair, "are the operatives who have gone missing. These are the files of the 'vanished'."

Jake shook his head. "Is that what all this is about? Stupid rumours?"

"Rumours based on facts," said Angel, tapping at the screen with her finger. "All these field operatives' files have been accessed by the mystery program and now they're all missing."

"Rumoured to be missing," corrected Jake. "I can't believe you're doing this, Angel," he said, angrily. "I'm in enough trouble as it is without being caught breaking curfew for some ridiculous gossip!"

"I'm trying to help you!" spat Angel defensively. She took a deep breath and regained her calm. "And there's something else, something else that is disturbing," she paused before speaking again. "Three of the four who are missing...were vanished...had..."

Jake could see Angel was struggling to find the right words. "Well?"

"Well, they didn't exactly have a smooth ride on the mission directly before they vanished."

"Just be honest Angel, you mean they cocked things up, like I did," said Jake harshly. "And so you assume I'm next for vanishing. It's so obvious. Why didn't I see it?"

"Three out of four Jake," argued Angel. "That's a seventy-five per cent probability."

"But it's not one hundred per cent, is it?" Jake was seething. He could feel his breathing was long and deep. His first thought was to turn round and go back to his room, hoping Routledge didn't catch him, but he could see the earnest look in Angel's eyes. Losing his temper with her was not going to resolve anything.

"Okay," he said finally, calming down a little. "Let's assume I believe you, what do you think is going on?"

"I don't know," admitted Angel. "The only evidence I have found for the program ever being on the system is one line of residual code that indicates that the program is called 'Void'."

"Not exactly concrete, is it?" said Jake. "And there's

a major flaw in your theory about it being linked to the 'vanished'. I'm not missing."

"I know," admitted Angel. "Neither is Clarkson, as far as we know, but his file was targeted as well."

"I'm sorry Angel," said Jake shaking his head. "This could all be coincidence. This Void thing could be something new to the system, something St. Margaret's is behind."

"I don't think so."

"But you don't know so," argued Jake quickly. "Do you?"

Angel shook her head solemnly, but she was in no mood to give up. "No, but what if you've been marked out for something and…" she cut herself off as the computer screen fired up a warning window. "Oh no," she said, "we're being tagged," and began to tap furiously at the keyboard.

"What?"

"Tagged!" said Angel, with more than a hint of panic in her voice. "The system has detected me and has activated the security protocol."

"And that's bad, is it?"

"Just a bit," hissed Angel. "If they get a trace fix on this computer they will know exactly what we've been doing, who is logged on, where we are. And that's really bad for us."

"*You.* I think you'll find you mean bad for you, Angel," grinned Jake.

Perspiration was beginning to bead on Angel's forehead. "It's not funny, Jake," she spat, her fingers hammering away on the keyboard. "It's…it's…just…not funny. Oh no, they've almost got us. I can't seem to shut the link down. They're going to get us…they're going to—" The computer screen went black.

"What? What?" gasped Angel, wide-eyed. "I don't understand!"

Jake leant forward and waved a length of electrical cable with a plug on the end of it in front of her. "Being brain damaged does have its advantages sometimes. You tend to look for the easy answers for a start."

Angel let out a huge sigh of relief and leant back in her chair. "How do you go through all that stress all the time?"

"You're making it sound like it's not fun," grinned Jake, dropping the lead. "But back to the problem in hand. If it is a problem. A rogue program has temporarily accessed several files, one of which was mine and may be linked to the possible disappearances of several operatives?"

"Yes," confirmed Angel. "That's how I see it."

"However, we can't prove any of it and, other than rumours, we have no evidence."

"Yes, but—"

"On the other hand," interrupted Jake, "I am up to my neck in it at the moment, unless I get caught tonight from which point on it will be six foot over my head?"

"I know how it looks, Jake, but I'm concerned. Something's not right. And what about the dart—"

"What's got into you, Angel? Conspiracy theories now? The Watkinson mission was my fault! Look, I'm grateful for your concern," smiled Jake, "but can't we please forget about all this until we know something for sure?"

Angel stared for a few seconds at Jake before reluctantly nodding her agreement.

"Great," smiled Jake, "because I could really do with

some sleep tonight. Are you going to be alright getting back to your room?"

"No problem," said Angel, lifting a hand-held video device. "I've got my own TV channel, don't forget!"

"I'll see you tomorrow," said Jake, unlocking the door.

"Oh that reminds me," said Angel, clicking her fingers. "I checked out the Headmaster's organiser, just to see if I could, really. You're down for an appointment with him at two tomorrow afternoon."

Jake shook his head. "Thanks, Angel, that'll really help me get a good night's rest."

REDEMPTION

Jake spent the next morning trawling through his lessons half-heartedly. His mind was more occupied with the possibility raised by Angel that he would be summoned to the Headmaster's office in the afternoon. He'd even spent the whole of his dinner time in the cold confines of the canteen, not noticing the discomfort, as he mentally rehearsed what might be said or done when, or if, he was invited to the historic room. He was trying to second guess whether he was in more trouble and, if he was, what he could do or say in his defence.

The first double period after dinner did, however, offer some respite from his self-absorbed wonderings. Jake enjoyed Modern Languages and, although they didn't come easy to him, he tried his best to grasp a subject that could lead to assignments in foreign countries in the future. He also had to admit that the teacher did a lot to help concentrate the mind.

Mademoiselle Felloux was the Academy pin-up. This wasn't a tall order as competition from the other female staff at the Academy wasn't exactly stiff. Among them was the school nurse, who rumour had it was so old she used to attend the ill at the Crimea and personally knew Florence Nightingale; the Headmaster's secretary Miss Fort, who on the rare occasions she left her office looked old enough to be the school nurse's mother; and Skidmarks, who was generally considered to be mental and dangerous, rather than attractive.

Mademoiselle Felloux could speak seven languages fluently – eight, the male students would say, if you included 'body' language – and she could hold a class's attention with a single look.

Jake's mind was so focused on trying to learn the latest French words written on the board that when his thoughts did eventually wander back to the possible appointment with the Headmaster, it was already twenty minutes past two. 'Well, Angel,' thought Jake, allowing himself a quick grin of relief. 'Computers still never wrong?'

Had the grin not already left Jake's face, it would have done for sure when there was a harsh knock on the classroom door. A split second later, Routledge burst in without waiting for permission to enter.

"Mademoiselle Felloux," announced the PTI in an obviously quieter tone than usual, which Jake assumed was his 'talking to ladies' voice. "The Headmaster wants to see Highfield in his office."

Jake could imagine the smug smile stretching across Angel's face, wherever she was. He imagined her saying something like, 'A twenty minute margin of error is acceptable.'

Mademoiselle Felloux looked at Routledge, who seemed to be wilting into his vest under her gaze. "Non, Monsieur. En Francais!"

"Yes, of course," replied Routledge remembering the language teacher's class rules that stated whatever language she was teaching was the only language allowed to be spoken in the room. "I mean...qui... of..." the PTI's bald head began to glow a delicate pink under the pressure. "Err...le...err...tête...master..." Routledge tried in vain, gradually turning the shade of a London bus.

Someone at the back of the class tittered. The PTI shot a glare as hard as cold steel in their direction, which had promises of quad circuits nailed to every centimetre of it.

"Le Principal?" offered Mademoiselle Felloux, with a sweet smile.

"Yes...I mean, oui...er...le..." stuttered Routledge. "Le principal..." Jake almost felt sorry for the crumbling man, but a twinge of pain from his aching leg muscles soon dismissed that. Suddenly Routledge could take no more humiliation; he needed to get this over with and escape as quickly as possible. "Highfield, dans le Principal's off-eece, por favor!"

The whole class erupted into laughter, careless of the fact that they knew Routledge would dish out his own brand of pain-inducing punishment under the guise of their next PT lesson. But seeing the man wither and break, defeated by a petite woman armed only with the French language, was worth every second.

"Thank you, God," muttered Jake under his breath, revelling in the revenge by proxy.

Mademoiselle Felloux hushed the class into silence, then turned to Jake. "Monsieur Highfield, le Principal, veut vous voir, s'il vous plaît."

"Oui, Mademoiselle," replied Jake, rising from his seat and walking toward Routledge, who sneered at him more deeply with every step he took.

"Bon après-midi," said Madame Felloux with a smile as they left.

"Bon après-midi, Mademoiselle," said Jake, with a slight wave. Routledge let out a small grunt, impatient to get out of the room before he was verbally assaulted again.

Out in the corridor, teacher and student stared at each other for a second. Jake got the feeling Routledge was trying to send a telepathic message threatening him never to mention this incident, ever, to anyone.

"Well, boy," barked Routledge, back up to his usual full volume. "What are you waiting for? Double time!" The PTI set off up the corridor.

"Yes, sir," replied Jake, shouldering his bag and falling in step.

*

Jake was familiar with the mind games the Headmaster played with students who were summoned to his domain. Sometimes he would have his head buried in a book; other times he would be gazing silently through St. Margaret's window. This time he was carefully pruning a Bonsai tree with the aid of a large magnifying glass and a pair of delicate scissors.

Jake, fighting to keep his breathing steady and imploring his heart to stop beating so loudly, stood before the desk. Behind him, he could feel Routledge standing stiffly 'at ease' as if waiting for the Queen to inspect the troops.

Eventually the Headmaster laid down the scissors, rose from his desk and placed the tiny, yet perfect, tree back into pride of place on the mantelpiece above the redundant fireplace. He was adjusting the position of the pot for a fourth time when he spoke without turning. "I have decided to give you another chance, Mr Highfield."

Jake felt like jumping up and punching the air. Instead he managed to offer a calm, "Thank you, sir," in reply, the knots in his stomach finally untying.

The Headmaster turned. "I would not go as far as thanking me yet," he said. "This is only a temporary state of affairs depending on how you shape up."

Jake lowered his head.

"You have caused the Academy a great deal of trouble with your gung-ho antics, Mr Highfield," explained the Headmaster, pacing over to his window. "We have had to spend a lot of time hiding your tracks, time that we could ill afford to waste on such things."

"Yes, sir," replied Jake quietly, keeping his head down. "Sorry, sir."

There was a long pause in which Jake did not need to look to know that the Headmaster would be staring out of his window and the sadist Routledge would be staring harshly into the back of his lowered head. Eventually, Jake's discomfort was broken by the Headmaster speaking again.

"I have decided to put you out in the field again, Mr Highfield. See how you do. Hopefully you have learned the error of your ways and will perform to the standard that St. Margaret's expects of you."

Jake lifted his head, consciously biting back the urge to smile with relief. "I won't let you down sir, I promise."

The Headmaster turned from the window and raised an eyebrow. "Promises are not the most effective defence against failure, Mr Highfield, which is why I have decided you will be subordinate to another operative on the mission."

Before he could stop himself, Jake protested. "But sir, I always work alone in the field, I—"

"Not this time," said the Headmaster firmly. "Those are my orders. That is the end of the matter. Mr Routledge, please escort the lucky, yet seemingly ungrateful, Mr Highfield back to his class."

"Sah!" barked Routledge and he forcefully dragged Jake out of the office and closed the door behind them. At the top of the stairs the PTI decided he would make his views on the subject clear too.

"If it was up to me, you maggot, I wouldn't have given you another chance." A vein began to stick out on Routledge's bald temple. "But be warned, Highfield, you cock this one up and I promise you, I promise you, I'll be there to see you vanish from this place for good."

Jake thought better than to turn the Headmaster's words of wisdom about promises against Routledge; besides, his stomach was busily knitting itself into a heavy weave at the mention of the words '...see you vanish from this place...'.

*

"I'm worried," said Angel, as she and Jake walked across the quad.

"Don't tell me," Jake said, with a sigh. "The vanishing thing again?"

"I can't help it, Jake, I really am worried."

"I thought we'd decided not to overreact to the rumours unless we got more evidence?" said Jake, forcefully.

Angel nodded. "Yeah, sorry, you're right and at least you're operational again, I suppose, and that's what you wanted."

"Not exactly what I wanted," corrected Jake. "I've got to prove myself worthy yet." He'd decided earlier not to mention Routledge's threatening speech outside the Headmaster's office door, which had included the word 'vanish'. The last thing he needed right now was to start Angel off on her conspiracy theory again.

"You'll be fine, Jake," said Angel quietly.

Jake could sense Angel was forcing herself to be positive for his benefit. "Of course I will," he said, his words full of bravado. "But I've never worked in the field under the direct control of someone else before and must admit I don't feel comfortable with it."

"On the plus side, you're back in the game," said Angel, keeping up her pretence. "Do you know who you're teamed up with yet? Maybe it will be one of the upper years?"

"If only," replied Jake. "I have a horrible suspicion it could be Routledge."

"Routledge?"

"Alright, Angel. Keep it down," said Jake, almost fearing the utterance of his name would summon him like a genie.

"Why would anyone in their right mind send 'Major Disaster' on a covert mission?" whispered Angel. "Unless…"

"As I said," interrupted Jake, before Angel could mention the Void again. "I don't actually know it is him for sure, it was just the things he said and the way he said them. I could be wrong and, God, do I hope I am," he finished, with a sigh.

"I'm not surprised. I can't imagine Routledge's army parade ground ways working too well in the field."

"I'll know for sure soon enough, anyway," said Jake, as he stopped and placed his hand on the double doors that led into the main building. "I'm getting briefed for the mission in twenty minutes and I've got to be kitted up and ready for the off by seven."

Angel stood next to him and Jake could see she wanted to take off into a massive speech about her fears for him, but instead she forced herself to simply say, "Good luck." She turned her back on him and walked across the quad.

"You know me," Jake called after her with a smile. "I don't need luck." Angel didn't respond or turn to face him. "See you tomorrow," he added, but Angel continued walking away in silence. He opened the door and walked into the corridor.

The 'basement', as the cavernous area carved beneath St. Margaret's was known to the students, was the heart of all pre-operation preparations for field operatives. It was here that all essential equipment was stored. It was a secure and controlled environment to ensure optimum efficiency of equipment when it was called upon to be used. Temperature and humidity were constantly monitored and kept within strict boundaries which were controlled by huge dry-air heaters that hummed in the background twenty-four hours a day.

Strong steel cages with electronic locking systems stood along the walls of the basement. They were lined with virtually indestructible glass and housed firing ranges and test sights for newly developed and experimental prototypes. Two large vaults sat next to each other. Neither would have looked out of place inside a large merchant bank, but instead of cash or jewels they were used to store weapons and other sensitive or dangerous equipment. At the far end of the basement a large steel shutter sealed off the area, behind which were the various specialist vehicles used during operations.

Jake took the final piece of his equipment. It had been laid out for him on a stainless steel counter before he had arrived in the basement. He carefully slid the night vision goggles into a black backpack. He turned at the sound of feet descending the metal stairs.

Routledge approached him, his bald head shining under the bright lighting in the basement, showing off his scar to great effect. "Ready for the off, Highfield?" he shouted, enthusiastically. "Once more unto the breach and all that...as some poofy poet once said."

Jake smiled with half of his mouth; partly at Routledge's macho overload and partly because down here in the bowels of the Academy, the subtle echo gave the impression that there were two obnoxious PTIs. 'Now that is scary', thought Jake, tugging the drawstring on his backpack tight.

"Yes, sir," he said, looking Routledge in the eye. "I won't let you down."

A grin spread across Routledge's mouth that was as friendly as a dose of flu. "Oh, I'm sure you will, Highfield. Losers like you always let people down."

Jake felt nervous enough about this mission without this kind of goading. He looked at his watch, then at the white-vested man in front of him. "I don't want to appear cheeky, sir, but it's ten to seven. Hadn't you better get ready?"

"Ready?" repeated Routledge, but the momentary confusion was soon replaced with yet another broad, dentally challenged grin. "I get it," he laughed. "You think I'm the one going with you. Oh, I can't wait to tell the Headmaster that one."

Jake was confused. He had been so obsessed with the thought that Routledge was going to be his chaperone that his mind refused to throw up any other possible candidates. Jake was beginning to really hate this feeling of uncertainty.

"I might not be able to speak all clever in French, Highfield, but I ain't stupid enough to be anywhere near you when things go pear-shaped." There was a second clomping of boots on the basement steps. "Perfect timing," said Routledge, his wide eyes bright with evil joy. "I reckon this is your partner for tonight's dance coming now, and I'm sure you're going to enjoy his company just as much as you would have mine."

Jake felt all his facial muscles collapse at once. "You," was the only word he could muster.

"Hello, Highfield," said Clarkson, calmly.

Jake declined to return the greeting, more through shock than anything else, if he was honest with himself.

"Well, this is nice," Routledge grinned, obviously enjoying the moment. "The two of you should get on like a house on fire…or at least a small petrol station."

"How's the running going?" asked Clarkson, filling his backpack as Jake had done. "Broken any records?"

"Not yet," said Jake, mimicking Clarkson's fake emotion. "But I do have plans to break a few other things in the near future."

"Really?" said Clarkson, tugging his backpack draw string with excessive force. "Well, I'm ready when you are."

"Now, now ladies," said Routledge, laying a hand on

each of the boys' shoulders. "You can sort out your little differences at playtime. Tonight, you have a job to do and we expect nothing but success. Do you both understand?"

Jake and Clarkson both nodded, neither taking their eyes off the other.

"Right, lock 'n' load, gentlemen," barked Routledge, slapping each boy on the back so hard they both nearly lost their footing. "See you in the morning, and don't be too late back; you know how your mother worries."

Routledge walked off with a deep chuckle rattling in his throat. "Me," he muttered. "Funniest thing I've heard in years."

"I don't like you and you don't like me," muttered Clarkson, as he and Jake made their way to one of the waiting vans. "But let's get this right. I can manage to suffer your incompetence for one night. What I need to know is, can you manage to do as you're told and not be too much of a screw up?"

Jake was grinding his teeth too tightly to talk but he managed a nod of agreement. As much as he hated it, his future at St. Margaret's was riding on the success of this mission and for that reason he had to take anything Clarkson wanted to hand out without kicking back.

"Good," Clarkson grinned. "You never know, maybe one day you will be able to come out from under my shadow."

"Maybe," agreed Jake, unable to keep himself from having one last verbal dig. "Though I reckon it would be easier to come out from under a hippo's shadow, given the choice."

Their boots hit the steel floor of the van in unison and, as required for covert operations, all spoken communication from that point on ceased.

BACK IN THE FIELD

The black van looked normal enough, right down to the writing, 'Speedy Build', on both sides of the vehicle. Someone with a sense of humour at the Academy had come up with the advertising motto 'You won't even know we've been'.

Inside the back of the van, secret panelling could be removed to fit it out with a veritable arsenal of weaponry and equipment, depending on the nature of the operation in hand. The bodywork was bulletproof and painted with a coating that was able to deflect radar and block infra-red sources. The chassis and flooring were strengthened to withstand high speed impacts and explosive charges that would normally shred a vehicle of this size. Below the bonnet, a four litre engine with nitrous-oxide boosters growled with awesome power but a special silencing system quietened the exhaust note to that of a smaller engine. This vehicle, quietly ticking over at traffic lights of any city or town, would attract no more attention than any other builder's van.

Jake and Clarkson had travelled for four hours in the back of the van, sat opposite each other on seats built more for practicality than comfort. Neither had broken the rule of silence that was imposed on operatives mobile in the field, but that hadn't stopped the rivals exchanging frequent hate-filled stares.

Jake and Clarkson had done a final check of the equipment in the backpacks when a small red light had flickered once in the dimly lit van. Now Jake's attention was grabbed once again by the light. This time it stayed on.

'T minus five,' thought Jake pulling his rucksack onto his back and slipping the ski mask over his head. Across from him, Clarkson did the same. They took their positions, crouched by the double doors at the back of the van.

As the red light went out and was replaced by a single flash from a green lens, Jake grabbed one of the handles of the door, Clarkson the other. For a second they looked at each other, nodded and then, as one, opened the back of the van and rolled out of the moving vehicle on to the tarmac of a small country road.

Jake was on his feet in a second, dashing for the cover of the overgrowth at the side of the road. He could hear the soft tapping of Clarkson's boots close behind. Jake lay still for a minute or two, silently cursing the nettles that had managed to slip their barbs between his sleeve and his glove. He couldn't help thinking that the drop-off drivers picked stretches of road with this kind of vicious foliage at the sides on purpose. He watched the tail-lights of the van disappear from view and then put all his efforts into scanning the countryside for signs of movement or noise. He knew Clarkson, lying a few metres to his left, would be doing the same thing but also, as he was the 'senior' operative on this mission he would be using the 'bat-ears', a hand held audio device that could hear a spider sneezing half a mile away. If for any reason Clarkson detected anything out of the ordinary, he could abort the mission and they would both have to lie there, frozen as if part of the natural environment and simply await the return of the van to pick them up. If that happened, the only chance Jake had to prove himself would be lost.

Several minutes passed before Jake felt Clarkson's hand on his shoulder. To his relief they were on the move. They had a two-mile jog across open farmland to their target. The heavy-clouded, wet night made the ground damp and hard going, but on the positive side, that gave them the cover of almost complete darkness. It would be nearly impossible for anyone to notice them unless they were actually looking for them. Jake shook his head clear of such thoughts, negativity being an operative's worst enemy against a mission's success.

Jake checked his watch again as he and Clarkson hit the ground and began to crawl towards a hedge of obviously manicured trees. 'Under twenty minutes from drop off', he thought. 'We're making good time.'

They were under the thinly-branched base of the trees, at the edge of a closely cut lawn, when Clarkson raised his clenched fist. Jake stopped. Clarkson placed a flat hand up to shade his eyes. Both operatives pulled the night vision goggles from the top of their backpacks and slipped them on. The dark featureless shadows of the night were washed away as the scene before them was made clear, bathed with a watery green tint.

Fifty metres from where he and Clarkson lay, across the open aspect of the lawn, stood an old Tudor house. Apart from the distorted colours the goggles offered, it was exactly as the pictures he'd been shown in the briefing room. Huge beams, buckled roof and leaded windows bowing with age. Jake couldn't help but think of the Headmaster staring out of his own precious leaded window at St. Margaret's.

Jake felt a tap on his shoulder and saw Clarkson pointing an insistent finger in the direction of the right-hand side of the house. He followed the direction of the finger and noticed a large area penned off with high wire fencing. 'Dogs,' thought Jake. 'Big ones too, judging by the size of their run.' Jake nodded at Clarkson to let him know he had seen the problem.

Clarkson paused for a moment, as if thinking through the situation.

'Skirt round the lawn with the hedge to our backs,' Jake tried to will into Clarkson's mind. 'Approach the pen from the blind side.'

Clarkson came to a decision and signalled with his hands exactly what Jake had been thinking.

With a crouching run, they moved to approach the dog pen from behind. 'Well done, numb nuts,' smirked Jake to himself. 'You'll make a half, well quarter, decent operative some day...maybe.'

Going to ground again as they reached the back of the cage, Jake could see a bulky dog asleep by the fence and another nearer the centre of the pen which, although also asleep, appeared more restless. He knew that dogs had been credited with the ability to dream, but he couldn't dismiss the possibility that the dog may have heard, or sensed, their presence in his domain and was waking up to protect it. The last thing they needed was agitated barking breaking the silence of the night.

He looked to Clarkson, who drew his hand across his

throat and although Jake couldn't see it under his ski mask he just knew the bully's face would be filled with psychotic joy. Jake clasped his hands as if praying then tilted his head onto them to indicate sleep, but Clarkson had made his twisted mind up. He tugged his sleeve back to reveal the wrist gun he was wearing.

The wrist gun was one of Jake's favourite pieces of kit the Academy had to offer. It was totally concealed by the sleeve, constructed from ceramics and rubber which not only made it durable but also invisible to any metal detector. Although quick to use, it was only accurate over very short distances. A thick rubber strap wrapped around the wrist while a small ceramic chamber and magazine sat neatly on the underside. Its functional parts were almost completely concealed, even when no sleeve was covering it. The gas propellant made it recoilless and silent in operation for each of its six-shot magazines. It was a basic point-and-fire weapon, but it required the use of two hands to discharge. The forefinger and thumb of the opposing hand had to be applied to two safety catches, one on either side of the gun. Then a quick snap of the wrist backwards released the dart. This overly complex method was employed to prevent accidental firing, but had the disadvantage of making the wrist gun very difficult to use on the move. Two types of dart could be fitted into the magazine. A white one, which caused instant unconsciousness and a black one, emblazoned with a small skull by a sick designer. This was known as 'the Terminator' for obvious reasons. Once released, the dart, made from a highly volatile substance, would last ten seconds in contact with the air before decomposing. Only an almost untraceable residue would be left on the target and a slight swelling where the hair thin dart had pierced the skin.

Unfortunately, for this mission the Headmaster had deemed Jake sufficiently untrustworthy to be issued with a wrist gun. In contrast, and much to Jake's annoyance, Clarkson had obviously been cleared to carry one.

Jake shook his head in disgust as Clarkson crawled up close to the mesh of the dogs' pen and fired at the nearest dog. It had been sleeping already so it made no movement but the second, more restless, dog raised its head as it heard the dart being spat from the gun. Clarkson took aim again. Gripping the safety releases, he flicked his wrist sharply back, there was another spit of gas and the second dog's head fell heavily back to the floor of the pen.

Clarkson raised himself to a crouch and beckoned Jake to join him. Jake scuttled forward and sneered with contempt under his mask as he saw the two black darts, one stuck in the neck of each dog, fizz and then disintegrate. He had the sneaking suspicion that there were many spiders minus limbs courtesy of Clarkson's warped thinking. If there was any justice in the world Jake could imagine, with some pleasure, arachnid and canine revenge being played out one day.

Half sprinting, half crouching, the operatives made their way to the rear of the house until they stood underneath the bright yellow alarm box that nestled high up on the wall just below the thatched roof. Clarkson indicated his intention to climb up to tackle the box and ordered Jake to keep a watchful eye out. Jake managed a slight nod, far from pleased with his role of understudy, which was doing little to help his confidence.

As Clarkson scaled the height, Jake watched with undisguised contempt etched on his face. The large figure lumbered from a first floor window ledge onto an iron drainpipe, which he dragged himself up in an ungainly fashion before struggling to haul his bulk onto the eaves of the roof. Jake half expected, half wished, Clarkson would wobble uncontrollably before plummeting back to earth. It was a strange feeling to watch another operative working in the field, doing what he felt he should be doing himself. Up until tonight Jake had always worked alone and now he found himself the unhappy junior in an enforced partnership. 'I'd have done it quicker,' he thought sulkily.

Jake pulled his eyes from Clarkson, as the inept gymnast hung himself over the lip of the roof to begin work on the alarm box, and concentrated on checking the perimeter for any signs of movement. Intelligence had stated that the property would be empty for at least two nights and by the look of things around the area, the information was right. The whole place, the building, the grounds, gave Jake the feeling of a graveyard, 'Especially there,' he thought, as his gaze swept past the dogs' pen. Jake had learned long ago to trust his gut feeling on missions. He felt like he had some kind of internal survival mechanism that watched his back all the time and tonight there were no blips on his instinct radar.

Boots scuffing against the wall brought Jake's attention back to Clarkson as he made his descent. Jake had to admit he'd made good time disabling the alarm. He only hoped he'd done it properly. The trick was to bypass the circuit board in the alarm system at exactly the right point, removing the need to cut any wires, to override the siren, any flashing lights and finally the all important link to the police station. In a few seconds Jake would know if his begrudged admiration for Clarkson's speed was misplaced or not.

Back at ground level, Clarkson indicated a window that was over a firm grassed area, flower beds being too easy to leave careless footprints in. He signalled for Jake to sort out their access point. Jake made quick work of the old window, easily slipping a thin blade between the frame and the casing which had warped over many years of weathering. Lifting the latch, he smiled to himself; 'Now that's slick, Clarkson.' The window swung open and the alarm stayed mute and lifeless. Clarkson had sorted the job properly and Jake almost felt disappointed. He raised a foot onto the window ledge, but was stopped as Clarkson grabbed his shoulder and indicated he would go in first. Jake stepped back out of the way without protest. Clarkson was determined to milk this temporary position of power for all it was worth.

Once inside the room, Jake's night goggles picked out the painting they were after. Ironically, it depicted the scene of a highwayman robbing a stagecoach full of helpless victims. Jake looked to Clarkson who stood by the room's only door. He gestured at Jake an order to proceed with this part of the operation. 'Watch it, fat boy,' thought Jake, 'you're missing out on some of the glory here.' He found the catch and the painting swung away from the wall like a cupboard door to reveal a sunken safe.

Jake reached into his backpack, removed the small x-ray screen and placed it against the grey steel door. He watched the tumblers of the lock fall into place one after the other as he turned the numbered dial carefully to the left and right. When he was done, he pulled on the handle with a satisfying clunk.

'Strange,' thought Jake, picking up a large bundle of cash with his right hand and several cases that were obviously jewellery boxes with his left. 'This isn't right. The briefing detailed blueprints for an electronic bugging device.' He turned to show Clarkson the items he'd found in the safe but as he did so his eyes burned with pain as blinding light flooded through his night vision goggles. Someone had turned the light on in the room. Jake dropped the loot and ripped the goggles off his face in an attempt to stop what felt like hot sand being blasted into his eyeballs.

Tears streamed down his face as Jake tried to focus on anything that might give him a clue as to what was going on. He was as good as blind and in a situation like this that could mean caught…or worse. Then he heard it, the telltale click of a wrist gun's safety catches being pressed into the primed position and a dart being selected.

Jake recovered enough blurry vision in time to see the unmasked face of Clarkson grinning like a lunatic, both arms levelled directly at him. 'I've got to…' was as far as Jake's thoughts took him before he heard the spit of compressed gas, felt the sting of a point in his neck and fell like a stone through water into a complete and cold darkness.

YOU'RE NICKED SONNY

Jake came round in the not unfamiliar setting of a police holding cell. Before being recruited into St. Margaret's he had spent several nights as a guest at Her Majesty's Hotel and he had to admit since that time, the facilities had not improved much. There was still no MTV and the beds were of the comfort level usually associated with a pool table, with the balls still on it.

The inside of his skull ached from the effects of the wrist gun dart and, touching his neck, he could just make out the raised entry wound. Moving his hand up his face he winced as he touched his cheekbone. 'Must have hit something when I collapsed,' he assumed. 'That or Clarkson got some easy revenge while I was out of it.'

Swinging his legs onto the floor, he gingerly stood up and swayed unsteadily. He was not one hundred per cent recovered from the drug; however, a chemical hangover was the least of his problems. His backpack was missing and a quick check of his covert operations suit told him that what little equipment he had been issued with had gone too. 'If the coppers have got that, I'm going to have some really awkward questions to answer.'

Before Jake could even begin to think through the events of the previous night, the cell door opened and a large policeman entered the sterile, white tiled environment.

"Good Morning, Sleeping Beauty," he growled, puffing out his enormous chest like an ape does, to prove he is the alpha male in the group.

Jake couldn't help but grin at this primitive display of dominance.

"Does that make you Buttons then? Or maybe you're the Dame?" said Jake, taking great delight in seeing the copper's top lip curl in anger. "No, I know," smiled Jake broadly. "You're the back end of the ass."

A vein on the constable's neck stood out so far it looked like it was going to rip through the collar of his white shirt. He took a step toward Jake, his right hand itching to form a fist, but at the last second he paused and a weak smile crept slowly onto his face.

"Keep it up, Sonny," hissed the constable. "Sarge enjoys a good story." He grabbed Jake roughly by the upper arm and marched him out of the cell.

Jake, keeping his neck loose as he was forced along the corridor, let his head appear to be bobbing in a randomly arrogant way, but his eyes devoured every piece of information his brain could absorb. Positions of doors, especially fire exits; the amount of staff, civilian and police, and where they were stationed; fire alarms, windows, light switches, everything that he may need to know in a hurry. As they passed a toilet, the door to which had been opened by a WPC returning to work, Jake managed to catch a glimpse of his face in a mirror. 'No wonder my face aches,' he thought, wincing. 'That's one hell of a bruise.' He also noticed, in the split second view of the toilets, that a window above the sinks was slightly open. Whether it was jammed in that position or would open further to allow escape he couldn't tell.

"In here," barked the constable, opening a door marked as 'Interview Room One' and shoving Jake in before him. "Sit down..." Jake opened his mouth to speak but the policeman wasn't in the mood for any more banter, "...and shut up. The Sergeant will be in soon."

"Could I have a drin—" began Jake, taking a seat, but the constable cut off his request by slamming the door.

'It looks like the staff are still as unhelpful as the last time I stayed in this hotel chain,' thought Jake with a grin that faded quickly as the movement made his wounded cheek sting.

Like cells, Jake was familiar with police station interview rooms. One desk, four chairs – two on each side of the desk, plain walls, ceiling the same except for one strip light, a solid door with a square of reinforced glass in the upper third for viewing the room's occupant through and a tape recorder, used during interviews or, if the coppers got their way, confessions.

"Everything in order," muttered Jake to himself, a little disappointed he hadn't found something a bit more out of the ordinary, a bit more helpful to his situation. His quick recce merely confirmed something he already knew. He had little chance of escaping from this windowless room. He needed to be in the main body of the police station where he had pinpointed several weaknesses waiting to be exploited.

A key slid into the lock and the door was opened by a tall, thin, middle-aged man. He had lost his hair from the centre and front of his head, but was making up for it with a thick moustache.

"Your wig's slipped," said Jake, touching the top of his own lip as the uniformed officer took a seat opposite him.

The sergeant looked at Jake and pinched his moustache between forefinger and thumb. "My God, so it has," he gasped sarcastically. "I hope no one else has noticed; I'll be the laughing stock of the force."

Jake grinned. This bloke wasn't going to be as easy to faze as the Constable. He was the experienced type; a man who had seen far too much of the bad things in life to be wound up by some kid with an attitude problem. He was here to do his job, clock off and go home to forget all about it until the next shift.

"My name is Sergeant Regard and I reckon a sensible kid like you wants to get this mess cleared up and be on your way as soon as possible, am I right?"

"Funnily enough," replied Jake, "I was just thinking the exact same thing myself."

"Great," smiled Regard warmly. "That's what I like, an easy day at the office. We'll start informally; can't stand the annoying hiss of the tape machine in the background. Then we can record your story, get it typed up, you sign it and we're done."

Jake sat silent and still.

"I'll take that as a maybe, shall I?" offered Regard, less than hopefully, as he saw his 'easy day at the office' take a nose dive off the top of a mountain of trouble. "How about we start with your name?"

Jake stared into the policeman's eyes. 'Chaos,' he thought to himself as he settled into his interrogation stance. From now on, no more chat, no more jokes, no more anything. They would have to get cutting gear to remove the mental weld he'd placed upon his lips.

Regard let the silence hang for a minute or two, hoping that the suspect would fill the empty void with something. "We could take prints," he said eventually. "No doubt you'll show up on our records; I have a feeling this isn't your debut at this kind of thing."

Jake leant back in his chair and rolled his head as if removing tension from his neck. He shot a quick glance at his hands under the desk. There were traces of ink, only slight traces as if they had been cleaned while he was out of it, but they were there.

Jake returned Regard's gaze. 'You've done that already, Copper,' he thought, almost daring the policeman to pick up his thoughts telepathically. 'And you still don't know who I am.' Jake could tell Regard was playing games with him, seeing if he would crack and tell his tale.

"Okay," sighed Regard, leaning back in his chair to mirror Jake's casual pose. "Maybe I should tell you what happened last night and I don't mind if you correct me or not, we've got plenty of evidence to get a conviction. You were caught so red-handed you're crimson up to the shoulders."

Jake said nothing but could feel his skin temperature rise. Whatever bull this man decided to spin, he could make it stick like snot to a jumper. Jake had no defence to offer at all and he couldn't tell the truth, because he didn't know it fully himself. After Clarkson had shot him with the wrist gun, the only fact he knew was that he had come round in a police cell. End of story.

"Last night," began Regard, "you decided it would be a jolly little prank to break into Sir Alminson's country residence and make off with his considerable stash of goodies. You got lucky too; the place was empty and apart from the dogs, which we will come back to later..." he paused to exercise a look of distaste at Jake, "...you had the run of the place to yourself. How am I doing so far?"

Jake offered nothing more than a deliberately slow blink in reply.

"So, off you trot to the back of the house and, armed with your trusty crowbar, you split open a window. A grade one listed window, by the way, and drop yourself into a piece of stunning British Heritage." Sergeant Regard leant forwards, his folded arms resting on the desk between him and Jake. "Except you didn't, did you? Instead, you catch your foot, or your tracksuit leg or something, and tumble in, smacking your head on the desk as a finale to your stunning acrobatic act. Then, and I like this bit, a couple of boys in blue doing their duty, despite what the media likes to say, show up on a routine check and while they're on their patrol around the property what should they find but you snoozing peacefully on Sir Alminson's carpet. And so we come to the final chapter where you find yourself in a cell and I've got a bestseller on my hands."

Jake kept his face immobile but inside his mind was running faster than a gazelle with a cheetah on its heels. The copper's story was all wrong. But Jake had a feeling it all sounded right too. The fact that Clarkson had darted him was proof of that. Setting him up for a fall as the police unexpectedly showed up would have been the easiest thing in the world to do while he lay unconscious.

"Couple of things I don't get, though," said Regard. "Why kill the dogs? I'm sure Sir Alminson wouldn't miss the odd grand, probably do him some good to get in touch with the common people at some level, but the dogs were penned up; they couldn't get to you, so why kill them? Poisoned meat a bit of a laugh with you is it? Speaking personally I hope you get more for that than the breaking and entering and I will be doing my best to see that you do." Regard let that sit with Jake for a second before speaking again. "And the other thing I don't like about this; I don't think you were working alone."

Jake swallowed, and couldn't help thinking of Clarkson.

"All that way out in the back of beyond on your own? I don't think so. I reckon you were, if you'll excuse the pun, the fall guy. Little Oliver Twist sent in to do big bad Bill Sykes' work," Regard smiled, pleased with his own powers of deduction and the literary link. "Once the blue lights and sirens started, he was off like a shot leaving you sparked out to take the rap for you and him both."

Jake squirmed inside. Regard's tale was way off the mark but the fact was that Clarkson had taken him down easily as if he'd planned it all along, but for what reason? 'Petty revenge is possible,' thought Jake. 'But in the middle of a mission? That's dense even for Clarkson.' His mind threw up another question; why had the safe been full of cash and jewellery? It was the kind of thing Jake expected people like Sir Alminson to hide from the taxman, but he had been sent in to copy plans for a surveillance device. The whole mission was clearly beginning to look like a setup from the start and there was only one person Jake could think of who had the power to arrange something like that...

A loud, single knock on the door disturbed Jake's worried wanderings and the Constable put his substantial head round the door. "Excuse me, Sarge, there's a bloke here to see you regarding the suspect."

"Can't he wait ten minutes, Constable?"

The door was barged open, making the large constable stumble aside.

"No, he can't," said a man in a suit, bursting into the room like he owned the whole place. "This is a matter of the utmost importance." He stared coldly at Regard. "Not that I would expect a village bobby to understand such things. I have the paperwork from your superiors explaining everything." The man held out an A4 manila envelope.

For a second, a flare of defiance shone in Regard's eyes. He accepted the envelope without looking at it, but the realisation that his easy day at the office was back on, courtesy of this intruder willing to take over his problem, soon quashed any desire to stand his ground. He forced a smile so broad that it almost lifted his ample moustache to touch his ears. "Right you are, sir, I'll leave him in your capable hands then."

The man in the suit nodded but said nothing more until the two uniformed men had left the room. He dropped his briefcase onto the desk and opened it. "Bit of a bad do this, isn't it, Highfield?"

It was only at the mention of his name that Jake studied the man and a memory from years back came to him.

"I believe your combat skills have improved somewhat since we last met," said Packard. "So I would really appreciate it if you didn't take a swing at me this time."

"Somewhat," admitted Jake, "and I will resist the temptation," he added with a smile.

"Good," said Packard, taking the tapes out of the recorder on the desk and tossing them into his briefcase. "Let's go then, Highfield."

Jake rose from his seat.

Packard closed his briefcase and turned towards the door before suddenly stopping. He put his hand into his jacket pocket and tossed what he had pulled out to Jake. "Put them on would you, got to keep up appearances and all that."

Jake caught the handcuffs and slipping them over his wrists clicked them into place.

"Nice and tight mind, can't let the officers think you're being busted out of jail." Then, with a wink, he opened the door and he and Jake walked calmly out of Interview Room One.

TAKE DOWN

Jake and Packard travelled several miles in silence, the only sound the purr of the Mercedes' engine in the background. Jake was dying to ask a whole list of questions, most of them about his previous night's misadventure, but he felt awkward bringing up a subject that would inevitably draw attention to mistakes on his part.

"Nice car," said Jake, finally breaking the ice.

"Not bad, I suppose," Packard admitted with a shrug. "But my wheels in Milan are really something else."

"Top of the range Beemer?" asked Jake.

"In Italy? Ferrari, of course."

Jake's mouth opened to form the next question.

"Red, before you ask," added Packard knowingly, with a broad smile.

Jake let a few seconds' silence pass as he built up the nerve to plunge head first into the next icy conversation piece. "It was Clarkson who took me down."

Packard nodded. "We know; wheels are in motion as we speak."

He indicated right and swung the car so quickly across the junction that the tyres gave a short squeal of protest. "Don't worry, we're good at sorting things like this out;

your 'get out of jail free' for example."

"Yeah," nodded Jake, "thanks for that."

"No problem, Highfield, just doing my job," said Packard, accelerating hard to beat a set of changing traffic lights.

"What exactly is your job?"

Packard took his eyes off the road to shoot Jake an emotionless, almost reptilian look. "If I tell you," he said slowly, "I will have to kill you."

Jake had a feeling Packard was joking but a cold grip tightened in his stomach nonetheless.

Packard withdrew his stare and suddenly laughed energetically, rolling a victorious drumbeat on the steering wheel with his open palms. "I never thought I'd get to say that to anyone; it felt great. Do you reckon I've got a career in the film industry when I'm too old for all this nonsense?"

Jake didn't reply, he just chuckled quietly and hoped Packard hadn't seen him swallow down a second or two of doubt.

"As we're playing truth or dare, I'm what you might call a caretaker. Not my official title, of course, but basically when anything goes wrong, I come along and take care of things," Packard's voice trailed off into whisper as he concentrated, taking another corner at speed.

"I see…" said Jake slowly, unable to stop himself thinking that 'things' probably included people.

"Take your recent escapade," said Packard, waving his left hand in the air.

"I told you," protested Jake, "Clarkson went mental."

"No, not that recent, the one when you gave the guard a beating."

"Oh," was all Jake could muster in reply, still ashamed of his conduct that night.

"Terrible cock-up that one, people running all over and under and up the place; trail as wide as the M1 pointing straight at the Academy. Gave me a few sleepless nights that mess, I can tell you."

Jake opened his mouth to apologise but even before it reached his throat, the word 'sorry' just didn't seem to cover it.

"Got it sorted though, mostly. One or two loose ends to tie off but once that's done, happy days are here again."

Jake felt uncomfortable at his mistake being brought up so easily in conversation. He was still having trouble swallowing his pride with that particularly sour meal, whether the 'caretaker' had taken care of it or not. For a while he sat in silence looking out at the countryside as it passed by the passenger window.

"Don't worry about it, Jake," said Packard, seemingly picking up on Jake's thoughts. "Even the best make mistakes now and then; it would be unnatural if you didn't." Packard paused for a second as he overtook a dawdling tractor. "I imagine the Headmaster is giving you a hard time at the moment but that's just his way; he'll get over it soon enough. If it was up to me, Jake, if I had the power, I'd have seen it as a little career hiccup, nothing more. There's no way I would let such a talented operative like you go to waste; you've got the ability to be the best," he smiled broadly. "Present company excepted of course."

Jake smiled weakly. Despite the compliments Packard was showering on him, he didn't feel like 'the best'; two missions, two cock-ups. He shifted in his seat, the handcuffs biting into his wrists. "Can I take these things off now?"

Packard looked at the cuffs. "Best not, Highfield. I always think a disguise is best left on until you're totally sure you don't need it any more." He accelerated across a four-way junction without bothering to slow down and check that it was clear. "I understand, you know, Highfield. You're desperate to get back in the fray. Prove your worth. Show them what a class act you are. All field operatives are the same at the Academy, desperate to get back in the action. Believe me, I know what you're feeling."

"You were at St. Margaret's?" asked Jake.

"Don't sound so surprised!" smirked Packard. "Loved nothing more than disappearing into the night to run about in the shadows and come home loaded with goodies. Best days of my life. I'd go back tomorrow if I could…I would miss the cars though." Packard swung the Mercedes into a small, obviously ill-maintained B-road that ran alongside a forest. "Slight detour. My bladder was stronger in those days."

Jake was buffeted around in his seat as the expensive car made hard work of the rough road. He couldn't help thinking what abuse the Ferrari in Milan suffered at the hands of Packard.

Packard turned again, this time up a forestry track that led into the heart of the trees themselves. Jake's gut nudged at him. 'Why didn't he take a leak back there by the road? There's no one around to see.'

Jake was getting edgy. This wasn't right and thoughts of his recent experience with Clarkson did not help him to feel any more confident. "I need a burst too," he said, "so you'll have to take the cuffs off."

Packard didn't reply and kept his eyes dead ahead on

the narrow road as branches scratched at the expensive car's paintwork, then he turned left into a crudely cut out passing point used by the loggers' trucks.

"Won't be a second, Highfield," he said as he turned the engine off and opened the door to get out.

Jake's instincts went into overdrive, screaming out to him that something was drastically wrong with this situation. 'Why here? Why here?' His eyes began to take in details; the spacing between the trees; the dips and drops in the terrain; the glint of the door handle. Jake's mind was going into survival-in-the-field mode like it had never done before. Everything was precise and clear.

As Packard was climbing out of the car, his suit jacket fell open and Jake saw the shoulder holster. His mind required no more data and it ordered his body to flee. Jake grabbed at the handle and thrust the door open, instantly rolling himself across the ground and onto his feet, sprinting into the cover offered by the trees. Jake's only hope was to put distance between him and Packard. All the questions that wanted to rush into his head to be answered would have to wait.

As he ran, Jake could hear Packard laughing loudly and obviously for his benefit. "Good man, Highfield. I thought you'd make it interesting; can't stand having things too easy. No fun in that at all."

Jake ignored the taunting and continued to run. Not being able to pump his arms because of the handcuffs was limiting his speed and balance and he crashed through the branches of the trees and dead wood on the floor like an elephant. A deaf man would have been able to follow his noisy escape attempt. He made the decision to hit cover and hide as soon as possible and luckily a tree, felled by high winds, offered its bowl of roots to him. With panic running through his system, he dropped to the ground, scooping dust, dirt and rotting foliage over himself as best he could with his pinioned hands. Then he held his breath and froze.

In the still of the forest, Packard's mocking voice carried easily to Jake's ears. "…ninety-nine…one hundred! Coming, ready or not!" Then there followed silence. Complete and utter silence. Jake was terrified. He tried to control his breathing but his lungs demanded air and took it in noisy stuttering rasps, however hard he tried to quieten them. Packard had told him he had been an operative once, so to his trained ears it would be like banging a drum.

There was a quick, dull 'thunk' next to Jake's head as a bullet caused a section of unearthed dead root to explode. "Bugger, missed," cursed Packard, loudly, with obvious enjoyment. "Must be longer than I thought since I was last at the firing range."

Jake was up and running again. Unarmed and disabled by the handcuffs, the only logical plan was to try and find cover and lay low again. He needed to shake Packard off his trail; hide and move out as soon as Packard passed by. Jake could just about hear the footfalls of his pursuer over his own clumsy flight. He dived onto his belly and snaked forward until he was lying as still as a corpse under an umbrella of wide fern leaves. Seconds later the ground just to the left of his head jumped up in an errupting ball of dust.

"Hey, Highfield," called Packard, "I have to inform you this situation is a little unfair."

Jake ignored the voice and rolled back onto his feet,

sprinting headlong, deeper into the trees.

"I know what you're trying to do and you're not wrong. Go to ground and wait for me to bumble past like a preoccupied rambler and then double back and you're away."

'Screw you,' thought Jake, attempting to muster mental defiance to take his mind off his aching legs.

"Only thing is," added Packard, "I'm afraid you're tagged. Not very fair, I know, but that's the way of things in life."

Jake's shock at this news split his concentration and his foot caught an exposed tree root, cannoning him face first into the ground, his restricted hands unable to cushion his fall. The skin on his forehead scuffed and stung as the dirt on the forest floor ground into his flesh.

Jake cursed silently. He could run as far as he liked and dig three metres down. Packard would still be able to find him as easily as if he was singing Karaoke under a spotlight. He looked at the cuffs on his wrists; no wonder Packard had been so insistent about him wearing them and not taking them off. While he was stuck in these things he didn't have a chance.

"Tell you what, Highfield," shouted Packard, even closer than before. "Let's make this game more interesting. Remember how you wanted to kick my kidneys out through my head a few years back? Do you fancy having another go?"

Jake spat out a mouthful of leaves. He had nothing to lose and he wasn't going quietly. "Yeah, right," replied Jake into the air, unable to see where Packard was through the dense trees. "Even with my hands cuffed, it still wouldn't be fair me picking on an old fart like you!"

"Oh, I don't know," cried Packard. "I'll take my chances."

Jake was listening carefully, not to the words – he knew they were worthless – but to the direction they came from. He was one hundred per cent sure that as soon as he showed himself to Packard it would be open season and he would be shot dead without a second thought. "Don't forget, I'm a trained operative now, not some wound up kid with an attitude."

Packard laughed. "Don't fool yourself, Highfield. That's all you'll ever be. But don't worry," he added, "that won't be for too much longer now."

Jake pinpointed the voice; it was coming from his left. Jumping to his feet, he sprinted across the path of where he had targeted Packard to be. He was rewarded by the sound of another shot whistling past him. "Come on then," he called out, lifting his feet high to avoid any more treacherous roots. "Keep up!" If he could keep Packard running, he had a chance for his plan to work.

Packard took the bait and gave chase. "You could have had it easy," he shouted, quickly shortening the distance between him and Jake. "But now I think I'll have to teach you a lesson in respecting your betters."

Jake had what he wanted, Packard bearing down on him. Verbal exchanges played no more part in his scheme. Just as he thought, the man in the suit could still run like the wind. Packard was gaining.

Packard saw Jake veer off the path and collide with a branch, "Got you now you little—"

Jake ran full tilt into the low hanging branch that was as thick as his leg, forcing his weight against it as hard as he could until he folded over it, his stomach muscles burning with the strain. Then, he relaxed. By the time Packard saw what was happening he was too committed to the chase to stop.

Jake was hurled backwards by the protesting branch and driven full force into the advancing Packard. A flash of pain erupted in Jake's head as the back of his skull was driven into Packard's face with the considerable force of their two body weights accelerating in completely opposite directions.

Jake rocked from side to side on the forest floor for a few seconds, totally absorbed by the pain in his head. It felt like it was about to implode. If his plan hadn't worked, he would be an easy target for Packard but there was no 'spit' from a silenced gun barrel.

Jake forced himself to struggle to his knees. He reached up to the back of his head with his bound hands and tugged out a piece of broken tooth from his scalp. Once removed, it unplugged a steady flow of blood. A metre to his right, Packard lay unmoving, his jaw hanging at a weird angle, obviously broken. Splinters of teeth, tipped with blood, were scattered around his head on the fallen leaves. They looked like stubborn snowflakes resisting a thaw.

Jake breathed out deeply, scanning the trees that surrounded him. At that moment, with all that had happened to him recently, he couldn't convince himself that they weren't plotting to turn their branches against him, too.

THE PRODIGAL RETURNS

A quick search of Packard's pockets gave up the key to the cuffs binding Jake's hands. Once released, his relief at having his wrists free again almost caused him to hurl the cuffs deep into the trees. However, he paused, realising he could use them against their owner. Packard's hands were obviously a deadly threat, but Jake reasoned it would be safer to bind his legs and thus immobilise the man, giving him the option of a quick retreat from any danger. Lifting up Packard's trouser legs, Jake clicked the cuffs in place around the man's ankles, making sure that they sat tight against the bone.

He spent the next few minutes trying to locate the handgun Packard had used against him, without success. It could have been anywhere in the tangle of exposed tree-roots, fallen leaves and knee-high ferns. His aching head did not thank him for being kept lowered during the search either. Blood pounded in his temples.

Even though Packard was down, out and quite badly injured, Jake could not afford to take any chances; from recent experience his life could, and did, depend on being thorough. Crouching at the side of the unmoving Packard, Jake searched him and discovered he was armed with a wrist gun. 'Old habits die hard,' he assumed as he unclipped the weapon and slipped it into his pocket. He removed the man's tie, belt and shoes, also emptying the contents of his pockets onto the forest floor. He had to assume that Packard could probably turn most things into a weapon and Jake had no desire to prove himself right on this point.

Dragging Packard across the thick carpet of leaves that padded the forest floor was exhausting work, but Jake wanted to keep his enemy close. Better to know his whereabouts for sure than leave him to possibly come round and disappear or worse still try to continue from where he'd left off. After a great deal of exertion, sweat and protest from his wounded head, he dropped the limp body next to the Mercedes.

At the car, Jake found the keys to the unlocked vehicle in the ignition; obviously Packard had been supremely confident in his ability to neutralize Jake with ease and return to the Mercedes for a casual getaway. He removed the keys from the ignition and opened the boot.

Inside there was nothing to suggest the car was owned by anyone other than an ordinary citizen. A suit in a transparent plastic cover sat next to the usual clutter of road maps, factory supplied tool kit, spare bulbs and fuses which could be found in the boot of any number of vehicles on the road. No weapons. No hi-tech gadgetry. A quick rummage through the normal contents was all Jake needed to find what he was looking for.

With the cable ties he had taken from the Mercedes' toolkit, he secured Packard's wrists to his cuffed ankles. He attached left to right and right to left, then, just to be on the ultra-safe side he linked them all together with a third and fourth cable tie, pulling each until he could not get another click from the plastic bonds. When he had finished, Packard looked like an Olympic diver who had been frozen halfway between the board and the water in a less than perfect half-pike position.

Returning to the boot, he began to strip it bare. He turfed the contents out into an untidy pile. Everything that was loose was pulled free, right down to the carpet and spare wheel. Minus the extras, the boot was nothing more than a cold metal box with a large, round dip in its centre. "The height of comfort," Jake grinned to himself. "Just what he deserves." He felt less like joking when he discovered trying to get a man, trussed like a Christmas turkey, into the boot of a car was no easy job. Eventually, with some more sweat and cursing, he managed to get the passenger settled into his first class accommodation. Using two more cable ties, he attached Packard to the lug used to secure the spare wheel. Then slammed the lid closed, tugging on it a few times to make sure it was well and truly shut.

Jake sat down heavily and leaned his back against the wheel arch of the car. With the immediate danger over, he could sense the aching tiredness in his limbs and his thoughts turned to his next course of action as he looked into the trees that faced him.

The loud 'caw' from a crow high up in the branches jolted Jake awake. His eyes struggled to focus on anything as his heavy eyelids opened and closed slowly, demanding he surrender to sleep again. It was still light, but the onset of dusk was already melting the trees' shadows into one dark blanket on the floor.

Jake jumped to his feet and shot a glance at the car's

boot. It was still closed tight. He stretched his arms wide and yawned with a creaking sigh, feeling the last numbness of sleep leaving his body. Falling asleep 'on duty' was an unforgivable mistake, but at least he felt sharper. His mind was clearer and as his eyes fell on the abandoned suit in its see-through carrier. A plan of action formed.

The shirt and jacket were obviously too big for him, but his covert operations suit, with its many pockets and loose fit design to allow free movement, helped bulk them out a bit. The simple disguise would probably do the job if he attracted any casual glances whilst driving. A young boy in such an expensive car would stick out like a beacon, but a young man dressed in a jacket and tie would register as 'respectable' enough for him to be ignored by most people. 'Or at least I hope that's how it works,' thought Jake, using the wing mirror to adjust his tie. He finished with a wink of good luck to himself.

As the sun finally set, adding the all-important cover of darkness to his disguise, Jake turned the key in the ignition and prepared to leave the seclusion of the Forestry Commission land. He ignored the car's audible warning for him to put his seatbelt on as he programmed a route to St. Margaret's into the sat-nav, selecting minor roads as much as possible. He would have loved to cruise about in a car like this, showing off to turn heads, but tonight he needed to be as invisible as possible. With a final tap on the button, the route was set and the insistent nagging voice from the dashboard fell silent as Jake put his seat belt on. He selected 'D' on the automatic gearbox and drove off. His head was feeling clearer, which was just as well because he had a long and careful drive ahead of him. He couldn't wait to see the grateful expression on the Headmaster's face as he handed over Packard. A smile crept along his mouth as he played over in his mind how he was going to be instantly rewritten back into the Headmaster's good books. All memories of his recent mistakes erased for good.

*

The familiar silhouette of St. Margaret's loomed out of the darkness as he broke free of the forest surrounding the Academy. Hints of its many windows sparkled with moonlight. Ordinarily, Jake felt reassured by the strong lines of the old building when returning from a mission, the view of it signalling the end of uncertainty and the return of security. Tonight he was having trouble shaking a nervous feeling deep in the pit of his stomach, despite the fact he was returning triumphant.

Two figures were walking down the main steps of St. Margaret's towards the gravel driveway, perfectly timed to meet the car's arrival. Even in this low light level, one was wearing what was easily recognisable as a white vest.

"Good evening, Mr Highfield," said the Headmaster, as Jake pulled the car alongside the figures.

Despite Jake's best efforts to keep his calm, he couldn't help himself and leapt from the car and exploded, "What the hell is going on?"

"We have had a few problems," said the Headmaster.

"I kind of gathered that. I've got one of them in the boot."

As if on cue, there was a dull thumping noise from the car's boot that caught both men's attention.

Jake walked round to the rear of the car, joined by the two men, where all three stood staring at the boot of the

Mercedes for a few moments. "He started doing that about five miles back," Jake said, breaking the silence.

"Are you ready, Mr Routledge?" asked the Headmaster in a calm voice.

"Sah," growled Routledge menacingly, rolling his broad shoulders round like an eager boxer about to start a new round.

"Mr Highfield," beckoned the Headmaster with a twitching finger. "If you would be so kind as to open the boot then step back. Mr Routledge will take it from there."

Jake approached the boot and inserted the key. He looked at Routledge, who gave him a nod of readiness.

Packard had been waiting. Even though he was still bound wrists to ankles he had somehow managed to detach himself from being anchored to the car. With an effort of athleticism, he managed to roll up and out of the boot to land heavily on the ground with a splash of gravel. He turned his face to the Headmaster and Jake noticed the wounded man desperately trying to move his broken jaw, trying to talk, but only able to make meaningless gurgles. Even as Packard's voice failed him, it was easy for Jake to see the pleading desperation in the man's eyes.

"You know what to do, Mr Routledge," said the Headmaster, eventually.

"Yes, Sah."

Routledge, with little effort, soon had Packard over his shoulders in a fireman's lift and was walking briskly across the grounds away from the main entrance. Wherever Packard was being taken, Jake could tell by the direction he was going in, it sure wasn't for medical attention at the infirmary.

"So, Mr Highfield," said the Headmaster. "Getting into a few scrapes lately, are we not?"

"Yes, sir," replied Jake, doing nothing to disguise the concern on his face. And then, before the Headmaster could utter another word, all the questions Jake had been holding back erupted. "What's going on, sir? Why did Packard try to kill me? Is he working with Clarkson?"

"Where would we be without the impatient, inquisitive mind of youth?" said the Headmaster calmly.

"Still waiting for the answers?" said Jake pointedly.

The Headmaster looked at his watch. "Not long before you are up again, Mr Highfield. I suggest you get some sleep." He tucked his hands behind his back, turned and walked up the main entrance steps.

"But sir—" Jake started, but the old door was already closing behind the Headmaster. "Thanks for that, sir. That puts my mind at rest," Jake muttered bitterly.

Walking up the steps, he gingerly touched the back of his injured head and found that the wound from Packard's tooth still stung to the touch but had at least scabbed, a sure sign it was healing well enough. 'I'll get it checked tomorrow,' he half promised himself.

Jake felt strange walking alone in the empty corridor at the front of St. Margaret's. During the day this was the busiest area of the Academy with students moving between lessons, the air alive with the babble of voices. Portraits of masters from the school's previous incarnation looked down at him from their lofty heights. Their frame tops were heavy with dust, their eyes watching this lone pupil, out after dark, with great suspicion. Jake wondered what the stern-faced old men would have made of him walking through their hallowed sanctuary dressed like a scarecrow. He couldn't resist pausing under one portrait of an ex-headmaster called 'Jeremiah Cronk 1860-1865' and sneering, "What you lookin' at, Grandad?" with a crooked grin. He was pretty sure he saw the old boy's eyes widen with outrage.

At the end of the corridor at the double doors, he turned right and made his way up to the first floor. The corridor here lacked any of the pomp and ceremony of the floor below and with the loss of that diversion, Jake's fatigued body made its way with automatic reflex to the door of his room. He turned the handle and grinned at the sight of his bed; he felt he was getting more and more pleased to see it each time lately. Using the fading light from the corridor as the door closed, he limped forward and fell face first onto it.

"I'll shower tomorrow," he told himself sleepily. "Good idea," he agreed with himself and rolled onto his side only to be snatched back from the arms of sleep as something dug into his leg.

Rolling over onto his other side he slid his hand into his pocket and retrieved the wrist gun he had taken off Packard. 'I'll hand this back tomorrow too,' he thought, dropping it off the side of the bed. 'Wrist gun…shower… tomorrow,' his mind repeated sensing the onward rush of sleep once more. Jake rolled onto his back and inched himself up the bed until his head was resting on the bottom half of the pillow. His eyes began to roll up to meet the falling lids coming in the opposite direction but in the split second before they met, Jake's optic nerve rang an alarm in his brain that switched his senses back on.

On the ceiling, directly above his pillow, was a note written in luminous ink that had been activated by the darkness. Jake sighed and rolled his head from side to side on the pillow in frustration. "Why me, why me?" he muttered as the words, 'WATCH UR BACK' burned down at him in a handwritten, lurid yellow.

INFORMATION OVERLOAD

Jake hadn't slept much; he'd been too occupied watching the warning on his ceiling fade away. It had obviously been written in one of a number of specialist inks the Academy produced and used. Wondering who was warning him, and why, added another reason for his insomnia. It then seemed just as he'd managed to close his eyes, the lights in his room started their flashing alarm call welcoming him to a new day of unpredictable excitement at St. Margaret's.

Jake found his morning classes hard to follow, his mind racing over and over the same questions, his stomach adding to the fun by throwing the odd nervous somersault. But above all that there was now a new dimension to his problems too. It was obvious St. Margaret's rumour machinery was in full flow. At first Jake had assumed he was just on edge a little, which didn't surprise him considering recent events, but more and more he started to notice he was the centre of attention. Groups would huddle closer and fall silent as he passed, only to begin hurried whispering as soon as they thought he was out of earshot. He could sense eyes burning into the back of his skull, yet when he turned, no one was prepared to meet his gaze. They preferred instead to turn their faces to scour the ground or suddenly notice some new fascinating detail of the Academy's roof that they had to point out to their friends.

Even Pete, when Jake jokingly asked him if he'd had any more ghost trouble, had barely managed to blurt out, "Everything's fine, Jake," before scuttling off to get as much distance between himself and Jake as possible.

By dinner time, Jake was almost looking forward to the discomfort of the canteen. At least then he could catch up with Angel and make a renewed contact with normality.

With his tray catching the food that overflowed off his plate, a meal he had little appetite to eat, Jake stood on tiptoe and searched through the heads of the seated diners. A smile twitched at his mouth as he caught sight of an elastic band straining to hold a mass of dark hair into an off-centre ponytail. As usual, Angel had her head down and was scribbling furiously at a notepad on the table.

"No dinner breaks in Geeksville, I see," said Jake, as he let his tray drop loudly onto the table.

Angel jumped, her pen scratching an unwanted line across her notes. "You stupid—" she stopped her outburst as she lifted her head and saw Jake.

Jake felt concern and fascination in equal parts as he watched the colour drain from her face. "Are you alright?" he said. "Shall I get you a plate of chips or something?" he joked, trying to lift Angel's expression without success.

"I...I..." stammered Angel, her eyes darting from left to right.

Jake sat down heavily. "Not you as well! What's going on, Angel? What is happening with everyone round here today?"

Angel was suddenly on her feet, her pen waving in

Jake's face like a rapier. "I've told you before, Highfield, leave me alone!" she bellowed. Every head in the canteen turned. "I...I...I'm not...I'm not your girlfriend, so get that into your thick head!"

Jake's mouth moved to let out a startled 'What?' But the word was hammered back down his throat by Angel's continuing outburst.

"I wouldn't be seen dead with someone as...as thick! In fact, you're thicker than this crud!" Angel punctuated her sentiments by digging her fork into her dinner and flicking it in Jake's direction.

Jake twisted his shoulders and most of the 'crud' splattered down the back of a boy seated on the table behind him, much to the hilarity of the innocent victim's friends.

Angel growled with frustration at her own failure to hit her target. "Stay away from me, Jake Highfield! Just stay away!" She snatched up her notepad and, leaving her dinner where it lay, stormed out of the canteen.

Jake could only stare at Angel's ponytail as it whipped from side to side in time with her angry marching until she slammed the canteen door behind her. All other eyes in the room stayed fixed on him. 'Okay', he thought, 'that was...interesting.' He looked about the room and, as had been the pattern of the day, one by one the faces that had been so intently nailed in his direction fell back to their plates.

Jake prodded his food with his fork and wondered what surprising joys the afternoon would hold for him. He was truly glad that his timetable didn't place him anywhere near the firing range today. Angel's dinner coming his way was one thing, bullets were another. Then, from somewhere beneath the intense unease, he felt a smile rise up and ambush his face. "Girlfriend?" he muttered to his meal. "She's lost the plot in a big way this time."

*

It was only a click, a tiny noise, but enough to snap Jake out of his frustrating dream. It had been something along the lines of him being trapped in a giant bath like a spider, struggling to get a grip on the smooth white enamel...but this was not the time for working out symbolism.

A column of light split the darkness of the room as the door was opened carefully by someone who did not wish to announce their arrival with the usual polite rituals such as knocking. Jake quietly slipped from his bed and positioned himself on the blind side of the door. Whoever was calling on him at this unsociable hour was in for more than a warm welcome.

As the figure entered the room, Jake stepped forward and threw his right arm around their neck, his forearm acting like a bar across their windpipe. Gripping the inside of his left elbow, he made a figure of four with his arms so that his left hand pushed against the back of the intruder's head. He merely had to roll his hands in opposite directions to apply a very effective choke hold.

The intruder, shocked at being touched, instinctively threw their hands up in an attempt to loosen the grip on their neck. Jake applied a little more pressure. "We can do this the easy way or we can do this the hard way," he hissed into the intruder's ear close to his mouth. "Personally speaking, I'm in the mood for the latter."

The intruder, unable to speak because of the barring arm, lowered their grasping arms and relaxed in Jake's grip. "Good," said Jake softly. "I'm quite comfortable like this myself so why don't we have a little chat before I decide to let you go or…" Jake's nose was tickled and on lifting his head up and back he noticed the thick crop of hair. "Angel?" he gasped, his shoulders dropping as he loosened the lock.

The intruder didn't need a second chance and as his grip relaxed across her throat Angel drove a thin, and very pointy, elbow into Jake's solar plexus, forcing the air from his lungs. He folded double, looking like a puppet with its strings cut.

"A fine way to greet a friend," said Angel, plonking herself down on the bed. "We can do this the easy way or the hard way, very macho."

"Friend?" gasped Jake, trying to suck down huge mouthfuls of air. "I thought I was thick?"

"And so you are," agreed Angel. "Surely you didn't think I was serious, did you? That was just some acting for the benefit of the audience in the canteen."

Jake straightened up, his breathing less laboured. "Roll out the red carpet and give the girl an Oscar." Angel smiled and Jake could tell she was secretly proud of her newly found thespian talents. She'd fooled him anyway.

"Come on, stop wasting time. I'm nervous enough as it is, breaking curfew again," ordered Angel, pulling out a small hand-held computer. The light from the screen painted the room a twilight blue.

"You come unannounced, assault me and don't even allow me the decency of putting something on over my boxer shorts."

"You're making a big deal out of nothing," grinned Angel, wickedly.

"Har-har," said Jake dryly, taking his tracksuit with 'St. Margaret's' emblazoned across the shoulders in gold thread from the wardrobe, putting it on and slipping his feet into his trainers.

"I take it you read my note," said Angel, tapping away at the handheld gizmo.

"'Watch your back', that was you?"

"Yet you still go strutting round like you own the place; typical."

"Hold on," said Jake, sitting on the bed beside Angel. "I've had my ass kicked from here to the back of beyond over the last few days for no reason that I can figure out and I'm supposed to have a blinding flash of inspiration from three bright yellow words written on my ceiling?"

"They were obviously brighter than you."

"Okay, so you've said. I'm thick," said Jake, tapping the side of his head. "You tell me what's going on then."

Angel looked up from the computer screen. "I can't."

"Hah," barked Jake in triumph.

"Not yet, not fully," she paused before dropping the next bombshell. "But I think your life may be in danger."

"No crap, Sherlock," said Jake, sarcastically.

Angel ignored him and pushed on. "We know Clarkson's file was infiltrated by the 'Void' program and we know he's gone missing; vanished, in other words. Logic dictates that because your file was also accessed, you could be next."

Jake put two and two together. "Is that why everyone is ignoring me? They think I'm going to vanish and they're frightened it might be contagious?"

"I know you don't believe in listening to rumours," said Angel defensively, "but yes, that's what most of the students believe."

Jake smiled. "In that case they're idiots. I had a little trouble with Clarkson—"

"Shot in the neck with a wrist gun dart, according to the rumours," offered Angel helpfully.

"Okay, yes," confirmed Jake, "the rumours about that are right. And I admit Packard gave me an even harder time, but I brought him in and the Headmaster dealt with it."

"Who's Packard?"

"So the on-the-ball gossip factory hasn't heard about that then?" said Jake in mock surprise. "Do you remember the bloke with me on our first night here?"

"Vaguely," said Angel. "I had my head down and my eyes full of tears most of the time."

"Well, him, anyway. I'm assuming he's lost it and gone rogue. The Headmaster isn't exactly being open about the details."

"When did you bring him in?" asked Angel.

"Last night...well, early this morning," explained Jake, correcting himself.

"In that case, it's not him. You're still in danger," said Angel calmly, as she tapped at the device in her hand. "Your records were accessed by the Void again at two o'clock this afternoon."

Jake fell silent as he thought through the situation before speaking again. "So you think there's more to this? Someone else is involved?"

"I do," she said bluntly. "For all we know, more than one someone." She took a deep breath and added quickly,

"I know you're not going to like this, Jake, but you've got to get away from St. Margaret's."

"What?"

"For now at least; it's not safe for you here."

Jake paused, almost struck dumb by Angel's suggestion. "Are you saying I should go AWOL?"

Angel looked Jake straight in the eyes and he could see her sincerity. "Yes, Jake. There is something very wrong going on here. I don't think many things are what they seem to be. Besides, it would be safer if you 'vanished' under your own terms, rather than theirs."

Jake frowned. "I don't know, Angel, we might be rushing things. We don't know anything for sure."

"The trouble is, Jake," said Angel, her face more serious than Jake had ever remembered seeing it since their first night at the Academy, being chased around the forest, "there're those who think you're part of it."

"What? Me?" gasped Jake. "They think I'm mixed up with this?" An unwelcome thought rammed into Jake's head but one that had to be verbalised anyway. "And what about you, Angel? What do you think?"

"Duh," said Angel. "I'm here aren't I?"

"Yes," said Jake, embarrassed he had raised the point. "I'm sorry."

"It's not a problem, apology accepted," said Angel. "I expected nothing less from you with your limited thought processes. But that still leaves the matter of what you are going to do."

Jake rubbed at his forehead. "Wait," he said eventually.

"Wait for what? For you to vanish one day? Or have an 'accident' on the assault course?"

"They're just rumours, Angel. We don't know for sure

if anything is the way you think it is. There's no positive proof. I can't risk everything without being one hundred per cent sure that something is going on." Jake paused. "St. Margaret's is all I've got, Angel. I can't throw it away so easily."

"I knew you'd think this way," said Angel, smiling. "And I don't blame you, but hear me out for a little longer." She closed the lid down on the small computer. "This is for you; keep it close at all times."

Jake took the gift and turned it over in his hands. "Very compact," he said.

"Oh, I nearly forgot; you'll need this." She pulled a small earpiece from her pocket. "I couldn't get an internal speaker and mic unit in, not enough space."

"Bluetooth as well," smiled Jake with an appreciative nod, turning the tiny earpiece over in his hand.

"It's a bit more sophisticated than that," rebuked Angel with a frown.

"Goldtooth?"

Angel's frown grew deeper before she continued. "If I get any further information, I'll get in touch with you and it's probably best if we keep up the pretence of a broken friendship for now. It'll give me the chance to snoop around without suspicious eyes watching me too closely."

"I can live with one less nutter in my life," smiled Jake, trying to make light of something that they both knew would be painful to do.

"One thing though," said Angel. "I can only set up a safe communication link from here. I can't guarantee the security of a source signal coming into St. Margaret's being undetectable."

"You mean I have to wait for you to call me?"

"Exactly," confirmed Angel. "Once the link is made it will be safe for us to talk."

"I see," said Jake, before a thought entered his mind. "Hold on, I thought we agreed I wasn't going to run?"

"It's just in case, Jake, that's all. It's got sat-nav too with a new tweak I've added that makes the triangulation of your position impossible. It uses frequency modulation technology, which means it switches randomly between satellites every five seconds and…"

"Er, that's great," said Jake, placing the device on the bedside cabinet, "but I'll know exactly where I am all the time, because I'll be right here."

"Promise me you'll get out if things get worse," pleaded Angel.

Jake nodded his head in agreement but Angel was not convinced of his sincerity.

"Promise me," she pushed.

"Okay, I promise," answered Jake, a tinge of annoyance to his voice.

"Good," said Angel, smiling broadly and rising from the bed. "Having an idiot like you around makes me look even more brilliant than I am already and I don't want that vanishing on me." She opened the door and popped her head into the corridor.

"Watch out for the professional insomniac," warned Jake. "No doubt he'll be doing his nocturnal rounds as usual."

"Is it true Routledge only sleeps two hours a night?" whispered Angel, checking her escape route was clear.

"The rumours are totally true on that one," confirmed Jake, "and he does it hanging upside down from a beam in the clock tower."

Angel smiled. "Take care Jake and…"

"…watch my back?" finished Jake.

"I was going to say put some clothes on before a lady calls round next time," grinned Angel as she left his room.

Jake picked up the computer and flipped the lid open. It was light and slim, no bigger than a mobile phone. He had to admit Angel was something special when it came to this kind of thing. He scrolled through the functions highlighted on the screen which numbered an impressive two; the promised sat-nav and a calculator.

'Splendid,' thought Jake, 'I can always catch up on my algebra between dodging bullets.' Nonetheless, Angel was obviously worried enough to risk breaking curfew to give him the device and he couldn't dismiss her findings out of hand, especially considering his recent experiences. 'But it's still rumour and speculation,' he argued with himself. 'To act without positive proof would be stupid.' He could see no sense in lighting a match in a fireworks factory until it was absolutely necessary. He did not want to have to face the Headmaster again, especially if he stank of gunpowder.

Outside in the corridor he heard footsteps. 'Routledge doing his rounds,' Jake thought, placing the computer into his bedside cabinet drawer. He was confident that Angel would be safely back in her room by now. The footsteps stopped directly outside his door and Jake listened intently, puzzled by the pause in the night time prowling. To his surprise there was a polite knock on his door.

Jake rose from the bed and reached for the handle. Surely the sadist didn't expect him to run the quad at this time of night? The instant he opened the door he was greeted by a fist in the face.

REALISATION

The force of the blow sent Jake rolling backwards over his bed. Instinctively he reached out to grab something to stop his fall and his right hand grasped at the curtains, pulling cloth and rail on top of him. Entangled like a camper whose tent had just collapsed on him, Jake struggled in panic to free himself of the ensnaring fabric. In this blind, tangled position he had no chance of defending himself against the onslaught he expected to follow.

Thrashing free of the clinging material and on his feet again, Jake took his fighting stance: his feet shoulder width apart, body angled at forty-five degrees to offer less of a target to his assailant, weight equally distributed between both feet so he could kick with either foot without having to shift his position, hands raised to protect his head.

The window, devoid of any coverings, let moonlight spray a silvery wash on the room, which only added to the underwater effect Jake was experiencing through his tear-filled eyes courtesy of the blow to his nose. The room was only small but shadows layered on top of each other to confuse Jake.

He knew he wasn't alone in the room, but he was having trouble pinpointing the intruder. Slowly reaching behind him with his left hand he touched the wall, which gave him the brief relief that at least no one was behind him.

"That was fun," said a voice from somewhere in the misty view to the front of Jake. "You didn't even see it coming." A brief laugh punctuated the mocking sentence.

Jake rolled his fingers until they were tight fists. This was a voice he knew and now he heard it again, a not-unpleasant feeling gripped him. There was a score to be settled. "Clarkson. I was hoping to meet you again." He blinked furiously, trying to clear the tears from his eyes so he could pinpoint the unwelcome intruder's exact location in the room.

"I thought you might be," sneered Clarkson, his voice coming from a slightly different angle. "But I'm not so sure you'll feel as happy when it's all over."

"Bring it on, lard arse," spat Jake, his eyes drying and his vision adjusting to the dim twilight. "Or are you going to wait for the easy option like last time?"

Clarkson laughed again, obviously enjoying the moment. "Yeah, sorry about that. Bit of a cock up, I admit."

"It sure was," sneered Jake, beginning to make out the dark edges of Clarkson's form.

"Funny how when you need a copper there's never one around, but when you could really do without them they're crawling all over the place."

Jake could now clearly see the outline of Clarkson gently moving sideways across the room in front of him like a large black crab. "I've got to hand it to you, you've got some balls coming back here; which by the way I'm going to take great pleasure in kicking into your throat."

"No, please don't," mocked Clarkson, in a quivering

high pitched voice. "You've got me shaking in my boots."

Jake's vision had cleared sufficiently to make him more confident of his situation. "One more thing before we start: how have you avoided being caught? Certain people have been rather anxious to have a word with you."

"Let's just say I'm well connected." Clarkson cracked his knuckles loudly. "Right, have we allowed enough time for your vision to clear? Can you see me alright, now?"

Jake swallowed. Clarkson couldn't beat him in an even match, but the bully seemed filled with arrogant confidence. Was he armed again? "I wasn't stalling," Jake lied. "I was just seeing how long it would take for you to use up your whole vocabulary in one conversation."

"I reckon about…NOW." Clarkson threw a left-handed punch that came with such speed that Jake only just managed to avoid it. He rolled sideways across the bed, landing off balance on the other side of the room. Before he could put up a strong guard again, Clarkson had leapt up onto the bed and driven a foot into his chest.

Jake folded up and slammed backwards into the door, most of the air in his lungs exploding out. There was no time to recover his breath. He had to move again and as he did, Clarkson's other foot hammered into the door with a crunch.

Jake saw the advantage of being at Clarkson's side and though still not totally solid in his stance, whipped out a right-handed back fist toward the exposed temple. The block that Clarkson raised was swift and accurate and to Jake it felt like his forearm had been hit by an iron bar.

Clarkson grinned. "Getting slow, aren't you, Highfield? Maybe you're still a bit sluggish because of the dart?"

Jake gritted his teeth and shot his left fist toward Clarkson's ribs, which Clarkson pushed harmlessly to one side with an open palm before driving his forehead into Jake's bruised cheekbone.

Jake's head snapped back as a flash of purple light robbed his vision to accompany the pain shooting through his face. He staggered two paces before regaining control of his body.

Clarkson stood where he'd been after his strike, seemingly not eager to follow up his obvious advantage. "Ready for the next round, or should I see if your girlfriend wants to fight for you for a change?"

The pain in Jake's chest and face fought to get attention from his brain, but his mind was racing with matters of more immediate concern. 'Come on,' he thought to himself. 'This is Clarkson. Seven bellies himself. He's never beaten you yet, and that's not going to change now.' Jake snorted like a bull and flicked his arms loosely before raising his guard again. He stormed in, throwing a right-handed feint whilst driving at Clarkson's knee with the heel of his foot. Clarkson merely pulled his leg out of range and at the same time drove the bottom of his fist onto Jake's collar bone. Luckily Jake saw it coming and managed to drop his body to lessen the impact and save the bone being broken, but in doing this, he left his jaw exposed. An easy target for Clarkson's left hook.

Jake's head snapped sideways and for a split second he felt as if he was going to be knocked unconscious by the blow. Even though his brain rebooted quickly, he still found himself dropped onto his backside with a jarring thud.

Jake expected Clarkson to move in and finish the fight,

but instead he stood over him for a second then backed away. 'He's enjoying this,' thought Jake, keeping his eyes on Clarkson as he got to his feet untidily. 'Toying with me, and why not? He's owed some payback.'

"You're fighting well," said Jake, spitting out a mouthful of blood thick with mucus. "Been paying attention in class lately?"

"Aww, didums. Is likkle Jake feeling tired?" retorted Clarkson. "Don't take it too hard, Highfield. You've had a rough time of it lately. Anyone would be off form after what you've been through. Luckily I'm not the kind of person to take advantage of someone's moment of weakness." The statement was heavily laced with sarcasm. "Besides," Clarkson continued, "it's not your fault."

"No, it isn't," agreed Jake. "It's yours, among others." Jake was breathing heavily, shakes of exhaustion running up and down his limbs. Clarkson was right; a scuffle like this would not ordinarily tire him to this extent. "But don't beat yourself up about it...let me do that for you."

"As always, Highfield, you're talking the talk but can you—"

Jake took the chance, as Clarkson revelled in his own blind self-confidence, and leapt forward throwing a right-handed punch. It was met in mid-air by Clarkson's left arm stopping it dead in its tracks, leaving it hanging, all its force spent. Turning through a hundred and eighty degrees on the ball of his left foot Clarkson spun his body until his back was pinned to Jake's chest; then using the strength in his legs he lifted Jake off his feet and rolled him across his shoulders. Jake was thrown upward until he was almost upside down in flight, only to be driven into the bed with such force that he bounced off the mattress and crumpled in a heap on the opposite side of the room.

Clarkson casually sauntered round the bed until he stood over Jake, who scrambled into a seated position, back against the wall, legs outstretched. "Well, all good things come to an end, Highfield," he said, his tone of voice flat and emotionless.

Jake could tell by the cold look in his eyes that Clarkson had the intention of finally ending this. 'If this is it,' Jake told himself, 'don't you dare make it easy.' Despite the pain he was in and the aching fatigue that commanded his body, he slid his hands across the floor in readiness to raise himself up again. He stopped short when his fingers brushed against something under his bed. 'There is a God,' he thought as he snatched up the wrist gun. Squeezing the sleeve of its construction to depress both of the safety buttons, Jake flicked his hand violently to release the dart.

Clarkson reacted quickly and twisted. The dart sped past his face, burying itself with a thud into the wooden door of the shower room. He brought his foot down onto Jake's forearm, pinning it to the floor until Jake was forced to relax his grip and the wrist gun fell from his hand.

"I suppose I would have deserved that," smiled Clarkson, pulling out a small bladed knife from behind his belt buckle. "But I think I'll do this the old-fashioned way myself if you don't m—" Clarkson took a small involuntary step backward as he tried to steady himself but his body buckled and he collapsed to his knees. A fraction of a second later the knife tumbled from Clarkson's hand and the blade buried itself into the floor, two inches from Jake's outstretched leg.

Jake frowned. He'd seen the dart miss.

Clarkson wobbled, not upright, not falling, looking like a nodding dog on a parcel shelf in the back of a car. A line appeared on his face, the trickle of blood showing black in the moonlight, marking out the scratch the dart had left as it had scraped past his face.

Jake took his chance and got to his feet in a flash, tugging the knife free from the wood of the floor and holding it to Clarkson's throat. "Still want to go with the old-fashioned way?"

Clarkson managed to tilt his head and look into Jake's eyes, but if there was any defiance or presence of fear, neither registered on the limp facial muscles, effected by the dart's toxins.

Much as he hated Clarkson, Jake sneered at his own unwillingness to do the deed. He tossed the knife onto his bed. "At least I'm still with the good guys, Clarkson. Besides, I bet the Academy has a better way to deal with traitors and I'm sure Packard will be happy to show you the ropes in that department."

Clarkson continued to stare through unfocused eyes, a lengthening thread of dribble hanging from the corner of his mouth.

Jake sat heavily on the side of his bed and ran his hands through his hair, unsure of what to do. 'Angel,' he suddenly realised, sitting up. 'I could do with her brain on this one'. He reached into his bedside cabinet and pulled out the palm-sized computer before remembering her speech about it being only a one-way communication device.

Footsteps approaching down the corridor attracted his attention and slipping the device into his pocket he moved to the door and opened it just enough so he could see through the crack. Approaching his room were the figures of the Headmaster and Routledge. Their faces grim, their strides stretched and filled with purpose.

"Okay, Clarkson, let's see your connections get you out of this one," Jake said, opening the door and stepping out into the corridor. The words froze in his throat as he saw with unencumbered sight that not only were the Headmaster and Routledge marching down the corridor, but in their wake was Packard, his jaw held in place with enough metal scaffolding for a small building site.

The men saw Jake. The Headmaster and Routledge exchanged a look. Packard's eyes fixed on Jake and narrowed, shooting him a metaphorical stream of pure hatred.

The Headmaster nodded and immediately Routledge broke into a jog ahead of the two other men.

Jake slammed the door and with one heave pulled his wardrobe, crashing down as a makeshift barricade. His sense of self-preservation hadn't let him down yet and this wasn't the time to stop trusting it. 'Wrist gun,' he thought to himself and diving to lie on the bed he reached down to retrieve it from where it lay.

The door rattled against the wardrobe blocking its usual movement. There was a loud knock. "Open the door," said Routledge, his voice straining to stay calmer than usual.

The handle to the door was tried again and Jake watched it, glued to the spot, his mind racing with questions. Strangely he found himself half convinced that he should push the wardrobe aside and find out the truth, whatever it was. That way, at least, all the trouble would be over one way or another. A slobbering noise behind him brought him back to the reality of the situation.

"Connections," gurgled Clarkson, who was back on his feet, though visibly unsteady. He even managed to half raise a smug smile despite the poison in his bloodstream. "Connections."

The door to his room thudded loudly against the wardrobe, shifting it a fraction to jam against the bed. The doorframe had split by the hinges under the assault. It wouldn't take much more effort from the men on the other side of the door to destroy the barrier between them and their quarry.

Jake turned his attention back to Clarkson. He could tell by the clearing look in the bully's eyes that the small dose of toxin his system had been hit with was beginning to wear off quickly and when it did he would have trouble on both sides of the door. 'Neither of which I'm sure I can handle,' he thought grimly, making a decision that had been forced upon him.

"Clarkson," Jake said, forcing himself to raise a polite smile. "Would you mind opening the window for me?" Jake ran as fast as he could across the room and rammed himself into Clarkson, grabbing him by the lapels, making sure to keep his elbows tucked in tightly as he pushed him back with all his strength. They hit the old wooden frame of the window with such force that it splintered without resistance. The glass shattered, spewing shards to land on the grass one storey below like a coating of winter frost.

Jake's stomach didn't even have time to flip before the quick descent was brought to a thudding halt, jarring his body. He felt the bend of ribs and heard the bully's whelp of pain at the impact as Clarkson's still limp body cushioned his fall.

Without hesitation, Jake leapt clear of Clarkson and

began sprinting away. He reached the mouth of the arch and dared himself to look back. No one was following him as yet, but it was only a matter of time before that changed.

Jake put his head down and ran for all his worth through the arch towards the edge of the forest surrounding St. Margaret's and the shadows it offered to keep him hidden and safe…assuming he got past Satan and Lucifer.

CELEBRITY

Jake shivered as another blast of cold night air found its way through the old walls. At least the crumbling building that had the look of once being a small factory unit was sufficient to keep the steady rain at bay. As long as he stayed underneath the third of charred roof that remained he would at least be dry. In the opposite corner of his hideout, the sleeping form of a man, whose thin paper duvet had been provided by the ramblings of the national press, shouted out and jerked his leg. One of the empty beer cans that surrounded him rattled across the concrete floor. Jake looked at the sleeping man, fascinated that his face appeared to be mostly made of beard. He noticed the tramp's matching pillow revealed the partial headline, '...FEELS 'FURRY' OF ANIMAL LOONIES'. Jake felt his stomach sink as he remembered the roasting he'd had in the Headmaster's office and drew his eyes away from the depressing bedding.

"Not exactly the Ritz," Jake muttered to himself, thinking of the relative comfort and better smelling company St. Margaret's had to offer. But he made no wishes to be back there; at least here he was safe for the time being.

Angel's mini-computer vibrated against his leg as the tiny electronic device fitted into his ear crackled. Jake eagerly pulled it from his pocket. Pushing a button, the bright blue screen was filled with Angel's familiar face. "You took your time," sneered Jake.

"Great to see you too," Angel snapped, obviously hurt. The video of her was slightly out of sync with the audio, giving the impression she was an actress in a badly dubbed foreign film.

Jake ran a hand through his hair and tugged on it for a second. "Sorry, I've had a rough couple of days."

Angel smiled sympathetically. "I can imagine. Still, I see you managed to get on the property ladder and find yourself a good tailor."

Jake's good humour was returning by the second, just to see Angel and hear a friendly voice was comforting. "Of course, I only shoplift at the best charity shops."

"Excellent, I'm glad to hear all your expensive training hasn't been wasted."

"I've got some older habits that are coming in quite useful at the moment, like knowing that a couple of two hundred year old women are unlikely to give chase for a hoody on sale for 30p at Oxfam," laughed Jake.

"Oxfam?" Angel grinned. "A superstar like you shops, sorry shoplifts, at Oxfam?"

"I felt like slumming it. You know, get back to my roots," smiled Jake, enjoying the banter with Angel. Being flippant was keeping the harsh reality of his situation at bay for just a little longer.

Angel's smile faded. "Well, you're going to get ripped up by the roots pretty soon if the Headmaster has his way."

"You want to be careful, Angel; I've heard snooping

around the Academy's computer system can be addictive."

"This is serious, Jake," chided Angel. "He's mobilised operatives to track you down and not just operatives from within the Academy either. You've even had the mission named in your honour, though you don't want to know the full title of it."

"I can guess," sighed Jake. "But you're right, I don't want to know. Things are going badly enough, thanks." Jake paused before asking the next question. He feared the wrong answer could finally shred the last of his nerve.

"Do you know how close they are to me?"

Angel turned her attention from the web cam and towards the computer in front of her and tapped at the keyboard. "As far as I can tell, and I've got a live tap in the system at the moment, they haven't got a clue."

Jake's shoulders dropped with relief.

"No sightings," continued Angel, "no trail, no idea to be honest. Oh, other than your Academy tracksuit, which apparently they found in a wheelie bin outside a house yesterday, twenty miles from St. Margaret's." Angel frowned as a sudden realisation jumped into her head. "Does that mean all our clothes are bugged?"

"What's up, Einstein," smirked Jake. "Someone got one over on you?"

Angel was grimacing. "What? All of our clothes?"

"Reckon so," grinned Jake, not believing this himself, but enjoying his friend's discomfort. "Looks like the Headmaster is not as trusting as we thought."

"That's sick," barked Angel. "Did you know about it?"

"Let's say after my nature ramble with Packard I got the feeling they might be."

"And you never told me?"

"Take it easy, Angel," pleaded Jake. "There are more important things going on than your underwear being modified."

Angel could only open her mouth in shock at the thought of it.

"Besides, I'm sure the tracking devices aren't activated until they're needed. There's no way they could monitor all the clothes in the Academy; it would take a whole new section to work the system."

Angel's face was a picture of anger. "Well, now I know what my next project is going to be—"

"Something to get the bugs out of your knickers?" interrupted Jake. "Great, but can we please sort out this slight mess I'm in first?"

Angel looked like she was ready to explode across the small screen Jake held in his hands. She took a few deep breaths and managed to calm herself. Her face paled from the puce it had been turning. "You're right...I'm sorry, what do you need?"

"First I need the address of..." Jake paused. "Are you sure we're secure?"

"One hundred per cent," smiled Angel, the way she always did just before she was about to illustrate her genius. "I told you last night, the frequency of the module changes every—"

"So you did," interrupted Jake, trying to stop her flow.

"But did I tell you I installed what I call 'Spaghetti'?" continued Angel, unperturbed by Jake's look of irritated boredom. "It's a system of simultaneously running feeds that lead nowhere. So if anyone is trying to locate the source of the signal, they waste valuable time tracking the tail of a false signal."

Jake stayed silent for a second, making sure Angel had finished her technical lecture. "So we're secure then?"

Angel nodded her head, making her thick hair bounce madly. "Yes, we're secure. No one can track the signal to either of us."

The drunk in the corner swore loudly in his sleep, finishing it off with a coughing fit that echoed about the empty space as loud as a herd of elephants with bronchitis.

"What was that?" asked Angel.

Jake turned the screen to face the corner where the man rolled fitfully, trying to reconstruct his flimsy covers. "Angel, meet Fug. Fug, Angel."

"Who is he?"

"Don't know," admitted Jake. "He was the sitting, well, lying and snoring, tenant when I moved in here a few hours back and it appears his favourite word is 'fug', or at least that's what it sounds like."

"Are you sure he's not a threat? He could be an undercover operative for someone; we don't know how far the Academy's influence goes."

"Believe me," smiled Jake, "his level of body odour takes more than a few years of expert training to achieve."

Angel wrinkled her nose. "I'll take your word for it. Right; shall we get…wait a second, I think I heard something. Wait there."

Jake was about to make some smart comment about having nowhere to go but Angel had stood up and moved out of the web cam's view. Even though she was off screen he knew she was still there from her supposedly cautious footsteps on the audio as she tried to creep around the room. 'Some field operative she would make,' thought Jake, shaking his head at the noise she was making.

A few seconds later Angel was back on the screen. "Sorry about that, thought I heard something. I don't know how you do this creepy, secretive stuff all the time, Jake; my nerves are on edge."

"That's why I do it," smiled Jake, knowing full well she would never understand that sentiment at all. "But before I lose the taste for it I need the address of the nearest holding cell, preferably suburban and occupied."

"Okay," said Angel, slowly tapping away at the keyboard as she spoke. "But why an occupied one?"

"Less likely that it will be under surveillance," explained Jake. "They know I know the location of one or two of the cells, having used them before, so they will cover them without doubt and I assume they'll also be watching the unoccupied ones on the off chance I show up there, it being the easy option, so…"

"So you're going to try for one of the harder ones," finished Angel. "Well, stupid as your plan sounds, the nearest one to you that fits your needs is fifteen miles away. I'll download the data to your handset now."

Jake smiled. "The nearest one to my location; who's the one doing the secret bugging now?"

Angel flushed with embarrassment. "That's a very expensive prototype you're holding, the only one there is in fact, and when you make a mess of all this I'd like to know where it is so I can collect it."

"Glad to see you've got my wellbeing as your first priority."

"Some things are irreplaceable," grinned Angel.

"And on that cheerful note, I'm off," said Jake. "Thanks

for this, Angel, you're saving my neck."

"Or helping you to break it," said Angel sadly. "What have you got planned, Jake?"

"I'm not sure yet," admitted Jake. "Things are still a little confused. Once I've picked up a few toys at least I'll feel happier about facing the situation."

Angel looked out of the screen for a few seconds as if she was searching for the perfect words to express herself. "Take care of yourself, Jake," she said eventually and reached forward to shut the system down.

The computer screen in Jake's hand went blank except for a flashing icon in the top left-hand corner. He scrolled the cursor over to it and double clicked. The screen filled with the sat-nav's map, a solid red dot indicating the position of the hand-held device and a flashing green arrow notifying Jake of the direction of the holding cell he needed to find.

"Fifteen miles," Jake muttered to himself, getting to his feet and slipping Angel's prototype into his pocket. "I'll need some transport."

Jake's attention was caught again by the tramp's twitching and grunting mumbles as his body acted out his dream. It was as if he was an old dog sleeping on the hearth before a fire. "Hey, Fug," he semi-whispered. "Would it be alright if I borrow your Bentley for a while?"

Fug grumbled deeply at the world in general.

"Thanks awfully, old chap," smiled Jake, flicking up his hood and stepping out into the rain.

TOOLED UP

Jake dumped the run-down and unalarmed Ford Fiesta he had 'borrowed' at the edge of the town. It looked rough enough and smelt bad enough to actually have been Fug's car. Following Angel's sat-nav, he began to jog the path marked out by the flashing green arrow. Occasionally, when his instinct tingled or he noticed something that made him suspicious, he would take a detour from the suggested route. He knew full well if the Academy wanted to find someone they would leave nothing to chance. It was possible that the whole country's CCTV system footage was being downloaded directly to St. Margaret's. Taking chances was not a luxury Jake could afford.

Two streets away from the green arrow on the screen was the blue dot, which denoted his destination. Jake switched off the machine. He was entering a 'black zone', a term used at the Academy to signify an area where enemy activity and surveillance were likely to be very high. He took a couple of deep breaths and mentally switched to 'Chaos' mode. Without his usual arsenal he was at a disadvantage but he could still prepare his mind to be totally ready for the task ahead.

Jake took in his surroundings one more time. He had

decided to use the park to his right as a shortcut to his objective, but first he wanted to make sure that this was his best option. To the north, on the corner of the street he needed to get to, was a brightly lit petrol station. He'd be far too visible in that much halogen; besides, most forecourts used video cameras to catch drive-offs. South was also too risky, a cul-de-sac that would mean garden-hopping along the back of at least fifteen properties. Too much chance of waking people or their dogs or falling into a newly dug, yet to be filled, fish pond which would not only be the end of his mission, but also highly embarrassing. This only left, as he first assumed, the park to the east.

With a short, quick run-up Jake sprang up and placed his left foot on one of the solid sandstone pillars of the park gate and pushed himself up at a forty-five degree angle over the ornate wrought iron railings. He landed on the other side as silently as a cat on the grass. For the first twenty metres his progress was covered by unkempt bushes and shrubs. He moved quickly, confident that he hadn't been seen or heard, even by the couple he'd nearly stood on in the dark. At the edge of the cover he stopped to assess the situation once more.

The open expanse of the field was daunting. At least four hundred metres of open ground, broken only by a children's play area, halfway across and off to the left of where he crouched. 'Do or die,' thought Jake, instantly wishing he could have thought of a more positive phrase to urge himself on. He pushed off at a sprint into an environment where luck counted for as much as skill or training.

A crash of glass to his left caught his attention. He didn't slow his pace, but he checked out the source and was relieved to find it was just some kid and his mates making the play area anything but a safe haven for toddlers. With each pounding beat of his heart and stretch of his legs, Jake ate away at the open distance until he slid, like a baseball player hitting home base, into the relative safety of the shrubs that mirrored those on the other side of the field.

Jake lay still, controlling his breathing and trying to hear above the blood that pumped in his ears. Something disturbed the leaves of a bush to his right. A hedgehog rambled past his feet. 'Are you following me?' he thought with a grin that was quickly replaced by a suspicious raise of eyebrows.

"Not from St. Margaret's, are you?" he mumbled, but the hedgehog didn't even glance in Jake's direction to confirm or deny the accusation.

At the far edge of the chaotically planted bushes, more wrought iron railings marked the end of the park. Beyond that was an ornate hedge, probably planted by the discerning owners of the houses opposite who had no desire to look out onto imprisoning black bars. Jake slipped over the railings and with two steps was crouched within the bushes, blending with the plant as if he had grown there too.

Jake checked the house numbers, "Sixty-six, sixty-eight, damn, too far along."

Carefully, not making any noise, Jake slipped free of the bushes and crept his way along between the railings and the hedge. He stopped every few metres to check the house numbers through the leaves which so perfectly broke up his form in the night's shadows. 'Ninety-six; this is it', thought Jake. 'Time to play for real.'

Slipping back into the body of the bush, crouching low, he checked out the objective. He saw what he expected: a normal three bedroom semi-detached property no grander than any other in the street. A car was parked up the driveway and a downstairs front room light was on. There was security on display, but only in the form of a brightly coloured burglar alarm box high up near the roof, exactly the same as almost every other house as far as Jake could see.

Jake checked out the road itself. To the left, the road ran up to the brightly lit garage and he could see that there was no one about, which helped his confidence. To the right, the scene was different. A few houses down from his objective, five lads hung about the junction box for cable TV. Two sat on the green tombstone-like object swinging their legs, the other three milled around, occasionally kicking out their feet as if they were dancing to a private tune in their heads. Hooded jackets or baseball caps hid their faces, but something about them didn't fit. 'They're too quiet,' noted Jake. Where was the horseplay? The fooling around, the shouting as if they were the most important thing in the whole world and everyone needed to hear them? It occurred to Jake, after he watched them for a few minutes, what they were up to. They were trying to hide the fact they were paying close attention to their surroundings. Trying to look uninterested but it was plainly obvious to him they were taking in every little detail. Jake decided that if they weren't from the Academy he would eat his own hoody…and theirs.

Jake ran through his options.

By the size and build of the gang he could tell they were young, possibly only into their first year, second at the most. For all Jake could tell, Pete Philips could quite easily be among them, worrying more about ghosts than anyone living turning up. They would have some training without doubt, but it would be new to them, untested and raw. He was confident that he could easily take them out, though a five-on-one encounter, whatever the inevitable outcome, would always generate noise and the possibility of one or more of them getting away to raise the alarm. He had to be more subtle, use the other skills he'd been taught.

At that moment the five boys stiffened as one and started to mutter to each other. Jake couldn't hear what they were saying but their body language was screaming out 'panic'. Jake followed their anxious stares up the road and spotted the police patrol car crawling from the direction of the petrol station. Perhaps a curtain-twitcher on the street had seen the youths hanging round and phoned in their concern. This could be his chance to clear one of his obstacles at least.

Scrabbling around frantically at his feet, Jake's fingers curled around a stone that weighed at least a kilo – perfect for the job if his aim was true. Turning the missile over in his hand, he waited until the patrol car had drawn slowly past him before standing up and hurling it as hard as he could at the rear windscreen of the car up the driveway of number ninety-eight, the house adjoining the holding cell.

The glass imploded with a loud hiss and an alarm broke the silence with a deafening, oscillating note. The unit of five boys, who until that moment had stood their ground hoping to bluff it out with the police, jumped in shock. Their first and natural reaction was to run.

Like a pack of wolves on the scent of wounded prey, they sprinted into the night as one. The patrol car added its siren to the bedlam and gave chase, tyres squealing as the accelerator was nailed to the floor in pursuit.

Within seconds several front doors had been flung open and concerned neighbours poured out into the street to see what was going on. The door to number ninety-six stayed shut, as Jake thought it would. It was unlikely his simple diversion would fool the occupant of the holding cell and the situation could be getting relayed to the Academy at this very second. He'd managed to remove one problem. Time was his next – and he had little of it to play with.

Jake waited for an opportunity when everyone was concentrating on the damaged car, then slipped from the hedge into the road and began to blend in with the milling people, all of whom were venting their disgust with the youth of today. One man in particular was swearing as though he'd just invented it. 'Obviously the owner,' thought Jake.

"Hey, mate," said Jake, with as much confidence as he could. "One of them went that way."

The man's expression filled with hateful anger and he raised a short, strong finger poking it towards Jake's face. "Did you do this?" he barked.

"No, no mate, it wasn't me," stammered Jake, not having to try too hard to show real concern for his wellbeing. "It was some lad and his mates. I think it was the same ones that gave me this last night." Jake pointed to his swollen and bruised cheek.

The man breathed out heavily through his nose, trying to suss out if he was being fed a line. "Do you know them?"

"No," replied Jake. "But one of them jumped over that house's side gate." He indicated number ninety-six.

"Right," said the man, clenching his fists. He stormed up the path and hammered on the front door. "Open up, Tony," he shouted. "We need to get into your garden, now!"

There was no answer.

"Open the door!" demanded the injured party, his voice cracking as he lost what little control he'd had to start with since he'd seen his damaged property.

The door of ninety-six opened slowly. "What is it?" said the occupant, who was dressed in blue striped pyjamas underneath an open dressing gown. "I was just off to bed."

"I need to check the back of your house to see if the little git that's just trashed my car is hiding there," explained the man, with little politeness towards his neighbour.

"Oh, I don't know..." said the man from ninety-six distractedly as he looked through the crowd of people that had descended onto his driveway. Jake knew he was scouting for him and hid behind a large woman in a pink housecoat and blue fluffy flip-flops. He couldn't help thinking he could probably wave his arms about and still not be seen round her ample form.

The car owner's tone turned even harsher. "What do you mean, you don't know? My car's wrecked and you don't know. I get the feeling you do know actually. I think you're hiding something!"

Pyjama man suddenly stopped his searching for a fugitive he'd never met, he didn't know and had only heard reports of, as the gravity of his own precarious situation became clear. He got as far as, "But I can't..." before the angered man on his step interrupted.

"Can't? You've always been a weird bugger!" he shouted and smacked him straight and hard in the nose.

This hadn't been exactly what Jake had planned but with the large helping of luck he'd had, it would do perfectly. The ghoulishly curious neighbours gathered in a circle round the fighting men as they rolled around the small piece of yellowing turf that passed as a front garden. It was a scene taken straight from any schoolyard and Jake was almost surprised not to hear the chant of 'Fight! Fight!' being taken up as he slipped unseen into the house.

Every residential holding cell was the same to the exact detail. There wasn't a need for elaborate hiding mechanisms, in fact that would negate the whole premise of the idea. The cells were designed for easy access in a situation that required instant equipping of an operative in the field.

Jake made his way towards the living room at the rear of the house but stopped as he approached the open door. A shadow running parallel to the back of the door caught his attention. Putting his hand into his pocket, he pulled out the wrist gun and making sure he had a white dart in the chamber, slipped it on. He kicked the door violently, rolling forward into the room across his shoulders and back up onto his feet to face the way he'd just come in. The middle-aged woman behind the door knew she was out of range to hit the intruder with the baton she held up at shoulder height, but she swung it anyway. Before the baton had a chance to finish its useless arc, she had collapsed on the carpet, a white dart sticking into her chest.

"I hope they haven't got kids," muttered Jake, as he turned and strode to the fireplace. Once there, he counted four bricks from the top left and two bricks down and struck it with the base of his fist. It spun round to reveal a phone-like keypad on its reverse side. Jake quickly tapped in 1-8-0-5 but nothing happened. He tried it again. "Crap!" he hissed. "I bet the old sod has changed all the numbers for my benefit." Jake could tell the fight on the front lawn was dying down. Some good Samaritan was trying, and succeeding, to be the voice of reason. "Think, Highfield, think. What would the old fart change it to?"

Outside someone said, "Come on now, shake hands."

"Shake his throat," Jake hissed. "I need more time. 1805? 1805? Battle of Trafalgar!" Jake suddenly exclaimed. "Of course, glory days of the British Empire." He tapped away at the key pad. 1-6-4-2, Jake had no idea why that sequence but he knew it was something important in history. "1899, The Boer War," he muttered, inputting the date to no avail. "Stupid sod, we lost that one," he rebuked himself, suddenly recalling some tedious lesson or other. "He's hardly likely to use that. Come on; think! Think!"

Jake heard the front door creak open and then slam shut. A voice that was obviously looking for sympathy called up the hall. "You'll never guess what that stupid big sod from next door has just done to—"

The man from number ninety-six walked into his living room, his dressing gown torn, his pyjamas streaked with blood. He looked at Jake, then down at the drugged middle-aged woman at his feet and then back at Jake.

"1815," said Jake with a smile, holding up a large black holdall.

"What?" said the man still obviously dazed from his punch up.

"1815, Battle of Waterloo," explained Jake. "Sweet dreams." The wrist gun did its job for the second time that night.

FIVE STAR

Jake considered torching the semi-detached holding cell purely to show a metaphoric middle finger to those who were hunting him down, but he quickly dismissed the idea. He had no idea if the victims of his wrist gun had had time to report his presence or not before he took them out, but lighting a beacon would surely attract unwanted attention. At the moment, as far as he knew, he was not on the Academy's radar and he had no desire to be, either.

Peeking through the heavy curtains on the front window he could see people still milling around the front of the house. They were revelling in the excitement of the events that had lifted the usual boredom of their night in the pleasant, quiet street. Some bickered with the man whose car had been damaged; others congratulated him for giving 'that bloke from ninety-six' exactly what he'd deserved for years. Whatever it was that was keeping them padding up and down in their slippers, Jake wasn't going to be able to slip out unnoticed the way he came in.

Throwing the holdall onto his shoulder, he made his way into the small conservatory at the rear of the house, the key to which was helpfully present in the lock to the double doors. A quick check of the garden beyond the glazed doors told him that no one had actually bothered to follow up his helpful suggestion that one of the car wreckers had jumped the side gate. Jake opened the door, quietly jogged to the end of the garden and scrambled over the back fence. Within minutes, Jake was a safe distance from the scene of his making.

Jake had to sort out a few things as quickly as possible before he could relax a little. He was still wary that contact with the Academy could have been made from the holding cell. He needed a place that was private, out of sight and lit well enough for him to see what he was doing – a car park, or a supermarket loading bay, or…

'A library,' thought Jake with a grin as he rounded a corner. Pretending to stop to tie his trainer's lace, he checked he wasn't being watched and hopped over the low stone wall. He skirted around the library and turned a corner of the building so he was hidden from the road. A security light lit up the car parking area at the back. In the right-hand corner was a security camera blinking its red power light dutifully, but its lens was pointing uselessly up into the night sky. Jake could tell by the rust on the bracket that it hadn't swept the area it was meant to protect in years. It had instead stayed fixed in one position, leading its own mission in the search for life on Mars. The security on this place was abysmally lax, but then again the black market for library books wasn't quite in the same league as the one for mobile phones or MP3 players.

Kneeling directly under the broken camera, his back to the supporting pole, Jake unzipped the holdall and began to haul its contents onto the stone paving, careful to make sure he opened all the side and internal pockets to remove each and every piece of equipment. Once it was all out he reached for the 'bug sweeper' and began to run it over each item in turn. Nothing was left out, even down to the triangular five centimetre blade of the knife hidden in the belt buckle. He only found one tracking device and as he suspected after his run in with Packard, it was in the collar of the covert suit. It was easily cut free and deactivated.

Jake began to sift through the array of equipment laid out before him, selecting those he thought he would need. Travelling light was essential. Anything too bulky or heavy was placed back in the holdall and could be dropped en masse should he need to make a quick escape. Items that he thought might prove useful and that were small and light enough were placed in the numerous pockets and pouches of the suit. When he got to the roll of cash containing various world currencies, he paused. As much as he would welcome the ease and comfort the money would bring, it would be easily traceable from the serial numbers and so it was left on the grey floor. 'You've survived without cash before,' he told himself. 'You can do it again.'

He stripped off his newly acquired tracksuit and reached down to pick up the covert suit but paused as his hand touched the cloth. His mind threw up the comment he had made to Angel and he looked at his underwear. Making sure he was not being watched, he quickly, and with some embarrassment, ran the bug sweeper over his boxer shorts. They were clean…of bugs anyway. 'Must tell Angel,' he thought, as a smile lifted his face, 'eventually.' He dressed in the covert suit and slipped the tracksuit over the top of it, finally crouching down to tightly tie the laces in his new boots.

With its job successfully done, Jake lifted the bug sweeper again and was about to place it in his pocket when he stopped. "How do you sweep a bug sweeper for bugs?" he wondered to himself quietly. It was the kind of sneaky practice that wasn't beyond the Academy, so the device was kicked into the corner of the car park, once it had received a little modification courtesy of the heel of Jake's left foot.

Jake slipped the repacked holdall onto his shoulder and, taking one more reluctant look at the roll of cash at his feet, hoping someone like Fug would find it, he rounded the municipal building and resumed his previous direction alongside the road.

As he walked, masking his alertness to avoid attracting attention, his mouth was ambushed by a long, wide yawn. He shook his head and blinked to clear the water in his eyes. 'That's not good,' he thought to himself, sniffing loudly.

Fatigue and pain, which adrenalin had helped him ignore until now, started to become the focus of his mind. His legs ached, his arms ached and the weight of the holdall bit into his shoulder. Lack of sleep and overexertion were beginning to take over his body and as strong as his will was, it would, sooner or later, lose this battle for sure.

There was no point in pushing on in this state. He would be an easy target for anyone. Weakened physically and mentally, he would make mistakes, get sloppy and get himself caught. It was only a matter of time. At this moment, more than any other in his life, he needed to be as strong and alert as possible. He knew he couldn't get the rest he needed spending another night in a condemned building, however congenial the company. What he did need was a meal, a shower and a bed, in that order. 'Time for the old pre-Academy skills again.' This simple thought brought enough adrenalin to fire his energy levels up for one last effort.

The meal was easy; there wasn't a takeaway owner in the land who was going to abandon his cash register to give chase to some thieving little brat. He would grab an ordered meal off the counter and leg it up the street without paying. Jake could live with the harmless, crude name-calling and spatula-waving that followed him through the night in exchange for a full stomach. He couldn't help thinking how envious Angel would be as he shovelled chips into his eager mouth.

Getting a shower and bed wasn't a new challenge to him either and it didn't take him long to find a hotel to his liking. All he needed was a secure drain pipe to climb and a screwdriver, which his holdall readily supplied.

Within an hour of his yawn he was fed, clean and lying back on a soft double bed finishing a Coke from the complimentary mini bar. Putting the lights on was out of the question in the supposedly occupant-free hotel room. The muted TV was the only illumination he could chance and even then, he rolled a towel up and laid it across the space under the door. The door itself was deadlocked from the inside to make sure no unwelcome visitors got in without him noticing during the night.

It was close to midnight by the time Jake sprawled on the bed, letting the waves of exhaustion wash over him without resistance. If Angel wanted to contact him tonight she'd better have fitted a program to wake the dead.

Jake grabbed the remote and set the TV for an alarm call at six a.m. Without warning, this action seemed to bring on a strange, new feeling. It wasn't fear or loneliness but it was unsettling, like there was something he was supposed to have done but hadn't and now he couldn't remember what it was. Jake looked at the four blandly decorated walls around him and wanted to escape from them. Run into the night outside, into more familiar territory. Here he was out of place but then again he had always been out of place, always the outsider. Except at...

Jake shook thoughts of St. Margaret's from his mind, lay back on the bed and pulled the luxury duvet over himself. He noticed how clean it smelled and how heavy and comforting it felt on his tired body, pinning him down gently into the soft mattress below. He wondered if this was what kids with happy family lives felt every night? Their parents would tuck them in with a kiss and they would drift off to sleep, filled with sweet dreams. Even if they dreamt of dark places and the bogey man, he would be quickly chased away by loving embraces and kind words of assurance that everything was okay. One thing Jake did know for sure was that any bogey man who chased them through their dreams would be gone by the morning, not still in the shadows breathing down their neck and waiting for the perfect moment to pounce. As he fell asleep, Jake felt an unmistakable pang of envy.

"Can't miss what you've never had, idiot," he muttered dismissively into the pillow.

HAVE WHEELS WILL TRAVEL

Jake had slept fitfully, spending the night being woken by the slightest sound, real or imagined, that the hotel threw up. He was awake and out of bed, showering and making full use of the complimentary coffee and biscuits before the TV's alarm call had the chance to carry out its programmed role for the morning.

As he towelled himself dry, he watched the local news programme on the muted television in the corner. His previous night's work was unlikely to make headlines – the Academy would see to that if necessary – but maybe the regional broadcast units would pick up a face he knew in the background. Some uninteresting report on the plight of a local charity or housing estate may give an indication to the activity going on beyond the walls of the room he'd stolen for the night.

Jake's eye was drawn to Angel's miniature electronic masterpiece which was vibrating, with a noise like a drill, on the bedside cabinet. His face broke into a huge smile as he fitted the earpiece and pressed a button on the handheld unit. "Morning, Angel. You're up early for a geek, considering you've probably spent all night surfing the net, playing Dungeons and Dragons with your cyberfriends." Jake's joy faded as he realised this wasn't a live link and the screen was filled with a short, unfriendly document instead.

'JAKE. THEY KNOW YOU'VE BEEN TO THE CELL. MISSED YOU BY MINUTES. STILL NO IDEA OF EXACT WHEREABOUTS BUT ASSUME YOU ARE IN LOCAL AREA. FOUND DAMAGED BUG SWEEPER. GOT TO GO. HIS MAJESTY WANTS TO SEE ME. ANGEL.'

He switched the machine off. 'Another "good luck" wouldn't have hurt,' thought Jake, suddenly wincing. 'Unlike my shoulder'.

Jake's body still ached from the various knocks he had taken and he stretched with some discomfort before pulling the holdall he had liberated from the holding cell from under the bed. Within half an hour he was dressed and, having checked for any unwanted witnesses, had descended the drainpipe and skirted round to the front of the hotel. His outward appearance hadn't changed from the night before. He still wore his 'borrowed' tracksuit, though underneath that, his covert suit was stuffed with as much of his field kit as he dared carry. The bulky holdall was left as a tip for the hotel's cleaning staff. Short of an alien invasion of earth, he was as prepared for anything as he could be, though considering his recent luck he half expected to see little green men land their flying saucer at any second.

He gingerly popped his head round the side of the wall and watched. It was too early for most of the residents of the hotel to be up and about, but the regular appearances of travelling salesmen in the car park, desperate to get an early start on the road, denied Jake any chance to get himself a car without a good chance of being seen.

A quick glance up also proved his suspicion that CCTV was in operation. Jake had no choice. He would have to find another, less open and busy place to 'shop' for transport.

Keeping close to the wall, he followed the building's outline. He came to an area at the side of the hotel where an extractor system filled the air with the delicious smell of cooked breakfast. Jake crouched and took in details. A single solid door led into the hotel's kitchens, entry to which was gained through the use of a numbered keypad. The windows to either side of it were steamed up from the heat of the cooking going on inside. Two cars and a scooter cluttered up the small area of tarmac that Jake had to assume was the kitchen staff's designated parking area. Obviously, the hotel management didn't see their employees' transport to be as important as their customers', as Jake was happy to see that no surveillance systems had been rigged up here.

Jake placed his hand into one of the pockets in his covert suit beneath the tracksuit and pulled out a piece of equipment. It had a long technical name, but was known by field operatives at the Academy as the 'SMK' or 'Santa's Magic Key'. There wasn't a lock made that required a key that this thing couldn't open. Jake knew the basic theory. The slim flat bar protruding from the black box was built up of a vast number of sections. Each was able to move independently of each other, rising and falling to mesh into a lock's tumbler system. Angel was fascinated by the workings behind this kind of thing; Jake was just happy to know that when you pressed the button, a red light went green and it worked. He didn't really care how, as long as it did.

Jake checked the area once more and then, keeping lower than the steamed windows and always watching the door, he scuttled across to the scooter. Within seconds the padlock securing the chain wrapped around its rear wheel had been opened. Jake carefully slid the chain free and inserted the SMK again, this time into the ignition barrel, and pressed the button. Jake listened to the device hum quietly, his eyes darting between the red light on the key and the door to the kitchen. Red turned green and Jake turned the unit to release the scooter's steering lock. As quietly as he could he wheeled the scooter round the corner.

Working quickly, Jake checked the scooter's carrying box and to his joy found a helmet. It was a little big for him but he discovered if he put the hood up on his tracksuit, it padded out his head sufficiently. 'Must be my lucky day,' thought Jake as he turned the SMK in the ignition barrel and the lights lit up on the dash. With one hard stamp on the kick-start the scooter buzzed into life and Jake wasted no time in putting distance between himself and his as-yet unsuspecting victim of theft.

He couldn't guess how long it would be before the scooter was reported stolen, but he'd given himself a maximum of four hours use before he would ditch it, however far he'd travelled.

Jake would have used Angel's sat-nav feature but there seemed no point; he didn't have a specific destination to head for. For now, anywhere, as long as it was further away from St. Margaret's, would do. He decided to rely on the roadside signs to guide him, picking names of places he liked the sound of. If he didn't know where he was going himself it would be hard for anyone to second guess his destination. His progress was slow in the morning traffic and he found the engine on the scooter was in dire need of a turbocharger or two. On the plus side this slow-motion metallic stampede acted as the perfect cover for his snail like escape. It would take some doing for the people looking for him to pick out a single scooter among the many vehicles struggling to get to places of work or doing the school run.

The longer he was in this thick traffic, the more it seemed to Jake that everyone was out to get him. It appeared he was more invisible than he hoped to be on the scooter. Several car drivers had almost knocked him out of their way into the gutter without the slightest indication that they had seen him. He soon discovered how ineffective it is to swear at someone from inside a helmet when they are in a car listening to a radio. That, however, did not stop him doing it every time anyway.

As he sat waiting for a set of lights to change, he noticed a police patrol car in his mirrors, two places behind him in the queue. The constable driving was talking and moving his head side to side as if trying to read something that the cars in front were obscuring. Jake cursed again, 'Is he trying to report the number plate on the scooter? That's all I need.' As he watched the police car in his mirrors, a sweat breaking out on his forehead, the lights on the roof burst into life. As soon as they did, Jake decided not to take any chances and wound the throttle of the scooter back, riding up between the lanes of waiting traffic. Whether it was him the copper was after or not, Jake wasn't going to wait around to find out.

Jake hit the front of the queue just as the lights turned amber and he swung left, causing a car to slam on its brakes to avoid hitting him. He could hear the blast of a horn as he accelerated down the side street. Within seconds the vastly more powerful patrol car was bearing down on him and Jake tried to wring out more speed from the scooter but it was useless. If he was going to get away he would have to think fast. To his right Jake spotted a one-way street and, swinging across the flow of traffic, headed down it. Much to his dismay the patrol car followed, weaving in and out of the oncoming traffic with great skill. 'Just what I need,' muttered Jake to himself, 'a copper who's a stuntman on his days off.'

The police car was so close to Jake now the only thing he could hear was the deafening pitch of the siren. He swung another left and then a right; the pursuing car stuck to him like glue. Jake was running blind in a strange town. He knew at any second he could run straight into a dead end or cul-de-sac. Worse still, the pursuing copper would radio ahead and get a road block set up. 'Come on, Jake, think. Think like Chaos.'

The patrol car gunned its engine and drew alongside Jake. He and the driver exchanged glances. Jake had the feeling he looked like a terrified rabbit caught in the headlights of an oncoming truck but he could see the copper was grinning like mad. The traffic cop was enjoying himself without a doubt and for that split second Jake could remember that feeling himself; the kick he used to get from playing on the side that was in control.

There was a blast of horn and the front end of the patrol car dipped as the policeman braked and swerved, falling back behind Jake to avoid an oncoming car. Jake took his opportunity and hurled his scooter down another side road but the grinning policeman was still on his tail.

Jake's attention flicked between the road ahead and the reflection of the patrol car in his mirrors, inches away from his back wheel. Suddenly the pursuing vehicle dropped back and pulled into the kerb before swinging a U-turn to speed away in the opposite direction, its sirens still shattering the air. Jake slowed the scooter to a stop and turned in his seat to watch the disappearing police car in amazement. 'Bigger fish to catch than a kid on a stolen scooter,' he assumed.

Before he had time to be thankful that his luck had held out yet again, a large black Range Rover, all four of its tyres squealing as if in pain, skidded sideways out of a side road less than fifty metres away. It slid across the two lanes before snaking its way at speed toward the stationary scooter. Jake got the feeling the 'bigger fish' had just arrived and it was him that they were trying to catch.

SHOP TIL YOU DROP

Jake wound the scooter's throttle, trying to wring any extra power out of the small engine. He paddled his feet along the floor in an effort to speed up the heart-stoppingly slow acceleration. Weaving wildly across the lane, Jake checked his mirror to find that not only had the Range Rover easily caught up with him, but also a second identical vehicle had appeared from its shadow and was speeding down the oncoming lane to cut him off.

Jake swung into the first road that offered itself without braking, and supported the sliding scooter with his outstretched leg. The machine bucked like a rodeo horse until he managed to force it back into a straight line. The screech of tyres behind him told Jake he was not alone in successfully negotiating the sharp change of direction.

The nose of the pursuing Range Rover rammed into the back of the underpowered scooter, jolting the machine forward and Jake backward, almost rolling him off the seat. Jake was thinking as fast as he could. He'd ridden into a high-walled back street, without a pavement; obviously it was not a busy road. The walls were dark and grubby and the lack of decoration and windows of any sort suggested he was at the back of retail premises, a road used for deliveries and little else.

The scooter was jolted forward again and the mirrors were full of the Range Rover's high front grille. He knew he couldn't brake, that would be suicide, and trying to outrun his pursuers was an obvious nonstarter. Ahead of him he saw the bulk of an articulated lorry pulling slowly away from a delivery bay where the road swept sharply to the right. 'If I can just squeeze between that and the wall...'

Jake's thoughts of escape were cut short as the engines behind him were gunned again, the higher note of the exhausts echoing about the claustrophobic walls. Looking into his mirrors, Jake saw the cars had repositioned themselves one either side of him. Sparks showered off their bodywork as they scraped down the walls each side of the street. Obviously, they too had seen his escape route and intended to cut him off from it by any means possible. At best they could pen him in until a dead end brought him to a forced stop. At worst, Jake was about to become the processed meat filling in a deadly metal sandwich.

As the delivery vehicle slowly ambled away from its drop off, it cleared the view of the loading bay shutter. It was rattling slowly down directly in front of the advancing trio of scooter and cars. Jake checked to his left and right; both Range Rovers' bonnets were already level with his shoulders and the grinding of metal on brickwork pitching higher than even the over-revved engines was almost deafening. Jake fixed his eyes on the descending shutter and forced himself to keep his nerve. He saw one last hope of escape, but he had to time it perfectly.

Too late or too early and the result would be the same: game over.

The Range Rover to his right screamed past him then skidded to a halt to block off the road as it swept to the right. The one on the left kept pace with him. 'The classic bottle and cork,' thought Jake. 'They know what they're doing. They've got to be working for the Academy.'

At that instant, Jake pulled hard on the left lever on the handlebars, locking the back brake and letting the rear wheel slide round so he could lay the scooter down and skid it across the tarmac in the direction of the descending shutter. With a few centimetres to spare, in a shower of shattering plastic, he and the scooter slid under the shutter. A split second later, the metal door was remodelled with a huge dent courtesy of a Range Rover unable to brake in time. Jake kicked himself free of the scooter. He removed his helmet and threw it across the floor. The faces of two of the warehouse staff looked at him with concern. Those of the men from the cars peered under the damaged shutter door with nothing but malice. 'Pit Bulls?' he thought, wondering if the whispers and rumours of St. Margaret's were more accurate than he'd given them credit for.

It was common knowledge, though no one could prove it, that the Academy used ex-military personnel, Special Forces veterans as the rumours had it, to handle situations that needed an instant, unsubtle response. These men could be called into the field with the minimum of briefing to sort out problems quickly, efficiently and with a great deal of tenacity; hence their canine nickname. If the scowling men staring at him under the shutter were indeed the legendary Pit Bulls, Jake was in trouble.

On the other hand, what was a little more grief on top of what he was already facing?

Jake couldn't help but plaster a grin onto his face and wink before leaping to his feet and sprinting away, more than a little pleased to hear a chorus of frustrated swearing and heavy blows being rained upon the damaged and jammed metal shutter.

Jake made quick work of leaving the warehouse area and emerged into the back of a large department store which was full of the usual browsing customers. He walked briskly across the shop floor to the glass doors and looked through them into a large mall. He checked his watch; ten forty-two. The place was lit brighter than a Christmas tree and wasn't exactly as packed as a football ground on match day, but there were enough people eager to sniff out bargains for him to try and blend in with.

Edging forward, careful to keep concealed as much as possible, he glanced about the building. 'Two storeys,' noted Jake, 'and enough security cameras to shoot a Hollywood blockbuster.' He ground down on his teeth as he thought through his options. He needed to get out of the shop. Staying here would only make him a target easier to find than a goldfish in a bowl, but his problem wasn't much different within the bigger complex itself. He didn't have a clue about the layout of the building. Exit points, other than the front of the building, which was no doubt being covered already, could be anywhere. Even if he did find one, it could be alarmed or locked and the last thing he needed was to attract even more attention by breaking out with a fanfare of alarms. To add to his problems he did not have the luxury of planning time; he had to move and he had to move quickly.

Flicking up his hood, he curled his shoulders and walked out into the open space. A few plastic palm trees dumped in concrete pots were dotted about the expanse randomly, their false leaves and spindly trunks offering no cover at all. He strode confidently, trying to look like any other teenage kid out to impose their presence on the building. Trying to sneak around in such a bright open area would have him spotted a mile off.

Keeping his head lowered and facing forwards Jake's eyes scanned the scene before him. Two pairs of escalators leaned on each other offering rides up to and down from the floor above. With a slight quickening of pace, Jake headed over to them and sprang lightly on one as it silently worked its way uphill. Behind him, Jake could hear the sound of hard-soled shoes clattering in a run on the tiled floor. He resisted the urge to look around and kept his head still, fixing his eyes on the point where the stairs of the escalator disappeared back into the workings. His throat was dry, his breathing long and stuttering.

Reaching the top, Jake took a couple of steps away from the escalator, then leaned against the glass barrier that ran along the edge of the upper tier giving him an almost total view of the level below him. He instantly spotted two of the Pit Bulls jogging across the wide floor, their heads turning from side to side as they searched for their quarry. One of them had his right hand tucked inside his suit jacket at chest height.

Jake forced himself to relax, draping himself over the handrail of the barrier as if he didn't have a care in the world. He watched from beneath his hood as two more men appeared from the shop he had just left and joined their colleagues in the search.

A scratch of static echoed in his ear. "Jake?" came Angel's voice. "Can you hear me, Jake?"

Jake straightened up, "Angel. Am I glad to hear you." Unfortunately his movement was not lost on the trained eyes below him and one of the dark-suited men put his finger to his ear and Jake could see him mouth something.

"Are you okay?" asked Angel.

Jake hissed out his frustration.

"There is no need for language like that," said Angel, tartly.

Jake moved away from the barrier as the men made their way towards the escalators and him. "Right at this moment, I think there is," he replied, flicking back his hood. He broke into a quick walk away from the moving staircase.

"Have you combed your hair today?" asked Angel.

"That's rich coming from…" Jake paused. "You can see me?" he said, realising the hand-held unit was closed and stowed in his pocket.

"Clear as day. Look up to your left."

Jake looked up and found himself staring directly into a lens of a CCTV camera. "You've hacked into the system?"

"It was easy. The level of security is quite—"

"Not now, Angel, get me out of here," interrupted Jake, speeding his legs into a run as his pursuers leapt from the escalators.

"Give me a second Jake and I'll bring up the schematics of the building." Angel went quiet.

Jake threw a glance over his shoulder and saw the men sprinting towards him. He suddenly had the unnerving feeling he was being herded like sheep towards a cliff edge. There had been two cars chasing him that meant there could be at least eight Pit Bulls after him. Four were running behind and the rest...Jake could only guess where they might be. There was no time for clever plans and subtleties. Jake reacted instead and sprinted into the nearest shop. He began to weave in and out of the aisles full of merchandise and then slid across the floor to hide under a rack of coats. He froze like a stone but his body was ready to move again in the blink of an eye.

From where he lay hidden, it was hard for Jake to see anything. His view was obscured by stands and piles of boxes, but he could hear the slow progress of the footfalls making their way towards the back of the store. He knew the men would sweep the area by spreading out, each of them taking a section as their own. Their weapon hands would be ready to react to the slightest abnormality with lightning speed.

Jake heard the click-clack on the tiles to his right and slowly turning his head, he saw the highly polished leather of a shoe crowned by black trouser cloth. He stared intently, willing the wearer to continue forward and away from his fragile fortress of ladies' winter wear. The shoe lifted, heel then toe, and moved out of Jake's peripheral vision.

"Jake," came Angel's voice in his ear, "I've got the plans."

The next sound Jake heard was the squeak of shoe leather twisting on the floor as the wearer turned around. With his cover blown, Jake had no choice but to leap up and sprint for the door, scattering the rack of coats, hoping his luck would hold and that all the Pit Bulls were behind him and caught off guard.

Jake exploded out of the shop door and forced his legs to pump as fast as they could. Behind him he heard the cries of the men all warning each other of his flight. "Angel!" shouted Jake. "Can you see me? Have you got visual?"

"I can't—" Angel began, but her voice quickly changed with a squeak of excitement. "Yes, I can see you Jake, I can see you."

"Well, get me the hell out of here!"

There was a pause.

"Angel!" screamed Jake, the sound of pounding feet so close behind him he imagined he could feel the breath of the chasing men on his neck.

"Take the next right," squealed Angel, "and go straight through the double fire doors at the end."

"What if they're locked?" demanded Jake, almost skidding off his feet on the smooth tiles as he rounded the corner. Behind him he could hear by the thud and the swearing that at least one of the Pit Bulls had not been so lucky.

"They won't be," assured Angel, "not by the time you get there anyway. They'll lead you into the outer service core of the building. If you make it to the stairwell there's a chance you'll get out before they secure it."

Jake threw himself at the double doors which burst open, slamming themselves against the wall, just as Angel had promised. "Which way?"

"Left," instructed Angel, "and then the second door on the right."

Jake sprinted along the windowless corridor. Compared to the welcoming white shine of the shopping centre interior, the dimly lit tunnel was much less friendly.

It was a rough concrete construction decorated with pipes and electrical cables tied up to metal frames. Jake glanced at the first door on his right as he passed it. A square green sign above it read 'EXIT' and showed a pictorial flight of stairs; he paid it little notice. Angel would have a good reason for him not using that way out.

The second door was only metres ahead for which Jake was thankful. He couldn't keep this up for much longer.

The single door gave way easily as Jake rammed his hands into the bar. His face filled with shock. He halted his headlong flight sharply to prevent colliding with a wall. He stumbled back a pace and realised he was in a room no bigger than three metres square, with no window and the only way out was the way he'd come in.

"It's a dead end, Angel!" He looked about quickly seeing some empty and discarded containers for cleaning agents. "Some kind of storeroom or something! Angel? Angel!"

The earpiece wasn't dead; Jake could hear her breathing, but he received no reply. "Angel!"

Then the open door was filled by the large shape of one of the Pit Bulls, a broad-shouldered man in his late forties with tightly cropped dark hair that was beginning to grey at the temples. His suit sleeves clung tightly to the muscles in his arms. Sweat ran freely from his forehead down his face, following the lines of his severe looking mouth to drip off his broad chin.

Jake raised his arm ready to fire his wrist gun but the man was surprisingly quick for his bulk and grabbed Jake's elbow with one hand whilst ripping the weapon free with the other. "I'll take that, if you don't mind," he said, pushing Jake back.

Jake stared at the man before him, but the shock on his

face was not because of his presence or because he had been disarmed so easily. He lowered his head to hide his moving lips. "Angel?" he whispered into the air, a quiet pleading in his voice.

"I'm sorry, Jake," replied Angel and a second later the telltale click of a communication link being broken echoed in Jake's ear.

The man in the doorway stepped forward and grinned. His colleagues stood three abreast behind him, just outside the room, making sure Jake didn't have the slightest crack to squirm his way through this time. "You're to come with us," said the man, his facial expression telling Jake that was all the information he was going to get.

Jake didn't answer. His arms hung loose and lifeless at his sides, his legs seemed to suck in the weight of the concrete that surrounded him and for an instant his body trembled with an intense, bone-deep cold.

BANG BANG YOU'RE DEAD

Jake offered no resistance as he was led by the arm in a vice-like grip. His head felt numb and his legs moved heavily, almost unable to support his weight. The men in suits stayed close to him, talking to each other sparingly, but Jake couldn't make out any of their words. To him their voices were as far away as if heard from the end of a long tunnel. He had no desire to eavesdrop on their conversation.

The party had reached the exit that Angel had failed to tell Jake about when he was jerked to a stop as the four men escorting him were challenged by an ancient looking security guard.

"What are you doing back here?" said the man. His peaked hat was far too big for his shrunken-looking head and his baggy blue shirt hung off his skeleton-like frame. A badge that read 'Officer Jenkins' was pinned to his chest at a forty-five-degree angle.

"Special Branch," said the man gripping Jake's arm. "We've just apprehended this suspect and we're taking him down to the station for questioning."

"Not that way you're not," said the guard, obviously not impressed. "That's for emergency use only."

"Listen, Officer…Jenkins," said the Pit Bull, trying to form a friendly professional link with the old man. "You don't understand—"

"No, you don't understand," interrupted the guard, fumbling with a thin old hand to free his radio from its belt holster. "That's a fire exit and you can only use it in the event of a fire."

The Pit Bull to the left of the one holding Jake reached inside his jacket. He looked to his superior for permission to act, but received a negative head-shake, so withdrew his hand and relaxed.

"Do you realise the amount of paperwork I would have to fill in if I allowed you to use that door?" continued the old guard. "And that's not counting the resetting of the whole alarm system, the cost of the Fire Brigade being called out to a false alarm, the endless…"

"Forget it," barked the Pit Bull, his patience worn out. "We'll take him back through the shopping centre." Jake was persuaded forward again as the Pit Bulls walked past the fussing old-timer.

Back down on the ground floor of the shopping centre, the group of men were met by two others dressed in exactly the same dark suits. They talked over Jake's head in tones that were obviously happy with their morning's work, tinted by the odd comment about stupid old buggers making life more difficult than it already was.

Jake lifted his face and caught sight of his reflection in the large glass window of a shop front. Staring back at him with dull eyes, he saw his pathetic figure hanging limp and lifeless, his mouth slack and emotionless, his shoulders hunched under the weight of treachery and defeat. The bruising on his left cheekbone stood out like a tribal marking of shame. Around his mirror image, the reflections of the taller men laughed and joked about their prize, about him, the pathetic loser kid who thought he could better them.

Jake lowered his gaze again and caught sight of the few centimetres of his covert suit that showed beneath his dirty tracksuit bottoms. In that second Jake became aware of his heart beating. It thudded in his chest once, twice. The blood in his veins that had felt like jelly, began to flow again, bringing feeling back to his limbs, feeding his brain and mind with the vitality they needed. Jake raised his face again to meet his reflected image and this time he looked back into a pair of eyes that shone with vitality. 'Going down without a fight, were you? Curling up and giving in?' Jake's mouth reflected as a stern straight line and his nostrils flared slightly as he pulled in a deep breath of air, slowly and deliberately.

Another peel of laughter from the men reached Jake's ears but he found no shared humour in their comments.

"His codename's Chaos, apparently," chortled one of his captors. "Funny name to give to a harmless kitten like him." His comrades joined in with appreciation of the joke.

Jake kept his head low, his eyes darting as his mind formulated a plan to get free of these clowns. His teeth came out from hiding as he grinned. 'You want Chaos?' he thought. 'Let's see how sharp this kitten's claws are.'

The shopping mall was much busier than before. It would be much easier for him to disappear into a crowd this size. He was searching out people; the frail old lady pulling the blue shopping trolley; the broad shouldered and fat bellied builder with the bright red beard; the tall youth in a business suit covered in flaky crumbs working his way through a pasty on the seats by the litter bin. He took in the signs pointing to exits, emergency and otherwise, that were placed on fake old-fashioned sign posts. He took in the noise, the feeling, the whole atmosphere of the place and let it soak into his mind until an answer revealed itself.

"Come on, Tiddles," said the Pit Bull, gripping Jake. "Time you were back in your kitty box."

Jake resisted and, taking a deep breath, screamed at the top of his lungs. "Help! Please, somebody help me!"

Instantly the man gripping Jake's arm tightened his grasp and the remaining Pit Bulls automatically closed in around him, ready to stop any attempt at breaking free. Jake kept on screaming. "Help! Please, they're hurting me!"

"Shut up!" ordered the head Pit Bull. Another tried to cover Jake's mouth with his hand and was rewarded for his effort by Jake clamping down with his teeth on the flesh between his thumb and forefinger. The man removed his hand and raised his fist ready to strike back at his assailant.

"What are you doing to that young man?" asked the old lady towing the blue shopping trolley behind her as she tapped at the Pit Bull's back with her rolled up umbrella. Several other shoppers' attention had also been drawn to the shouting youth in the middle of the huddle.

"Nothing to do with you, madam," was the gruff reply. "Go about your business."

The woman ignored the rebuke, tilting and bobbing her head to look at Jake in the centre of the men.

"Are you alright, dear?"

"No, they're trying to take me out of here," sniffed Jake, even pleasing himself with the amount of panic he had laced his voice with. "My dad will be back at any minute but they won't listen. I'm scared…I'm really scared they're going to hurt me."

"Take no notice of him," argued the Pit Bull, gripping Jake's arm so tightly that the knuckles on his hand were white. "He's up to no good. He's lying, he was…shoplifting."

"In that case," said the woman, with a defiant look in her wrinkled face, "we can wait for the police to arrive, can't we? They can sort it out."

"Look, lady, this has got nothing to do with you," and the man pushed her gently away. The lady staggered back and gave out a high-pitched yelp of distress.

"Oi! Who do you think you're pushing?" said the red-bearded builder, striding over to stand aggressively in front of the old woman as protection. Much to Jake's pleasure he did not look as easy an opponent for the Pit Bulls as the old lady had been.

The suited man's face did not disguise the anger that was welling up in him. "Sir, do not do anything you might regret."

"Oh yeah?" replied the building worker, flicking up his arms in a 'bring it on' motion. "Like what?"

Jake checked his captors. The situation was perfect; all their attention was focused on the problem being generated beyond their circle. People's attention in the shopping centre was turning in their direction and they did not like it. At that moment he was way down on their list of priorities. The situation was spiralling beyond their control. Raising his right foot, he kicked back slamming the heel of his boot into the shin of the Pit Bull and forced it down the bone until his foot hammered onto the man's instep, protected only by a thin barrier of shoe leather and sock. The crippling pain instantly caused the Pit Bull's grip to loosen enough for Jake to shoulder-charge forward with all his weight and break through the blockade of men in front of him.

The builder mistook the suited man's stumble forward as an act of aggression and instantly responded with a perfectly delivered right hook to the chin. The Pit Bull lurched backwards, colliding with another of his colleagues and their combined weight sent them both crashing to the floor.

Jake was free but he needed to put distance and obstacles between himself and the men. They would soon gain control of the situation and switch back to operational mode. Then nothing, interfering old women and chivalrous building workers included, would stop them completing their mission. Glancing up, he saw what he needed. He ran to the marble-effect pillar between two shops and slammed his elbow into the fire alarm. A tinny bell filled the air of the shopping mall with its clanging warning. The shoppers stopped for an instant, raised their heads as one, trying to locate the source of the sound and then began a quick, but orderly, exit.

Jake glanced at the Pit Bulls again. To the side of their group the red bearded man lay rolling on the floor, clutching at his groin. Their attention was focused back on him. He took a few steps backwards; he needed to time his escape to perfection and for that he needed to make sure the conditions were right. He was gambling for the highest of stakes: his life. 'Come on,' he thought to himself, staring at the men walking toward him, 'play the ace.'

"Not bad for a kitten, hey?" said Jake with a smirk, "I'm sure you'll be talking about this for years back at your kennels."

One of the Pit Bulls reached inside his jacket, tired of playing games with a mouthy kid and pulled out a Taser gun. He levelled it at Jake's chest. 'At last,' thought Jake. He swallowed hard at the sight of the weapon, knowing full well his plan could collapse right now, and him with it, at the mercy of tens of thousands of volts.

"Say good night, kitty," mocked the man.

"Terrorists! They've got a bomb!" shouted Jake as he sprinted away.

The Pit Bull stalled, his finger frozen on the trigger. Shoppers close to the man holding the Taser took notice of him and saw the drawn weapon. Even if the Pit Bull had tried to argue that he wasn't a terrorist, the damage was already done. New voices shouted out warnings above the wail of the fire alarms, echoing Jake's subterfuge. Panic spread.

People gave up their orderly evacuation and rushed toward the exit. They ran, pushed, scrambled and shoved their way forward to get as far away from the potential disaster as quickly as possible, all to a soundtrack of shouts and screams. Within seconds, a mass of people crushed together in the aisle between the shops that led to the main entrance.

Jake buried himself in the throng, forcing his way into the centre as each person fought their own selfish battle to escape. Behind him, caught off guard by the sudden mayhem, Jake could see the Pit Bulls trying to get to him. Now their size was a disadvantage. They became one with the flow, carried wherever it took them. His smaller, lighter frame made it easy for him to squirm between the gaps in the human tide and worm his way forward.

As the main entrance to the shopping complex got closer, the pressure became less as people spilled out into the street. Ahead of him, Jake could see another solitary Pit Bull, obviously posted to keep an eye on the exit. He grabbed at any kid that passed him, checking for a positive identification before shoving them away. His colleagues may have been trapped back in the mass evacuation but it didn't mean they hadn't had the foresight to radio their situation in.

This was no time for subtleties. It wouldn't be long before the men in the shopping mall worked their way out; Jake had to act quickly. He found himself with just enough space to pick up pace and began to jog forward, taking measured strides, gauging the distance between him and the obstacle like an athlete judging the first hurdle in a race. 'Steady,' he told himself, 'he hasn't seen you yet.'

The Pit Bull's head was turning frantically, but suddenly he stopped and fixed his stern gaze. Jake stared back at the Pit Bull, unblinking. He knew he'd been seen but it wasn't a problem, it was too late for the man ahead of him.

The man reached inside his suit jacket as Jake dropped onto his side and slid feet first along the tiled floor. The soles of his boots made contact with the man's knees before he could withdraw his weapon hand. Jake covered his head with his arms as the man flipped forward, his face hitting the ground with a crack. The sickening, jarring sound reached Jake's ears but he had no time for sympathy or damage assessment. He pushed himself off the floor and took to his feet again. The Pit Bull remained still, as rushing feet stepped over, around and on him to make good their escape.

Outside the shopping centre, people were still jostling to get as far away as possible in the shortest possible time. They were blocking the road in front of the building so a traffic jam had built up. Frustrated drivers with no knowledge of the supposed terrorist situation blasted their horns in anger at their inertia. Jake left the flow of people as soon as he cleared the doors and looked quickly about. Assessing his options, he discovered he only really had two: left or right. The outpouring of people filling the pavement opposite meant he could find himself snagged and trapped in the mass. He chose left and sprinted down the road until he came to another left turning which he decided was as good as any to take. Without a plan, random direction changes were as effective for losing someone as they were for getting lost.

He ran for several more minutes turning left and right, into streets and alleys that ran between buildings until his adrenalin started wearing off. He began to feel the pain in his chest and legs and a stitch was beginning to knot itself under his ribs. He stumbled into one more road and then put his back to the wall and slid down it to sit on his heels, gasping for breath, his pounding head glad of the cooling touch of the bricks.

His rest was too short-lived as he glanced left and realised he was at the top of the road he had been chased down on the scooter. At the bottom he could see two

Range Rovers, one of which still had its nose buried in the metal shutter. 'Jesus,' he thought, 'when your luck turns bad...' He stood up again, all thoughts of the stitch wiped from his mind. He slipped back round the corner he'd just come from and pressed himself against the wall, wishing he hadn't been so sloppy in his flight, cursing himself for not paying more attention to the direction in which he was fleeing. The sound of running shoes caught his attention. He stayed still, inching his head into different positions as he tried to pinpoint the direction the noise was coming from. There was a chance it wasn't the Pit Bulls trying to track him down but there was also a chance it was.

Jake risked a look down the road that led to the shutter. Next to the cars Jake could make out a figure pacing back and forth, obviously having been given orders to guard that exit of the shopping centre.

'Think, Highfield, think,' Jake urged silently to himself. The area had become too hot and he needed to get away, to put some distance between himself and the Pit Bulls. What he needed was a diversion.

Crouching low, he shot his head round the corner again, taking in as much detail as he could in a glance. Heroics were never encouraged by the Academy; it was a given fact that most foolhardy acts were followed by a funeral, but Jake did not have the luxury of playing by the rules any more.

He pulled his head back once more, took three deep breaths to fill his lungs and bolster his nerves, then sprinted round the corner as fast as he dared whilst trying to keep his footfalls as silent as possible.

The Pit Bull at the end of the street had his back turned, his focus firmly fixed on the damaged shutter.

'Remember your orders; remember your orders,' chanted Jake to himself, willing the man to keep his back to him just long enough for him to reach the cover he was aiming for.

The Pit Bull turned his head slowly from left to right, studying the shutter.

'A few more strides; just a few more.'

The man began to turn, slowly, raising his arms and arching his back as he stretched.

Jake reached the back of the crashed Range Rover and ducked down out of sight, looking at the legs of the Pit Bull from under the bodywork. His feet were facing up the street but stayed static. He hadn't seen Jake. As he watched, the Pit Bull turned his attention back to the metal shutter. Jake lifted himself up ready to put the next part of his plan into action. The solitary Pit Bull suddenly put his finger to his ear. "Delta Four, receiving," he said.

Jake dropped quickly back into cover.

"Yeah, don't worry, if the slippery bugger has doubled back and comes out this way his ass will be grass…yeah, no problem, I'm ready for him, Delta Four out."

As the man lowered his hand from his ear, Jake stepped up in front of him and, not allowing him time to react to the intrusion of personal space, reached inside his jacket pocket and discharged the Taser gun whilst still in its holster. The dart shot down and lodged in the man's upper thigh. He collapsed in a trembling heap onto the road before even the faintest gasp of surprise could pass his lips.

"Not that ready, were you?" said Jake, coldly.

He moved quickly and opened the door of the Range Rover that wasn't stuck in the twisted shutter door. It faced back up the street and the keys were still in the ignition. His luck was holding. The vehicle was probably modified to the normal St. Margaret's specifications, strategically strengthened to withstand firearms and high explosive attacks from the outside. Jake popped the bonnet open to reveal the highly tuned motor. 'No wonder the scooter had some problems getting away,' he thought as he delved into a pouch of his covert suit. He pulled out what looked like a coil of modelling clay. It was in fact what field operatives called exploding string. It was so effective at precision blasting it could be used to wrap round a tree and fell it in one go when discharged. Carefully, Jake wound it around the engine block. The outside may be bombproof, but this would be a blast going the other way. As he finished weaving the pliable charge, he retrieved a small metal torpedo-shaped device and twisted it to the left. It sprang open to reveal a timing mechanism. Jake pressed the timer until the display read sixty seconds and pushed the silver detonator into the exploding string before shutting the bonnet.

As he neared the unconscious man lying on the street, he heard a crackle. Pulling the man's earpiece free he could hear requests for 'Delta Four' to report in. Time was running out fast. The remaining Pit Bulls would realise there was something wrong.

Running back to the driver's door, he turned the key and fired up the powerful engine. He reached into his pocket and pulled out the computer unit Angel had given him. "This time you can be of help," he muttered bitterly as he placed the device on the accelerator pedal and wedged it in place against the side of the foot well. The engine roared uncomfortably at full revs.

Slipping his left leg into the vehicle and across the driver's seat Jake pushed his foot down on the brake pedal and pulled back the gear selector until it slotted into 'D'.

The 'goldtooth' device in his ear gave out a hiss of static. A familiar voice broke through, barely audible over the howling engine.

"Jake? Can you hear me, Jake? I know you can. It's Angel, I..."

Jake' face twisted with rage as he pulled the earpiece free and threw it onto the passenger seat; at the same time he lifted his foot off the brake pedal and leapt clear of the car. The tyres squealed in protest before the spinning rubber found its bite on the worn tarmac and hurled the heavy car forwards bouncing it left and right off the walls of the narrow street.

The Range Rover burst out onto the busy road at the top, glancing off one car before hammering into a lamppost. The rear wheels lifted off the ground with the force of the impact before slamming back down to carry on screeching as the engine continued to try and drive the trapped vehicle forward. Five seconds later the exploding rope did its job, tearing the bonnet in half like paper and filling the engine cavity with flames that burned ten feet high.

Jake could hear the screams and shocked exclamations of witnesses to the crash and resulting fireball. He'd known it would not be a big explosion, he just wanted to raise some attention. If the area was under scrutiny, the Pit Bulls would have to watch their step to avoid attracting suspicion from other agencies like the police who would obviously be working close by. It was breathing space he was after and it looked like he was going to get it.

Repeated cries for 'Delta Four' to respond and explain what the hell was going on poured out of the Pit Bull's earpiece. The worried caller, it seemed, was close enough to have seen, or at least heard, the explosion.

Jake looked at the burning vehicle at the end of the street. It wouldn't take long for anyone interested in his whereabouts to realise he, or his body, wasn't in the wreckage and that the explosion had been rigged to cover his escape. The familiar sirens of the emergency services approaching proved that his plan would work; people would be paying attention to this area, giving him a chance to disappear into deep cover again. He decided going back up the street was his best course of action. He could head past the burning car, which was already attracting a crowd of ghoulish onlookers in which he could mingle. He stepped forward, but just then, the sole of his boot tapping on metal gave him a better idea.

TURNING POINT

The smell in the sewer system was almost unbearable. Jake felt like the flesh on the inside of his nostrils was being burned by the noxious gases. He repeatedly found himself doubled over in a coughing fit he felt sure would end with him literally vomiting his guts up. But it wasn't just the stench.

Every one of his senses was being assaulted. His eyes watered; his tongue, even though he made sure to keep his mouth shut, could taste the rancid fumes which reminded him of sour milk and every inch of his skin crawled as he waded, at times chest deep, through the thick soup-like waste. Even his hearing was being tricked in the edgeless dark by the drips and splashes that echoed about him as if from all directions at once.

The small penlight that he dug out of his covert suit gave little support in this complete darkness; a pinpoint of hope that made Jake feel like he was looking at this strange, subterranean world down the tube of a toilet roll. He walked slowly and carefully, his left hand always brushing the wall. He soon learned to switch his imagination off when his fingers came into contact with unknown substances which clung to the bricks and squashed under his touch.

He swung the torch left to right, which at least warned him of the approach of dead ends. He alternated taking left and right turns in an effort to avoid walking round in circles in this unforgiving environment. He slid his feet forward, rather than stepping, before putting weight on them, to eliminate the chance of being surprised by any sudden drop or structural damage in the sewer floor. His ears were keen to pick out any hint of the hiss of rushing water that meant there was a drop in the level somewhere ahead of him. Even so, his careful progress did not negate all risks and several times he found himself tripping forward into the rancid liquid. Thankfully each time he managed to keep his head from submerging into the gunk.

Jake passed numerous shafts that led up, back into the outside world by means of iron ladders bolted to the wall but despite the discomfort of his situation and his senses begging him to get out, he knew down here was safer than up there for the time being. He needed to cover as much distance as possible before emerging back into the open and on view for possible capture, or worse.

As he settled into a steady rhythm, the adrenalin rush of his encounter with the Pit Bulls leaving his system, Jake's mind ploughed over all the things that he had been victim to over the past few days. Unnerving as the thought was, he was going to have to make a decision that would change his life forever.

He was alone and friendless, and Jake was surprised to find himself uncomfortable with this thought. Three years ago, before St. Margaret's, that was how he accepted his life was, that was the normal state of affairs. Jake Highfield, on his own, looking out for himself and happy about it.

He smirked in the darkness. 'Of course, three years ago I didn't have carloads of nutters chasing me, trying to make me vanish.'

His smile faded as he thought of Angel and how she had let him down. No, not let him down, pushed him down. Betrayed him. 'You don't say "sorry" unless you've done something to be sorry for,' thought Jake, darkly.

Whilst he couldn't think of any allies he could rely on, his list of enemies was not so short and each was linked directly to the Academy. The Headmaster, Packard, Clarkson, Routledge. The last two Jake could understand. From his arrival at St. Margaret's they had been on his case, bullies both, but the Headmaster had suddenly seemed to turn against him. He accepted he'd botched up the Watkinson mission and he felt guilty for doing so, but surely that alone didn't warrant being vanished? He'd proved his ability often enough in the field to negate one mistake, hadn't he?

'The real trouble started after Angel shared her discovery of the Void Program with me,' thought Jake. 'Maybe that's at the centre of all this.' Jake's expression darkened as thoughts of his ex-friend's treachery filled his head again. 'Maybe she's at the centre of all this?'

"Holding a grudge isn't going to get me out of this," he said out loud to himself, the words echoing off the curved walls of the sewer. "I've got to forget the past and think ahead, think my way beyond this place," he gagged, as a more pungent odour filtered out of a side tunnel he passed. "Especially this bloody place."

'The Void,' thought Jake, forcing his mind to ignore his physical discomfort. 'That is at the centre of all this mess. But how?'

He realised all he knew about this mysterious program was that it seemed to worm its way into St. Margaret's computer systems without resistance...or so he'd been told. Then there was the link between the Void and the vanishings. This was a theory he had to accept now, especially given his own experience. But why? What did the vanishings achieve for whoever was behind the program? Perhaps there was an enemy of the Academy picking off the students one by one? It was a possible answer, but who and for what reason? Surely such high profile activity would not be taken lying down by the Headmaster; unless...'

Jake's train of thought was derailed as he slipped on something and skidded backwards with a splash that seemed to have a thousand echoes before it stopped. Jake picked himself up and cursed as he shook his arms, violently trying to loosen whatever it was soaking through his sleeves to chill his arms.

"The biggest problem is," said Jake, finding the sound of his own voice in the darkness comforting, "the Void is invisible. A computer program. I can hardly ambush it in cyberspace and strangle the life out of it." He swore again in frustration, kicking the liquid at his feet so it showed up like a silver fan in the dimming light of his torch.

He moved on slower than before, checking his steps with even more care. The only fact he could be sure of was that all this unholy mess centred on the Academy and those within its walls, which left him with one decision to make and it was one that was far from easy. Whichever route he picked would be filled with lethal danger. But he knew that he had to make a choice: fight or flight.

The small point of light in front of him was closing,

shrinking. The batteries in his torch were giving up their battle against the endless, claustrophobic dark around him. At the next shaft leading up, Jake made his ascent from the subterranean gloom.

It was night when Jake emerged from the sewer but compared with the pitch black he had been moving about in for hours, this was much less oppressive. The first conscious thing he did was open his mouth wide and draw in a deep breath of clean air. Nothing had ever tasted so sweet and the steady rain that was falling only added to its cleansing purity.

Jake looked around and found he had emerged on industrial wasteland and was thankful for it. Operational CCTV here was unlikely, as were prying eyes spotting him, though at this moment Jake didn't care as long as he could breathe fresh air. Where he was exactly he had no idea, but he could find that out easily enough later from road signs and street names. For now he was happy that he was able to relax again, for a while at least. Pulling the rest of his body free of the circular drop, he sat down on the rubble-strewn ground, leaning back on his hands to let the rain attempt to wash away some of the filth he was caked in. He dropped his head forward. The cold raindrops dived between his neck and collar, sending a chill down his spine.

Jake stood up and looked about him. A car hissed by just beyond the metal fence at the perimeter of the waste ground, its wet roof shining orange, then black, then orange again as it drove under the lights lining the road. Jake's suspicious gaze never left it until it had crept out of his range of vision. He frowned.

'Is this it for me?' he thought. 'Always on the look out,

suspicious of everything, never sleeping soundly for fear of who may come for me in the night?' The grinding sound of a rolling bottle on concrete to his right made Jake flinch and freeze, ready to react. He stood still, alert, until the figure of a feral cat appeared for a moment before disappearing back into the shadows. Jake relaxed once more.

"Great, I'm scared of moggies now," Jake muttered to himself with disgust. "That'll look good on my CV." He imagined the words. 'Chaos – highly trained for any covert operation as long as he doesn't have to break into your granny's flat'.

Stripping off the tracksuit, the rancid smell of which was beginning to filter into his nose again, Jake checked what equipment he had left in the pockets of the covert suit. 'Not perfect' he thought, 'but it'll have to do. I'm sure there's enough stuff here for me to—'

At that instant Jake realised he had no choice; hadn't had a choice for the last three years. He was a puppet and whoever held the strings could make him dance or take some scissors and 'snip', let him drop lifeless. He was running for his life and still he was under the influence of those who were chasing him, those who had trained him. He had become St. Margaret's property and she refused to let him go.

He straightened himself, a defiant look in his eyes, and headed towards the fence and the road beyond. 'If they want Chaos,' he grinned to himself, his heart pounding with a mix of adrenaline, fear and excitement, 'then Chaos they shall have. But on my terms and my terms alone.'

HOME SWEET HOME

Jake wasted no time during the remainder of the night in covering the ground between him and St. Margaret's. He kept to the suburbs, avoiding town and city centres, anywhere there may be cameras that could pick up his image and put the Pit Bulls back on his trail again. He stole several cars from the paths of houses, sure to take nothing too flashy or distinctive, and ditched each exactly one hour after he had started them up. The only thing he kept between cars was the map that the first car's glove compartment had provided him with. He used it to plan his route using only minor roads whenever possible.

By five in the morning he was within ten miles of his objective, familiar territory. He ditched the final car on the main road of a small village. He greeted a milkman with a confident 'Good morning' as he got out of the car, then pretended to lock it up.

He left the map on the passenger seat, taking a fleece jacket that had been in the boot as a swap, though by the condition of the thin, torn garment he was the loser in this transaction. By seven he was buried under a pile of cardboard at the back of an empty unit on a little-used rural industrial estate, trying to get some sleep so he was prepared mentally and physically alert for the night to come.

By midday he had slept little, and fitfully, and had to accept there was little chance of a good rest, not only because of his location and discomfort but also because his mind would not stop racing through plans and ideas for what lay ahead.

He joined the queue at the mobile café van that was used by the workers on the industrial estate. The woman smiled over the counter at Jake in a motherly way and commented on the fact that she'd never seen him before and that he looked too young to be at work. Jake told her it was his first day on work experience and that he was really sorry, but he'd left his dinner money on the table in the hall.

"Don't you worry, love," the woman said, her smile getting even bigger. "You have that on me."

All Jake had to suffer in return was a long, sentimental tale about how she remembered her son's first days at work. In truth Jake didn't mind; he was short on friends and anyone taking his side, even with just the offer of a free bacon butty, was more than welcome.

Jake spent the next few hours huddled under his pile of loose cardboard examining the equipment he had left. His initial stock check the night before had been on the optimistic side. The explosives and detonators, which were only small in amount and designed for blowing locks, had been soaked beyond use in the sewer system. It seemed the same fate had been dealt to most of the electronic hardware, except the night vision goggles, but even they only functioned through the right-hand lens and then the image flickered in and out. After Jake had eliminated the damaged and useless equipment, all he had on the ground before him was a multi-blade penknife, the almost drained torch, a roll of thin wire and the damaged night-vision goggles. He swore repeatedly as he packed what was left of his equipment away.

By eight the sun had long since set and Jake still had not decided on a plan to get him inside St. Margaret's undetected but he had made himself a promise and he was not about to back down. If he turned and ran now, he would spend the rest of his life, until he was inevitably caught, facing the same thing day, after day, after day. He set off on foot at a jog, a steady pace he knew would get him to the perimeter of the Academy within two hours.

Jake prowled along the top of the high outer wall that cut off the trees' advance toward the unsuspecting outside world. He checked for the movement of any of Routledge's four-legged sentries. He waited patiently for a sign of their presence, letting caution be his guide. Jake's guts told him this was wrong; the dogs were always there, they lived there, only ever approaching the edge of the forest to be fed. Once you knew the pattern of their patrols, they were easy to avoid but tonight they were not where they were supposed to be. The dogs had pens close to the buildings but he'd only ever seen one of them there when it was ill. If the dogs weren't patrolling their territory it was because someone had a reason for wanting them out of the way. This realisation didn't sit well with him but Jake had no choice. If there was ever a night he had to take rash chances, this was it. He dropped off the wall silently and crept into the shadows of the trees.

At the edge of the forest, looking at the outline of the Academy against the night sky, Jake had to accept he was walking into a trap. The place was lifeless. Still. Not one light was burning through any of the windows. Nothing at all was moving in the grounds. The only word that kept echoing around Jake's head was 'abandoned'. It was highly probable and well within the Headmaster's powers for him to have the whole place emptied under the pretence of some form of exercise or field trip. He looked again through the night-vision goggles but the flickering, magnified image that ghosted in and out of focus added nothing to his information. The few drops of rain that had started to fall added more interference to the scene. Jake's frustration and impatience got the better of him and he threw the useless goggles away to his side.

He continued to watch without the aid of the equipment. Fixing his gaze on a single window, he tried to pick out the slightest twitch of movement, but at this distance it was impossible to tell if anyone was moving around. Jake was beginning to get nervous. The situation felt utterly wrong. Had this been a mission, he would have aborted it and withdrawn. No one would have blamed him for it; it would be the right thing to do. Taking risks in the field was one thing, but not when information was lacking and the odds were heavily stacked against success. Jake bit his lip. The only trouble with that argument was that this wasn't a sanctioned mission and this time he was playing against the people who wrote the rules.

A shiver ran over his body and he could feel the hairs on his arms stand to attention. 'Jake Highfield might turn and run,' his thoughts told him, 'and keep on running, but not Chaos. Chaos would see this through to the end.' He felt like a switch had been thrown in his brain, committing him to the action that lay ahead. He found himself looking at the sky, noticing the crescent moon was shedding little light through the gathering cover of the clouds that rolled in on the breeze. He pinpointed the closest point of the buildings to him – the corner of the science block. He estimated the distance to cover was just under two hundred metres and before Jake Highfield could try to talk him out of it, Chaos was sprinting forward, his mind set on one thing. He had a mission to complete.

Jake pressed his back against the wall of the single-storey building, breathing heavily from the exertion of the run. He had to assume he had been seen and therefore had to keep moving quickly to regain cover and maintain the element of surprise in some form. Lifting one foot onto a windowsill, he pushed up, catching hold of the lip of the flat roof, and hoisted himself up in one smooth movement. Half crouching, he scuttled across the roof to the skylight and using the blade of his knife, worked the catch open. Holding onto the frame he lowered himself in and dropped to the floor. He stayed motionless, his breathing controlled and quiet as his ears strained to pick up the slightest of sounds.

Keeping low, he made his way to the door of the classroom. He gradually raised himself up, resting on the left-hand side of the frame until he could see through the door's glass panel at an angle down the length of the corridor beyond. It looked clear but would it stay that way and for how long? Suddenly he heard the unmistakable sound of footsteps. He dropped his head again and moving to the right-hand side of the doorframe, slowly raised his head once more. This time he saw two figures.

They were at the far end of the corridor, which turned off to the left and right, and were obviously talking something over because of their animated arm movements. From that distance, and because of the closed door, Jake had no chance of hearing what was being said. He guessed his name would not be too far from the topic of conversation. Jake pushed his face hard against the glass trying to get a better angle, to get a better view of the figures. One was considerably taller than the other but in the limited light other details were lacking. However, as the figures turned in opposite directions and walked off, Jake saw the telltale swing of a ponytail.

"Angel," he said softly through gritted teeth, his breath steaming up the glass.

He sniffed and swallowed hard as the pain of raw emotions burned his throat. Forcing himself to forget her, he tried to concentrate on who she had been talking to. Who was he up against? The same names flowed into his head: the Headmaster, Routledge, Packard, Clarkson. It could have been any one of them. 'Does it matter?' he asked himself. 'I'm here to make a martyr out of St. Margaret herself, take her down for good.'

Jake counted to ten slowly before daring to inch the door open and slip into the corridor beyond. He needed to make his way to the main building as quickly as possible; it was only from there that he could gain access to the main stores in the basement. The Academy, devoid of students, felt dead and seeing the building like this Jake could well understand how the stories of ghosts had such a strong hold. He would not have been surprised if there was a spectral army waiting to open and slam every door and window in the place in unison to announce his arrival.

At the double doors, Jake checked the way was clear and pushed through, sprinting down the corridor, keeping close to the wall and so as far away from the windows as possible.

Ahead of him, a door to a classroom suddenly opened, but it was too late for Jake to stop or take evasive action. An arm, locked out straight, was thrust out in front of him, slamming across his chest and shoulders, knocking his upper torso back and lifting his feet off the ground. Jake slammed, spread-eagled onto the hard floor. The impact knocked the wind from his lungs. Before he could regain control to react, his arms were pinned by the knees of someone dropping their whole body weight onto his chest. Jake looked up into a familiar, unwelcome face.

Clarkson smiled, pulling back his fist.

"Wait," ordered a second voice in a harsh whisper from behind Clarkson, grasping the thug's wrist to confirm his seriousness.

Jake looked past Clarkson to see who it was who had just saved his teeth.

THE TRUTH IS TOLD

"Humpty?" gasped Jake.

"Humphrey!" snarled the small man as loudly as he dared, his face twisted into an expression that Jake had never seen in the round face before. It was undoubtedly anger. "And I'm in no mood to take any of your smart lip, Highfield, or I may just let Clarkson here have his fun."

Despite his threat Humphrey pulled at Clarkson. The boy got to his feet, but not without pressing his body weight, through his hand, into Jake's stomach to do so.

Jake stood up, fighting the urge to clutch at his gut, not wanting to give Clarkson the satisfaction of seeing that he'd hurt him. "I don't get it; what are you doing here?" he whispered, hurriedly.

"Some training you've had," said Humphrey with contempt, jerking his head toward the nearest door. "Is it your habit to stand around in the open, waiting to be caught?"

Jake's head was spinning and he numbly followed Humphrey into the room, allowing Clarkson to take up the rear and close the door behind them.

"What's going on?" he asked in a hoarse whisper. "What are you doing here? What is…"

Humphrey raised his hand to stem the flow of questions. "You're more ignorant than even I had given you credit for, Highfield."

Jake closed his mouth but did nothing to hide the look of contempt on his face for the small man who stood before him. Humpty was sweating freely under the tension of the situation and seemed to be swallowing between every other word he spoke.

"Things are not what they seem at St. Margaret's," said Humphrey, looking out of the windows of the classroom nervously.

"You don't say," sneered Jake, finding it hard to drop his old habits when in Humpty's presence.

Humphrey let out a short humourless 'Ha'. "Same old Jake, I see; too quick with the mouth, too slow with the ears. I'm surprised anything has ever got into that thick head of yours…but that may change before the night is over." He reached his hand inside his jacket.

Jake took a step back. He knew a threat when he heard one and he had a feeling the thing that would get into his 'thick head' could well be a bullet.

Humphrey pulled out a white handkerchief and wiped the sweat off his forehead, but he had noticed Jake flinch. "What were you expecting Jake, a gun?" he whispered. His nerves were clearly too tense to mock the boy who had been the pain in his neck for so many years. "You've got it all wrong. I—" He corrected himself and pointed his thumb over his shoulder to indicate Clarkson, who stood barring the door. "*We* are the good guys. It's the Headmaster who's the problem."

Jake would have agreed in an instant but he kept his silence. He wanted to know more from Humpty before he added anything to the growing intrigue.

"You need some background, Jake. I know seeing me again must be somewhat of a surprise," said Humphrey, dabbing again at his leaking brow. "I'm what is known as a 'Feeder'. It's my job to handpick students for St. Margaret's and deliver them safely here. It's also up to me, once they are here, to make them invisible to the outside world; remove any trace of their past, their family history and, especially in your case, any criminal record."

"You've been in on this since the start?" hissed Jake quietly. "You knew where I was going three years ago?"

"From your point of view, yes," confirmed Humphrey, "but usually that's it. Once a student is here they are the responsibility of the Academy and I have nothing more to do with them. I simply move on to the next case; choosing another…shall we say 'gifted' misfit who won't be missed by society."

"So, why the sudden personal call tonight? Interested in seeing how us misfits are doing?"

"If you will let me speak without interruption," said Humphrey, a little louder than he had meant to; he checked the windows in case he'd been heard, then paused and took a breath to gather what little nerve he had left before speaking again in a whisper. "The so-called Headmaster of this institution has turned renegade. In short, he's using St. Margaret's for his own ends and the people in charge know about it and believe me, they are far from happy."

"Go on," prompted Jake, still unwilling to share any of his thoughts or suspicions.

Humphrey dabbed at his face again. "The Headmaster is trying to build an empire with himself at the centre, all-powerful and answerable to no one. Hidden within the safe boundaries of the system, he intends to run a collective of trained mercenaries to carry out the work of the highest bidder, without any thought to the consequences of his actions to allies or enemies alike."

Jake nodded absent-mindedly; the revelation had a truth about it. If there was one thing the Headmaster would want, it was an empire. An empire for an emperor to survey from his precious window.

"So our problem is," said Humphrey, his voice seeming to drop even quieter, "we have to stop the Headmaster and it has to be done with the minimum of fuss and without attracting any attention, hence the two-man army. The last thing we need is an event out in the open for the world to see."

"So you're here to take him out?" asked Jake, bluntly.

"That was a possibility, depending on how things were going," hissed Humphrey. "Of course, we were also hoping that you would show up, that we'd get to you first, before the Headmaster did." Humphrey let that thought hang in the air for a second. "And now, like the ever present pain in the neck you are, you're here and I have a feeling you could be useful for the first time in your life. Have you ever heard the phrase 'the Void'?"

Jake was confused. He was standing in a room in front of a man he had only ever seen as a bumbling care worker, and feet away from a bully who had made two attempts to take him down. His thoughts raced round his brain. Lines between enemy and friend that had, until recently, been solidly drawn were melting and blurring. "I may have heard it mentioned," he said defensively.

"Of course, your friend, the technical genius, Angel

Dunne," Humphrey sneered with obvious distaste. "One of the 'chosen few'."

"The chosen few?" repeated Jake.

"The Headmaster has a system in place, a circle within a circle. Those that he keeps close and are part of his scheme."

"And that's got something to do with the Void?" asked Jake.

"He, they, are the Void," explained Humphrey. "Using the Academy as a front for their operations. Believe me, Jake," whispered Humphrey sincerely, "Angel Dunne is no friend of yours."

Jake said nothing but he could not keep the scowl off his face.

"I can tell by your face that you're asking yourself why she did it," said Humphrey, interrupting Jake's troubled thinking. "The Headmaster's no fool; we mustn't forget that and everyone has their price."

Jake shook his head. "She wouldn't have sold out for money. Do you know the reason she was sent here in the first place?"

"I'm well aware of her computer related fiscal skills," smiled Humphrey, "but nonetheless she did sell out. Not all problems can be removed with cash; different people have different desires. Take you for example, what has the Headmaster got to offer you?"

Jake could only answer with a puzzled expression.

"Not much, I would…" Humpty paused his whisper as he checked again through the windows and stepped further back from their view, "…say. You're too proud nowadays, proud of your status at St. Margaret's, proud of what you do. So what can he offer?"

Jake did not respond.

"Nothing, that's what," said Humphrey. "You wouldn't swap this for the world, which leaves him one choice." Humpty paused to let the obvious sink in. "Good as you are at what you do, you can be a problem at times and the last thing the Headmaster needs hanging around to mess his plans up is a proud operative, committed to doing his job."

Jake had to admit it was plausible; he already knew the Headmaster wasn't what he seemed to be. "Okay, Humpty, if that's the case then answer this. Why did Lard Boy over there shoot a dart into my neck?"

Humphrey smiled broadly; he was clearly enjoying having the upper hand over Jake for once. "The bigger picture, Jake. You're still not seeing the bigger picture. We knew that you were marked for..." Humphrey paused, dabbing the sweat from the folds of his generous chin, "...vanishing, I believe it's known as around here, and the chance to save you landed right into our lap."

"Clarkson was ordered to do the dirty work on the mission we were sent on," stated Jake flatly.

"You're catching on, Jake. I'm impressed. You were supposed to take the hit as the Headmaster wanted. But Clarkson was actually going to bring you to me," explained Humphrey. "The plan was to fill you in with the details of the problem then, instead of having this rather last minute briefing now. After that, I would have kept you in safety until all this had blown over. Clarkson here, having apparently successfully carried out the Headmaster's mission, would have gone back into the Academy undercover. We could have sorted this mess out with the minimum of fuss; nipped it in the bud from the inside. Unfortunately, the police showed up unexpectedly and the rest you know."

"So the Headmaster sends Packard to take me out? That I can understand. But why, when that failed, would the Headmaster use him again?" said Jake, nodding his head toward Clarkson. "Why would he trust him to do it, and here at the Academy?"

"Because—" began Humphrey.

"He's in the Headmaster's inner circle," finished Jake, shaking his head.

"Exactly. He couldn't return from the mission with you being held by the police and still a potential threat, but when you got away from Packard and came back to St. Margaret's…well, it was the perfect opportunity for the Headmaster. Let Clarkson finish his work, dispose of the evidence and then feed a rumour into the Academy that you'd run away, unable to take the shame of two failed missions."

Jake nodded his head. "I get that Clarkson is playing a double game, working for you and the Headmaster at the same time. But one thing I don't get is why the Headmaster picked him for the inner circle and not me. I'm by far the better operative."

"Maybe he thought your ego was too much of a problem," said Clarkson in a tone that showed he too, like Humpty, was revelling in Jake's anxiety. "Even though you were knackered, the night I paid you a visit, you were still big headed enough to think you could beat me easily."

"In case you've forgotten, I did beat you," replied Jake sarcastically.

"Yeah but you took your time about it and how easy did you expect me to make it for you?"

Jake frowned. "Are you trying to say you let me win?"

Clarkson shrugged his shoulders.

"No way," said Jake shaking his head. "You couldn't have known about the wrist gun."

"I must admit it didn't go exactly as I planned but the result was the same. And to see the look of fear in your eyes when the blade came out, Highfield, that was well worth the bruised ribs."

Jake lowered his head, his frown deepened as his mind took in this new, stomach knotting, information. Clarkson had let him win. The obnoxious bully had easily got one over on him and he had fallen for it like a complete amateur. 'If he'd really wanted to take me out, he could have just waited until I was asleep,' thought Jake, his body burning with the heat of shameful realisation. 'He wanted to scare me off, make me run and like a bloody idiot that's exactly what I did.'

"Don't take it so hard," said Clarkson, "I'm sure it will all be forgotten about in a few years or so."

The sound of Clarkson's gloating tone raised Jake's anger. "If you're one of the chosen few," he spat angrily, "why did you change sides and work for Humpty? Surely you'll be sitting pretty with the Headmaster anyway?"

"It's like Mr Humphrey said: everyone has their price," answered Clarkson levelly, "and the offer he made was better than anything the Headmaster could offer me."

Clarkson's face was hidden in shadow so Jake couldn't see the smug grin, but he knew it was there.

"What do we do now then?" Jake directed bluntly at Humpty.

OLD FRIENDS NEW WOUNDS

Jake padded carefully to the end of the corridor and turned to look over his shoulder. He saw Humpty and Clarkson disappearing from view around the opposite corner. Jake's mouth curled into a half grin as he watched his overweight ex-caseworker doing an awkward and poor impression of sneaking. The image of a fat duck on a frozen pond sprang to mind.

Their designated part of the plan was to track down the Headmaster and 'apprehend him' – Humpty's exact words. Jake had noticed the caseworker was taking great, if very nervous, delight in playing cops and robbers for real. Jake, on the other hand, had been sent to keep an eye on things in the quad. It was a lame excuse to keep him out of the way, and an order he had no intention of obeying.

Humpty's explanation of the situation at the Academy was feasible. All the pieces fitted together perfectly and made complete sense but Jake hadn't thrown off the puppet strings of St. Margaret's just to get hung up on the next set that came along. After all, Humpty's tale was just another collection of words neatly packaged together and thrown for him to digest without question. Jake felt as if he was getting all the bedtime stories he had never had read to him at once. He was determined not to swallow all the fairy-tale bull without some proof. He needed to find out the facts for himself before he knew whose side, if anyone's, to make his stand on.

Waiting a few moments for Humpty and Clarkson to be safely out of the way, Jake doubled back down the main corridor. He threw a quick glance up the stairs leading to the Headmaster's office, half expecting to see the man striding down them, and pushed his way through the double doors at the end.

In this newer part of the Academy he was still vulnerable. The row of windows on his right looked out onto the front aspect as they did along the main corridor and the classroom doors on his left would almost certainly be locked. They were not impassable, given time, but utterly useless to make a quick escape from this exposed position. Being sure to keep himself below the windows, he used his hands and feet, moving like a beetle, to propel himself along.

It was hard work to move in such a cramped style. By the time he reached the Tech department door at the end of the Perspex tunnel, his heart was pounding and his self-control was working overtime to keep his breathing quiet. At last he could straighten up and let the blood flow back into his numbing limbs. He gripped the door handle tightly in a sweaty palm and forced it slowly and silently down. The door inched open without a sound and whilst closing it with the same precise care, he saw computer terminals in the room flickering with life. Someone stood in front of one of them hunched over the keyboard, their silhouette seeming to throb with the pulsing light thrown from the monitor. Jake knew in an instant who the lone geek pulling the night shift was.

He crept up behind the figure and slipped his arm across her exposed throat whilst pushing his left fist into the small of her back, taking her off balance.

Angel tried to resist the attack but with her back arched she could not use the strength in her legs. She drove her elbow backwards but Jake had been sure to keep his body in total alignment with hers, not leaving any exposed area open to attack.

"Not this time," he whispered into Angel's ear. "You won't catch me out the same way twice."

Angel relaxed. "Jake? Is that you Jake?"

"Expecting someone else?" hissed Jake. "One of your inner circle buddies, perhaps?" His pushed his fist harder into Angel's back, making her enforced stance even more uncomfortable.

"What are you talk—" gasped Angel. "Stop it! You're hurting me!"

"Shame," said Jake, coldly.

"I know what you're thinking about me," Angel said between short breaths, "but you've got it wrong."

"Really?" With Angel helpless, Jake was taking stock of the situation. It looked like every terminal in the room was active. Each was filling its screen with page after page of flashing information, as if they got instantly bored with the data displayed and moved onto the next. "Seems like everyone thinks I've got things wrong lately. I'm no genius," continued Jake, "as you like to point out, but it appears to me you're trying to get rid of something. Having a bit of a clean out, are you?"

"Clean out?"

"Don't play stupid with me," said Jake, applying more pressure to his choke hold. "It's me that's the idiot round here. The brain-dead field operative, remember?" He didn't wait to, or want to, hear any more protesting. "This could look like you're getting rid of the evidence of the Void before the whole thing is exposed and your precious plans fall apart. It would fit rather neatly into the story I was told by Humpty about you and the rest of the chosen few and how your scheme is meant to fall into place."

"Who, or what, the hell is Humpty?" rasped Angel, swallowing hard.

"You won't know him," sneered Jake. "In fact it turns out I didn't know him properly either, but it appears he may be the good guy."

"Do you mean Humphrey?" Angel forced from her throat. "The man who sent you to St. Margaret's in the first place? He's the good guy now is he?" Angel's voice was laced with as much sarcasm as she could muster given her restricted vocal cords.

Jake could not hide the surprise. "You know him?"

"Not personally, just from tracking down the Void…the creation of which he is more than likely involved with."

Jake relaxed his grip slightly on Angel's neck. "Go on," he instructed.

"I managed to get some tracking software attached to the program and I'm trying to trace it back to source right now, but I'm finding it hard to think of anything but the pain in my spine at the moment. Will you please let me sit down?"

Jake steered her towards a chair and dropped her into it. "One wrong move," he said with sincerity and he could see in Angel's eyes that she knew he meant it.

Angel massaged her neck with her fingers. "Thank you," she said, bitterly.

"The Void?" pushed Jake.

"After I talked to you about it in your room, I dug deeper and discovered every vanishing was definitely linked to the Void. Just before an operative would disappear the rogue program had made an almost untraceable link to the student's file, seeming to mark them out. Sometimes as little as a week passed after the link; up to a month or even two in some cases. But eventually, every one of them ended up vanished and always in the field. I discovered the source was set up within the Academy's system itself but it was also accessed externally through a coded file called 'H'. We think it's H for Humphrey."

"Or Headmaster," argued Jake with an unfriendly smile. "Don't take this the wrong way, Angel, but I'm having trouble believing you. I'm only going by your recent track record at giving out false directions."

"I had no choice in that," protested Angel, her face flushed with anger. "Ask the Headmaster if you don't believe me."

"He's not exactly at the top of my 'people to see' list," said Jake. "Not yet, anyway." He reached into an open box of tools and pulled out a screwdriver.

Angel stared wide-eyed. "What are you going to do with that?" she asked nervously.

Jake shook his head. "I'm not the backstabber here, Angel. Remember?"

"How many times do I have to tell you? I had no choice, Jake," said Angel. "The Headmaster explained everything to me once he realised I was aware of the presence of the Void on the system and said it was for your own safety that you be brought back to St. Margaret's. You'd been at risk for too long in the field. That's why I did it, Jake, for your own good, to get you back to safety."

Jake barely managed to rein in his anger enough to talk. "Really?" he said. "Well, here I am and funnily enough I still don't feel too safe. But I will soon, once I bring this mission to an end. And I don't care if the Headmaster, Humpty or you and the precious chosen few are here to go down with the Academy as I do it."

Angel sat bolt upright at this news. "Humphrey is here, now?"

Jake walked back towards the door and began to unscrew the fasteners in the handle. "Wow, something you didn't know. That must be a first."

"We've got to find the Headmaster," said Angel, standing up. "We've got to warn him about Humphrey."

"Sit down," barked Jake, waiting until she had before continuing to work at the screws.

"What if you're wrong, Jake? What if Humphrey is behind all this and I'm telling the truth?"

Jake ignored Angel's pleading and removed the last screw from the door handle. He then turned his attention to the fuse box hanging on the wall. He flicked the securing catch up and opened the box to reveal a line of electrical trip switches.

"What are you doing, Jake?" asked Angel, the panic evident in her voice and eyes. "If you cut the power to the computers I may never be able to trace the Void back to its central source. That's why I'm still here, Jake. The Headmaster needs to know for sure who is behind the vanishings."

"Does he really?" said Jake. "Funny thing is, there

are people who already think they know who's behind them and the more I see, the more I am tending to agree with them. Which just leaves you…" he pulled the main trip switch out of the board, killing the power to all the computers in an instant, "…in the dark, doesn't it?"

Angel ran both of her hands through her hair. "Jake, you really are a bloody idiot at times!"

"So you keep telling me," snarled Jake, slipping the fuse into his pocket. "But let's see how Miss Brain-box thinks her way out of this one." Jake opened the door, jamming it with his foot and with a sharp tug, pulled the loosened handle away from the wood. "Oops, best not leave this bit in either," he noted, removing the square shaft from the exposed mechanism. "Don't want to make it too easy for you."

"Jake," said Angel, a note of pleading in her tone. "Find the Headmaster, please."

"I don't need to find anyone, Angel," replied Jake. "It's me out for myself. Just like it was before I got put in this dump."

"Humphrey is involved with the Void," pushed Angel. "He's the one you should be fighting against."

"Maybe," said Jake, stepping across the threshold of the Tech Department, "but right now he's the only one who hasn't tried to kill me or sell me out." He winked at Angel. "You'd know all about that though, wouldn't you? See ya later…maybe," he said with forced cheerfulness and closed the door with a click.

'More words, more lies,' he thought. 'Did she honestly think I'd be stupid enough to trust her again?'

A DAY AT THE OFFICE

Jake made his way back down the corridor the way he had come. He was starting to worry that his luck might run out. The enclosed surroundings offered little in the way of cover or exit points should he need one in a hurry. The first heavier drops of falling rain had started to streak the glass with silver scars and the grounds beyond looked empty. He opened the catch and slid the sash frame up until there was a gap big enough to allow him to slip through. He dropped silently and lay flat on the cropped grass, ignoring the chill that greeted his body. Jake froze for a second, letting his eyes adjust to the lower light level and to check for any sign of movement.

He intended to keep below window height and close to the wall, to follow the exterior of St. Margaret's structure and make his way back inside through the main front door. It was a more direct and less risky route than using the corridors to reach his destination: the Headmaster's office. For several days he had been ignorant of any reliable intelligence, running on his wits alone to survive. Now he found himself in a worse situation, conflicting reports giving him too much information. Half of which, at least, had to be lies. Which half, however, he could only guess.

Something moved to his left and Jake froze. Two ghostly green dots hung in the air. His first thought was it was one of the Academy's dogs, its eyes reflecting the little light the night had to offer. He held his breath, trying not to blink as drops of rain flicked against his face, but he relaxed as he picked out a familiar form from the shadows. 'Bloody wildlife will be the death of me one day,' he thought with relief.

The fox lost interest in the prone human in the rain and returned to its more pressing desire of hunting in the bins full of food waste. Jake too returned to his mission, his senses even more heightened by the innocent encounter. He began to drag himself along on his elbows, commando style, covered by the line of ornamental shrubs that ran along the front of the building up to the steps of the main entrance.

He was about to reach up to pull himself over the edging wall when he heard approaching footsteps and one of the large double doors being opened. He pushed his back hard into the corner and froze.

He couldn't see from his position, but he could hear two sets of footfalls, walking almost carelessly, making their way down onto the crunching gravel path. "Are you sure he's here, Sah?"

Jake instantly recognised Routledge's distinctive parade ground voice.

"Without a doubt," came the Headmaster's clipped tones. "Everything is going to plan. We will be tying up the loose ends in a very tidy knot before the night is out."

Jake listened to the crunching march until it faded so much he couldn't hear it anymore. 'We'll see how tidy your knot is,' thought Jake, heaving himself over the wall onto the top stone step. He pushed slowly against the door and slipped inside St. Margaret's foyer. 'Frayed ends all round is more what I had in mind.'

Jake wasted no time. He sprinted towards the stairs that led to the Headmaster's office, his progress watched only by the disapproving gazes from the dark canvas portraits of the ex-Headmasters. He leapt up the stairs three at a time, the wet soles of his boots squeaking against the old wood, and stopped outside the familiar oak door.

He hesitated a second, almost nervous to enter without knocking. His stomach knotted at the thought of what he was about to do. Fighting his urge to turn away, he reached for the handle and thrust the door open, rolling into the room. The Headmaster wouldn't be there, but that didn't mean the room would be empty.

Jake scanned the room quickly, his arms raised ready to fight. The light was on, burning the picture of St. Margaret in lurid stained glass colours onto the grass of the quadrant below, but the room was empty. How long the situation would remain like that was guesswork. Time was of the essence.

For a second Jake stalled. It was one thing to gain access to a building or room on a mission when you knew where you needed to look, and what you were looking for. But this was like trying to find a grain of black sand on a beach at midnight. He had to start somewhere so he made his way quickly behind the desk and tried the drawers. They were all locked. He reached for the Samurai dagger. It rested on a cradle at the front of the desk and served as the Headmaster's letter-opener. He was about to jam it in the gap between the top drawer and the desk's surface, when he heard someone climbing the stairs towards the office.

Jake tilted his head and listened. The steps were slow and measured. Someone was trying, and failing, to mask their arrival. Jake's mind raced. The single door that served as entrance and exit to the office was out of the question for escape and the elaborate window opened out onto a sheer drop that offered nothing but injury at best. The steps fell nearer. His eyes fell on the large open fireplace.

Jake was surprised to hear that the door was opened violently, probably kicked. He could imagine the scene of a gun being levelled into the room ready to blast whatever moved. He pushed his hands and feet harder into the rough brickwork of the chimney lining, suspended like a starfish above the hearth only a metre below.

The footsteps quickened, thudding heavily on the thick carpet, as the intruder realised, as Jake had on his entrance, that the office was empty and contained no immediate threat. He heard the footsteps come close to the fire and stop. He held his breath, expecting a gun to be shoved up the chimney and a sarcastic voice to sing, 'Come out, come out, wherever you are'. But instead the light from below dulled as the painting of Rourke's Drift which hung proudly on the chimney breast was removed and placed on the floor covering a portion of the open grate.

Then Jake heard a sound so familiar he almost cursed aloud at his stupidity, it was the clicking of a safe's combination wheel being turned and tumblers falling into place.

Gingerly he moved his left hand and, taking the extra strain through his three remaining limbs, he brushed gently over the brickwork in front of his torso. His fingers met the telltale smooth chill of steel; the back of a secure box. 'A safe behind the painting,' he thought angrily. 'So obvious, yet I missed it.'

A clunk echoed about the confines of the chimney as the safe's locking handle was pulled down and the metal hinge whined as the safe door was swung open. A slight rasp told the story of the safe's contents being removed and the thud and clank gave fanfare to a successful heist. Finally, more light filled the lower area of the chimney again as the painting was lifted and hung back in place once more.

There was small electronic beep. 'Speed dial,' thought Jake. A voice broke the silence.

"Yes, I've got it…it was exactly where you said it would be…"

Humpty!

"Listen, this is getting more dangerous by the second. I nearly walked headlong into…yes, I know you can deal with it but I don't think I…yes, I know, okay I'll do it…"

Jake was in the perfect surveillance position, the chimney's tight confines acting like an amplifier. He only wished he could hear the voice on the other end of the phone. Humphrey's voice grew more agitated.

"St. Margaret's will be mine, that was the deal…good, but let's get this over with quickly…"

Jake's throat was beginning to dry out in the dusty atmosphere. He swallowed as much spit from his mouth as he could to stifle a cough that threatened to give away his position.

"What, both of them? Highfield I can understand, I have no problem with that at all; but Clarkson? He's been useful, could be again…okay, okay, I know. No trail. No loose ends…"

'No loose ends,' thought Jake, a scowl growing on his face. Jake heard the dull clap of plastic on plastic, a mobile phone being closed. His heart was telling him to let the pressure in his arms and legs go, to drop down into the room and face Humpty there and then.

"Oh, I've got plans for you," Humphrey's excited voice rolled up the chimney like a trail of smug smoke. "New desk, more space, light, a huge cheese plant over there and as for this bloody stupid window…"

"Who are you talking to?" said a different voice, softly.

Jake hadn't heard a single noise betraying the new arrival's entrance. Whoever had entered the room was no untrained amateur like Humpty.

"Er…" stuttered Humphrey with embarrassment before regaining his control. "I told you to keep a watch out."

"I did; there wasn't anything to watch. There's more life in a grave."

Clarkson!

"Don't you worry," assured Humphrey. "There will be soon enough."

"We had a deal," argued Clarkson. "Something I could have already collected on tonight, if you hadn't stopped me."

"Listen," snapped Humphrey. "Remember who is going to be who when this is all over. It's better to have friends in high places than enemies."

Clarkson didn't answer.

"Good. I'm glad we understand each other," said Humphrey, his tone edged with anger, but it was only there in an effort to hide an underlying fear. "I want you to stay here and make sure no one comes into this room…

and if they do I want you to make sure they don't come out. Got it?"

There was no reply again.

"I'll be back as soon as I've finished," said Humphrey, his heavy feet stomping across the room toward the door. "I need to know you'll be here in the Headma— in my office."

'I bet you do,' thought Jake as the door to the Headmaster's office clicked shut. 'It's easier to dispose of things if you know where to find them.'

"Prat," muttered Clarkson, unknowingly giving voice to Jake's exact thoughts.

Jake had to get out, but with Clarkson playing sentry, leaving through the office door was, once again, not an option. He looked up into the darkness that seemed to start at the top of his head and go on forever above him; it wouldn't be a long climb onto the roof, but it sure as hell would be a tough one.

TIME TO DIE

Jake hauled himself clear of the chimney with a final effort and sat on the lip, his legs dangling into the void. He stayed there for a moment, trying to catch his breath and clear his lungs of the stale, soot-filled air. The rain washed streaks into the black dust that covered his face as he inspected his hands. Blood dripped from under several of his fingernails which had taken much of the strain of the climb, forced to grip the coarse bricks and thick, crumbling mortar joints.

He looked across to the opposite skyline at the clock tower that would be his way back in. The roof was steep and looked too treacherous in this wet weather to try and descend in the hope of finding an open window on the top floor. It would only take one slip to turn the Welsh slate tiles of the roof into a deadly water slide.

Jake brought his legs up out of the chimney and swung them over to dangle on the outer skin of bricks. Using his arms' strength, he lowered himself onto the apex of the roof so he had one foot either side of the ridge tiles. This way, if either of his feet slipped at least he wouldn't fall to the quadrant below, though he could end up doing a very painful version of the splits. With arms outstretched like a tightrope walker, he began to move across the roof. He moved his feet quickly so as not to put too much of his bodyweight on any one point for too long.

As he approached the first of the two corners he needed to overcome, Jake's foot fell too heavily onto the roof's brittle covering and the slate below his foot shattered and slipped away. Jake dropped like a stone, only just managing to thrust his hands down in time to save his groin taking the full impact of the fall. He watched wide-eyed as the remnants of the damaged tile skittered down the steep gradient toward the edge. If they fell onto the quadrant he might as well stand up and start singing to make sure everyone knew his whereabouts. Jake held his breath, watching the skidding debris as it neared the lip of the roof. He couldn't believe his luck when they dipped sharply and lodged in the iron guttering with a click. He closed his eyes and puffed out a breath filled with relief. His heart was beating, as if trying to break through his ribs and away from the tension of the situation.

The rain was falling steadily. Thick droplets burst on the tiles and the roof was greased by a film of flowing water. Jake decided against trying to walk upright the remainder of the way, instead opting for the slower but safer method of shuffling along on his backside, using his arms to pull himself forward.

By the time he reached the clock tower Jake was breathing heavily, his body giving off steam as its heat collided with the cold air around it. With his left hand he grabbed the ornate wooden rail that ran round the lower portion of the clock tower; then he stood up and vaulted over. He felt a welcome relief to have a dry, level surface under his feet again as he ducked low to prevent being spotted.

The clock tower was small, a little more than two metres square. A ladder lay on the floor, used to access the clock's mechanism higher up. It was yet another of the Headmaster's foibles that the clock had to be accurate at all times and it was expected to be maintained to an almost paranoid degree by the students who were allocated the 'honour'.

A short flight of bare wooden stairs led down from the platform to a door onto the second floor corridor. This was the only floor at this section of St. Margaret's, the two lower floors being broken by the arch below, and Jake knew that the door leading onto it would not be locked or secured by any means.

The clock tower, like so many places in the Academy, laid claim to its own ghost story. It concerned a maid from the first days of the old school who had locked herself in the tower before leaping to a messy death on the quadrant below. The reasons why she did it varied, depending on who was telling the story, but all the storytellers agreed on one thing – it was now an unarguable tradition that the clock tower's door was never locked. And to prevent this, so the story went, the locking mechanism had been removed the very night of the maid's death and never replaced to prevent such a tragedy ever happening again. An image of Pete Philips wetting himself with fright came to Jake's mind.

He trod carefully on the worn wooden stairs. If any steps were going to creak in St. Margaret's, he was sure it would be these 'haunted' ones. He put his foot on the last step which butted up against the door and reached for the handle. As his fingers brushed against the cold brass he felt it move and he withdrew his hand as if he'd received an

Alec Sillifant

electric shock. 'Back', his mind commanded. 'Go back'.

Without turning, he moved quickly backwards and, turning at the top, pressed his back against the wall to the side, hidden from the bottom of the stairs. Jake heard the door creak open and then click shut again. Someone began to ascend. They were taking slow, deliberate steps. Jake had a feeling whoever was on their way up knew he was there and more worryingly didn't care if he knew they were coming.

"Oh, Highfield," came a mocking voice. "Do you know what time it is?"

It wasn't the most welcome voice Jake could have hoped to hear but he decided on a head-on approach to this situation. He stepped out from his cover to stand defiant at the top of the stairs. "It's time we had a talk, Clarkson."

Clarkson stopped halfway up the stairs. "How did you know it was me? I was hoping you'd think I was the ghost of poor old heartbroken Fanny Crowley, back from the grave. That way you'd scare yourself to death," he grinned, "just to save me the effort."

Jake kept his face stern, his mind ready. He wasn't going to make the mistake of thinking Clarkson was a pushover this time. "They're going to double-cross you, Clarkson. I overheard Humpty on his mobile talking to the Headmaster about tidying up loose ends. Me and you being two of them."

"Is that so?" replied Clarkson. "And what do you expect now, a big hug and then we stand back-to-back fighting together to the last man? I don't think so. You missed your chance to be on the right side, Highfield. I'm afraid that deal has been withdrawn." A smile crept onto Clarkson's face.

276

"Nice work on the roof by the way. I especially liked the bit when you kicked the tile down into the guttering, hell of a sound show. Amazing view I had too, watching you shimmy along like a girl the rest of the way. Thought I'd come along and congratulate you personally on a job well done."

"Listen to me, Clarkson. Humpty is playing you for a fool. I can understand you not believing me," said Jake, realising he was stating the painfully obvious. "But at the moment—"

Clarkson sprang up the stairs.

Jake raised his leg to kick out but Clarkson was too quick for him and caught his foot, trapping it against his chest between both of his arms before he could straighten his knee and deliver any power to the attack. Clarkson's weight advantage enabled him to push forwards, throwing Jake off balance, tipping him onto his back to slide across the floor of the clock tower.

Clarkson pressed his advantage, cleared the last two steps and moved in. His intention was to cause maximum damage to his victim, but his foot fell onto the carelessly abandoned ladder causing his leg to buckle. Jake took what might be his only chance and swung his right leg in an arc, driving his shin into Clarkson's thigh. Clarkson's weakened leg folded further. Jake then raised his lower body by leaning on his elbow, and drove his left foot into the side of Clarkson's head with all the force he could.

Clarkson's body obeyed the rule of anatomical physics. 'Wherever the head goes, the rest follows.' It folded over, his body weight landing heavily onto the clock tower's guard railings. The old upright spindles sheered under the pressure and Clarkson cartwheeled head first onto the steep sloped roof.

Jake didn't think; he just reacted. Rolling forward he thrust out his hand and grabbed Clarkson's trailing ankle, halting the inevitable slide. Clarkson raised his head and stared up at Jake, his eyes burning with rage. Then he looked over his shoulder beyond the lip of the wet roof, into the quadrant below.

"Don't move," said Jake, struggling to hold Clarkson's weight with one hand, his other gripping what was left of the railings and praying they wouldn't break to release both of them onto the merciless angle of the slippery roof.

Clarkson was breathing heavily through flared nostrils. A mixture of loathing for Jake and fear for his situation twisted his face into a tight expression. "Why don't you let go?" he hissed through gritted teeth. "I would if it was the other way round."

"No doubt," gasped Jake. The strain on his arms was like someone pushing hot pokers into his muscles. "But—" Jake stopped, distracted by something.

"What?" growled Clarkson.

"There are two people in the quadrant," explained Jake between grunts of exertion. "They're looking up. I think they've seen us."

Clarkson had no desire to look back down again. "Who?"

"I think it's Humpty and…I think he's with the Headma—"

A slate tile erupted to the left of Clarkson's arm. "Jesus! They're shooting at us!"

Jake's instincts told him to get his head down but he had to see what was going on. Another tile erupted into dust next to Clarkson who flinched at the sharp cracking noise of the bullet's impact. "Hold still," demanded Jake.

"I can barely hold on to you as it is."

Two more tiles burst apart in quick succession, one so close to Clarkson he had to spit slate dust from his mouth. Jake could see it was Humpty who was doing the shooting whilst the Headmaster watched, his hands, as usual, calmly held behind his back.

"You're going to have to help," shouted Jake, realising the need for silence was irrelevant at this point. "After three…one…"

A bullet thudded into the wooden frame of the clock tower and neither Jake nor Clarkson waited for 'two' before taking the strain. Jake cried out with effort as he pulled, both of his shoulders threatening to separate from his body. Slowly he raised Clarkson far enough back up the roof for him to be able to fold himself forward from the waist and flail wildly with his arms in a desperate bid to grab at the corner pillar of the rails. On the second attempt he did it and heaved himself into cover as more rounds smashed tiles and ripped wood into large splinters.

"Still want me to take a lie detector test?" asked Jake, his chest heaving as he hunched over to keep his head out of the line of fire. "Or would you rather wait for the autopsy reports instead?"

Clarkson slowly raised his head to look Jake coldly in the eye. "What the hell is going on?"

"You're asking me!" gasped Jake. "You're the one in the Headmaster's inner circle!"

Clarkson's gaze wavered for a split second.

Jake grinned at his own stupidity. "It's all bull, isn't it? There's no inner circle. You're just working for Humpty; you always were. Everything he fed to me is a pack of lies."

"The Great Jake Highfield comes through again," sneered Clarkson.

"You reckon?" spat Jake. "That still doesn't explain why Humpty is down there *with* the Headmaster, his sworn enemy, taking pot shots at us."

Clarkson's face dropped its defiant look as his brain tried to fathom the information.

"Face the facts, Clarkson, we're both up to our ears in the same vat of crap," pointed out Jake with an anger that was directed at himself as much as anyone else. "We've been manipulated from the start, played for fools; shoved around in any direction that Humpty and the Headmaster wanted us to go."

Clarkson shook his head. "But I was told everything would be fine once the Headmaster was out of the way. I would be top dog at the Academy."

"Don't you see? The Headmaster is always behind everything in this place. He's down there now still in control. Humpty lied to you and you fell for it," said Jake before quickly adding, "*I* fell for it. I don't think either of us is up for a pat on the back from anyone in the near future...unless they're holding a baseball bat."

Clarkson's face told a story of self pity. "You should have let me drop," he said quietly.

"Probably," replied Jake, "but that would have left me back at square one. On my own and still fighting against... God knows who."

Clarkson stared at Jake. "Are you suggesting we team up?" he said, making a face as if he'd just smelt soured milk.

"I don't like it any more than you," admitted Jake.

"Especially since I now know for sure you were actually trying to take me out, both times."

Clarkson did not insult Jake by attempting to deny the fact.

'Tried and failed,' thought Jake smugly but this was not the time or place for petty gloating or revenge. "As it is," he said, "we've both got the same fate lined up for us and that leaves us with two choices."

"And they are?"

"Sit here and wait for Humpty, the Headmaster, whoever, to come up here and finish the job properly or," Jake paused, trying to gauge Clarkson's reaction, "we kick back. Take the fight to them. Teach *them* a lesson for a change."

Clarkson nodded slowly in agreement.

"Either way," continued Jake, "our chances are pretty slim. They're ready for us and, unlike us, they're armed."

"I may be able to even the odds out a bit on that count," said Clarkson, his mind made up, moving towards the flight of stairs at the back of the tower. He stopped and turned. "Listen, Highfield, we're stuck together for now but once this mess is over—"

"I expected nothing less," replied Jake. "But let's get out of this first, hey?"

GARDEN PARTY

"What's happening?" grunted Clarkson as he turned over the mattress on the bed in his room.

Jake stood to the side of the ground floor window. "They're both still standing there at the centre of the quad."

"That's why they didn't chase us down: they're waiting for someone." Clarkson pulled the short-bladed knife from behind the buckle in his belt.

"Maybe," said Jake, ducking back as the Headmaster's gaze fell in his direction. "Who though? If Humpty and the Headmaster are working together, who are they waiting for?"

Clarkson dragged the knife across the stitched seam of the mattress, slicing through the cotton. "Beats me," he said, slipping his hand into the cut.

'Nothing new there then,' thought Jake. But said out loud, "Maybe it's us; maybe they're hoping to draw us out into the open for an easy kill?"

"Here," said Clarkson, throwing something across the room which Jake caught.

"Wrist gun," smiled Jake, turning the device over in his hand. "To be handed back in to the supply department at the end of every mission, I believe?"

"Turns out to be handy for us that I've lost a couple of them over the years then," said Clarkson, strapping his to his wrist.

"Sure is," said Jake, fitting the weapon. He returned his attention to the two figures in the rain. "We need to be sure there's not going to be any more surprises for us before we go out there. Did Humpty bring anyone else in with you?"

Clarkson joined Jake at the window, standing on the opposite side of the frame. "The so-called 'vanished' are watching the perimeter but they've got orders to stay put, whatever happens until relieved."

"Assuming they haven't been relieved of their duties permanently already," said Jake.

Clarkson nodded his agreement. "Well, either way, it's unlikely they're going to pose an immediate threat. I haven't seen anyone else in the buildings or the grounds; what about you?"

"I heard the Headmaster talking to Routledge and…" Jake stopped himself before mentioning Angel.

"And?" said Clarkson sharply.

"And that's all I know for sure. I haven't seen anyone else."

"That's all we need, Vest-Man charging in to join the party," frowned Clarkson. "Still, at least we'll hear him coming and then…" he tapped the dart-firing weapon on his wrist, "…payback for thousands of push-ups."

Jake looked at his wrist gun. All four darts were the same colour. "Are you packing whites too?"

"Unfortunately," sneered Clarkson, his gaze fixed on the men outside. "They tend to be much more diligent on Terminators being returned. On the other hand, just think of the fun we can have when they come round tied to a chair in the boiler house, hey?"

Jake noticed an evil grin crawl across Clarkson's face. He was enjoying that thought far too much.

"Are we ready then?"

"Suppose so," said Clarkson. He raised his hand in a sweeping gesture, "After you, Highfield."

Jake frowned. "No offence, Clarkson, but I would rather you took the lead. I've worked with you before, remember?"

Clarkson shrugged. "Mistrust is not a good quality to develop, Highfield, but I'll go ahead. Probably do you good anyway. You can pick up some tips on how to do the job properly from me."

'As long as I don't pick up any more drugged tips from you, that will be a bonus,' thought Jake as he followed Clarkson through the door and down the corridor.

Jake and Clarkson hid at the edge of the shadow the arch offered them, looking out at the two men on the grass of the quadrant. The only advantage they seemed to have over Humpty and the Headmaster was shelter from the rain. They'd skirted round the outside of St. Margaret's and now this arch was the last piece of cover between them and the open space before them. Jake couldn't help thinking the pitch at Wembley would probably have looked smaller to him right at this minute.

Jake looked at Clarkson who pointed with two fingers at his own eyes followed by a circular motion with his forefinger and then a flat hand shot out in Humphrey's direction. 'Wonderful plan,' thought Jake, shaking his head in disagreement. Waiting for them both to turn their backs and rush them was suicide.

Clarkson turned his palms up and shrugged.

Jake chewed his lip in thought. As much as he hated the plan, Clarkson was right. What choice did they have? They could sit here waiting for someone to find them or take their chance with a mad rush into the open. Jake could see why the two men had chosen this place. No one could approach them from any side unnoticed. He nodded sharply once to Clarkson, who gave the thumbs up and turned his attention to waiting for the perfect moment to move.

Jake turned his gaze towards the two men. The communication between him and Clarkson was over. A plan had been decided on and it would be acted on without hesitation. He relaxed his body and focused his mind on the one goal ahead of him with complete confidence that Clarkson would be doing the exact same thing. They were both ready for action as soon as the time was right. And the timing had to be perfect. They had to wait until the attention of both men was directed away from their intended route of assault. Then they had to cover enough ground to get within an effective firing range for their wrist guns. Otherwise they might as well stroll out into plain view with targets painted on their chests and a marching band in tow.

Jake watched, his eyes beginning to water under the strain, but he didn't dare blink, dared not to miss the moment to react. He and Clarkson had to move as one, at the exact same moment. If one or the other lagged behind for more than a split second the chances of success dropped dramatically. Once up and running, they would each have their own target. Clarkson had insisted on Humpty after being shot at on the roof. Jake hadn't argued; revenge was as good a reason as any and it was the one that had made him happy to be targeting the Headmaster.

Humpty was the more animated of the two. He looked as nervous as a full waiting room at the dentist. His eyes were darting from point to point, rarely resting on any one place for more than a few seconds. The Headmaster, in contrast, kept his head less mobile, moving it slightly and purposefully to momentarily pause on one particular field of vision and study it before returning his gaze back to the same spot. To Jake's distress this was right down into the Archway. He was getting the uncomfortable feeling that the Headmaster knew they were there and was daring them to show themselves, to challenge him. All the while his hands remained tucked behind his back, as if hiding some deadly weapon that would make him victorious whatever the odds.

Minutes passed and the opportunity to move did not come. Jake knew he could not take his eyes off the scene to object again about the credibility of this plan. Clarkson was locked and ready to go and the slightest break in his concentration to get Clarkson's attention could make him miss the opportunity they both waited for.

Then there was a noise, a door being closed inside the building. Humpty and the Headmaster both turned their heads and Jake pushed off with his back leg. He was sprinting, the sound of his feet muffled by the damp grass. To his right he could feel the presence of Clarkson running level alongside him. Time seemed to slow as Jake's senses pitched higher than they'd ever been before. He saw the Headmaster begin to turn his head back. Jake felt as if he was watching a slow motion scene in a movie. Centimetre by centimetre the grey haired head, with its lined face, turned. A blink of the Headmaster's eyelids slowed to last what felt like a minute. Any second now they would be discovered, but if he could just cover a few more metres then the wrist gun would be accurate.

Out of the corner of his eye, Jake could see Clarkson was raising his arms, sacrificing speed and balance for the chance to get off an early shot. He was too far away, moving too fast. The compressed air spat the dart forwards missing Humpty by half a metre. Clarkson grimaced at the wasted shot and aimed again.

Jake decided it was all or nothing; he had to keep running, cover the distance, keep his cool and make sure the shot he made counted first time. He looked at his target, the Headmaster, and Jake saw to his horror the man looking at him. The Headmaster was staring directly into his eyes, his face emotionless and still. 'Why isn't he shouting? Warning Humpty?'

A single gun shot rang out and Clarkson spun. His left leg flailed, rising up into the air as he was robbed of his balance and forward momentum, to be thrown onto the wet grass. Jake watched Clarkson's body bounce and the drops of water caught in the blades of grass rose up like a fountain about him, each silver droplet hanging in an arc of slow motion perfection.

Jake's senses were shocked back into less forgiving real time, as his mind informed him they'd failed in their objective.

"Don't move a muscle!" commanded Humpty.

Jake stopped, his hands half raised in a lacklustre surrender position. He knew he was still too far away to get a clean shot with the wrist gun and his chances of taking out Humpty and the Headmaster before being gunned down were close enough to zero to make him pause. He looked back at Clarkson, motionless on the ground. 'Almost zero,' he thought to himself, 'but not zero.'

Jake's arm had only twitched when Humpty shouted, "Ah! Let's lose the hardware shall we…slowly. Even I'm a good shot from this distance as I'm sure Clarkson would testify to…if he could."

The adrenalin of the attack was leaving Jake's body and brain. His thoughts began to branch out again, extending beyond combat mode. 'Another way,' he told himself, 'another chance. I'm still standing. I'll get another chance'. Jake slowly moved his left hand to his right wrist and removed the weapon.

"Now lose it," said Humpty, flicking his head to one side.

Jake threw the wrist gun across the quadrant.

"And now his," continued Humpty, pointing his gun at the prone Clarkson.

Jake stepped backwards slowly and leant over Clarkson. Blood was mixing with the rainwater, staining the wet blades of grass pale red at his side. Jake reached down to undo the wrist gun and as he did he could feel a pulse beneath the weapon's strap. His eyes darted to take a rapid look at the boy's face.

Clarkson opened one eye. "Be ready," he whispered.

Jake threw the second wrist gun across the grass before standing in a defiant slouch facing Humpty and the Headmaster. "Anything else?"

Humpty snorted with disgust. "Still so sure of yourself aren't you, Highfield? Still the same big-mouthed joker? I am really going to enjoy settling the score with you." He wiped at the rain running down his forehead with the back of his hand. "I can't wait to wipe the smile off your face."

Jake didn't feel like smiling much right now anyway. He swallowed. He'd never seen Humpty as a threat before and it was a feeling he didn't like. He remembered a man who had made stress a career and now he was pointing a gun at him. Nervous fingers did not make reliable trigger ones.

"You not got anything to add," said Jake, addressing the silent Headmaster adding a drawn out, disrespectful, "sir?"

The Headmaster remained silent for a little longer, his facial hair collecting more rain into large droplets before releasing them onto the ground. "What are you expecting, Mr Highfield, an apology? Perhaps you think you deserve a civil discussion regarding the reasoning behind my actions? Over afternoon tea perhaps?"

Jake, even though he knew he was in mortal danger, could feel the anger beginning to burn at his temples.

"Why did you do it?" he barked, jabbing at the air between him and the Headmaster with an accusing finger. "One mistake and you turned against me! Turfed me out! Hunted me down!"

The Headmaster coughed to clear his throat before speaking. "I think maybe you should pay more attention to the situation at hand—"

"Both of you shut up!" interrupted Humphrey. "All this bull is irrelevant!"

The double doors at the east side of the quadrant burst open, slamming hard against the walls to rattle loudly. "Stop! Put down your weapon! One twitch and I'll decorate the night with your brains, sunshine!"

PICKING SIDES

At this moment the last thing Jake thought he would be happy to see was Routledge and his vest.

"Put the weapon on the ground!" ordered Routledge again. "Now!"

Jake could see the terror in Humpty's wide eyes. "I'll shoot them both if you come one step closer," he said, trying his best to disguise the squeak of nerves in his voice. "I've already killed Clarkson."

A shot was fired and the grass at Humphrey's feet exploded, throwing mud onto the polished caps of his shoes. "This is your last warning!"

Jake saw a second figure come through the double doors. He also carried a handgun, his head held within the confines of a metal frame. Packard strode forward and stood next to Routledge, training his weapon on Humphrey as well. 'What the hell is going on?' thought Jake. 'Packard and Routledge are the Headmasters' men…aren't they?'

Humphrey's arm twitched as if trying to build up the nerve to turn his gun on the two men who had him locked in their sights. "I wouldn't try it," hissed Packard, his wired jaw only allowing him to speak through gritted teeth. "Do as he says."

Humphrey paused for a second then, bending forward, placed his gun on the ground before taking a step back from it. Routledge and Packard moved forward with quick steps, their guns never dropping from their line with Humphrey's head. Routledge took an extra step forward and crouched down to retrieve the weapon. As he did so, Packard raised his gun up above his head.

Jake's mouth opened to shout a warning, but the base of Packard's pistol had already swung down to clash with its target before he could form the words. Routledge's knees buckled and he fell face first onto the grass without uttering a sound.

"What are you waiting for? Grab the guns," hissed Packard, "and keep them both covered."

Jake turned to the Headmaster, waiting for him to step forward and collect the weapons but to his surprise it was Humpty who reacted. Yet again he found himself looking down the barrel of a gun held in the fat swollen hand, but this time so was the Headmaster.

"Catching on yet, Mr Highfield?" said the Headmaster, turning slightly to expose the cable ties that secured his hands behind his back.

Packard stood up, having secured Routledge's wrists in the same fashion. "Is he still secure?" he said, a ball of spittle forming between his clamped teeth. Humpty spun the Headmaster, checked the bindings and nodded his affirmative answer. "Good. That just leaves our friend Jake here."

"Are we going to do it here?" asked Humphrey.

"Not losing your nerve, are you…Headmaster?" said Packard, raising the best smile he could given his wired jaw.

"No, I…" stammered Humphrey.

"Don't worry; I won't make a mess of your playground," said Packard. "I just want to know if Jake is in or out first. I think he's proved his worth. He could be useful, don't you think?" Packard turned to Jake. "Well? It's up to you?"

"No," shouted Humphrey. "Not him. He's nothing but trouble; a loose cannon. Beyond anyone's control."

Packard slowly turned to face Humphrey again. "Jake's not the same lad I drove to St. Margaret's three years ago. He's changed. He's disciplined and skilled." He tapped at the frame that held his jaw in place. "I can vouch for that personally. He's an asset I don't want to waste."

"You promised I would be Headmaster and I will not have him in my institution!"

"Don't," barked Packard, "you ever try to pull rank on me. You are only going to be Headmaster because I am going to let you be Headmaster. I am in charge." He stared into Humphrey's face, "Do we understand each other? I'll be training Jake myself and you'll have nothing to do with him."

Humphrey nodded his submissive agreement, his eyes looking at the floor.

"Is this what it has been all about," said the Headmaster, calmly. "An old grudge?"

Humphrey turned and jammed one of the guns he held under the Headmaster's chin. "I should have been Headmaster and you know that! If it hadn't been for you and your high-flying connections, I would have been too!"

"Hardly," replied the Headmaster, seemingly unworried by the weapon pointed directly at his brain. "You do not have the backbone to run St. Margaret's and it stands out a mile. Always has. Even when we were students you were always weak, unable to see anything through to the end, bitter or otherwise. There was no way on God's good earth that you would have made it, even if you had been blessed with royal connections."

Humphrey began to laugh. "Weak? Not so weak to stop me having the upper hand over you for once! I have the job now. And without having to resort to 'special handshakes' and who Daddy went to school with. Your connections don't matter anymore. The only connections you'll have soon are going to be the highest you can get," he paused. "With the angels I mean."

"Yes," said the Headmaster slowly. "I get it, thank you."

"Is the happy reunion over?" said Packard, struggling to speak clearly.

Humphrey took a step back, holding his gun up as if daring the Headmaster to make a move. "I win."

The Headmaster ignored the small man's baiting. "So then, Mr Packard, it appears you are the viper at my bosom after all."

Packard let out a throaty laugh through his closely wired jaw. "You almost managed to say that as if you didn't already know," he said. "I didn't imagine for one second I could start snatching operatives from under your nose with impunity. You may be old but I wasn't going to make the mistake of taking you for a fool that wouldn't react to an attack on your precious St. Margaret's. But what did surprise me was the time it has taken for you to fight back. Not like you at all, Headmaster. Especially since we both know you've been suspicious of me for a good length of time now. And as for pretending to swallow my story about Jake losing it in the forest... well, I was beginning to wonder if you would ever make a stand?"

"Suspicion and fact are two different things, Mr Packard," explained the Headmaster. "And it was evident that you had to have someone working with you. Even with your skills it would be hard for you to be in two places at once. I needed to make sure you had weaved enough rope for me to hang you with."

"You let him try and kill me and you knew he was a traitor!" shouted Jake, striding forward.

"Ah-ah," said Packard. "That's far enough until we know whose side you're on."

"Suspected, Mr Highfield," reiterated the Headmaster, "not knew. And as I explained when you joined us," he continued levelly, "everyone here is expected to make certain sacrifices. Individuals are not as important as the whole at St. Margaret's. However, unlike certain other parties, I did not underestimate your abilities to survive a challenge."

"See, Jake," said Packard, "that's the kind of man you're dealing with. He was willing to sacrifice you without a second thought."

Jake looked to the Headmaster almost hoping for a denial, but he remained silent, merely blinking as drops of rain made his eyes flicker.

"On the other hand," continued Packard, "if you join me..."

"Join you!" spat Jake. "So you can drive me off into another forest and use me as target practice again?"

"Believe me, Jake, if I had been trying to kill you, you'd be dead." The matter-of-fact tone in Packard's voice was proof enough for Jake to know that he was telling the truth about that at least. "I was merely trying to scare you off; get you out of the way until all this was over and then I could bring you back in to work for me. The fact that you managed to defend yourself so well was yet another testament to your valuable, and highly marketable, skills."

"And I suppose it was you who got Humpty to send Clarkson to try and finish off the job you had started," pushed Jake, finally fitting the pieces together.

"I was angry then," shrugged Packard. "You'd just rearranged my face and I was letting my feelings get the better of me. Hot-headed revenge is always very unprofessional, as I'm sure the Headmaster will agree. However, the fact that you are here tonight has reassured me of your undeniable value again and earned you a second chance to make the right decision."

Jake looked at Packard and then at the Headmaster, his head spinning. There was more crossing going on in the quadrant of St. Margaret's at this moment then went on at the Vatican in a year.

Packard continued to push his sales pitch. "Just think Jake, that Ferrari we talked about, it could be yours. Money, travel, excitement, it could all be yours for the taking."

"As could a bullet," said the Headmaster.

"You're really starting to hack me off, old man," said Packard, swinging his gun to join Humphrey's, pointing at the Headmaster. "Once you've been removed from the equation and Humphrey is running this place, I'll have access to the finest army of covert mercenaries the world has ever seen. St. Margaret's will join the twenty-first century and enter a marketplace that is willing to pay any price for her services and there's nothing you can do about it."

"You can replace me, that is true, but do you think the old boys from the Academy are just going to sit back and let this all happen?" said the Headmaster. "St. Margaret's is protected, you know that. They are not going to ignore the violation of the institution that made them what they are."

"The old boys," said Packard, with obvious distaste, "will have no choice. They will simply have to lie back and let it happen. Apparently that's all a corpse can do."

"I see," said the Headmaster. "But how are you going to get to them? We know the Void failed to find any trace of their records and they were removed from the system as soon as we discovered the program's presence."

Packard laughed deep in his throat, his frozen jaw making him look mentally unstable. "That's why I had my colleague take the system data disc from your office safe. It must be hard to live a life when the only person you can really trust is yourself."

"Not wanting to spoil your delight in your own intelligence," said the Headmaster, "but unless you enjoy the band of the Coldstream Guards I am afraid you will get little pleasure from the disc Mr Humphrey has in his possession."

Packard smiled. "Nice try, but I'm not that stupid."

"I know you are not, Mr Packard," smiled the Headmaster, "but you really cannot trust anyone but yourself to do a job properly."

Packard frowned at Humphrey. "Tell me you checked it out?"

"I..." stuttered Humphrey.

"I know, technically, it is illegal to copy commercial music discs," continued the Headmaster, "but I find it is always prudent to make a backup, you never know what might happen to the original."

Humphrey had removed the disc from his jacket pocket and was looking at it as if its silver surface would play in thin air. "I was going to check it out but there was no time and then you told me to get him and…"

"And? And? And?" strained Packard, through his gritted teeth. "I can see I'm going to have to keep a close eye on you, Humphrey. It could be that you're not the right man for the job at St. Margaret's after—"

He turned his attention back to the Headmaster, a sudden calm commanding his eyes. "Very good, Headmaster, divide and conquer. Feed the enemy false information and watch their ranks crumble. 'The Art of War' if I'm not mistaken?"

"You always were a fast learner," nodded the Headmaster, his voice laced with sarcasm.

"Put the disc away, Humphrey," ordered Packard. "Whatever's on it doesn't matter. He's probably bluffing, but even if he's telling the truth we will have enough time to trace the files ourselves once he's out of the way. Besides it might be therapeutic to do it with some background music. The more pressing matter is our boy here. Well, Jake, where do you stand?"

"Is there a 'two hundred miles away from here' option?" asked Jake.

"I like you, Jake. You remind me of me when I was your age," said Packard.

'Wet, cold, confused and scared stiff?' thought Jake. But he said, "It looks like I'm in the middle of two psychopaths who really don't care much about my ability to breathe." In his peripheral vision, Jake noticed a figure crouching in the open double doors that Packard and Routledge had entered the quad through. He kept speaking without pause. "And I've got to make a choice between nutter one and nutter two. Well, I suppose I'll have to choo—"

At that moment a thundering bang echoed around the quadrant.

BACK FROM THE DEAD

Shards of silver shrapnel flew across the quadrant, glittering brightly under the halogen lights that lit the area and in a split second the scene that had been almost static, exploded into life before Jake's eyes.

Packard grunted, his clamped mouth unable to let out the full cry of pain. Sharp plastic icicles buried themselves into his right arm and shoulder, causing a reflex reaction that forced him to drop his weapon.

Humpty, distracted by the cry, turned his head away from the Headmaster who swiftly stepped forward and kicked him in the stomach. He dropped his body onto the folded man and pinned him face down to the ground where he struggled without success, gasping for air.

From behind Jake, a figure raced forward, his right arm hanging uselessly at his side. Clarkson was back on his feet, rushing towards the injured Packard, who was pulling the largest of the vicious splinters from the back of his hand. "Come on, Highfield," he shouted. "Time we got that payback."

Jake leapt forwards, glancing at the figure in the doorway. Their outline was barely visible in the shadow but it looked to him like they were reloading whatever weird weapon they had fired already. There was no time to work out whose side they were on – more immediate threats had to be negated first.

Clarkson jumped toward Packard, executing a flying kick at his target's sternum, a devastating attack that could break bones and cause internal damage. But Packard was too quick. With a slight step to the side and slicing across and down his body with his left arm he diverted the power of the kick into thin air. The momentum carried Clarkson on, making him land off balance. Packard merely had to tug at the boy's shoulder to spin him and lock his neck into a strangle hold. With a sadistic grin on his face, Packard pushed two of the fingers of his right hand into the fresh bullet wound Humpty had given the boy. Clarkson screamed.

Jake launched himself and grabbed at the frame around Packard's head. Gripping with both hands he swung his legs out and round, his whole body off the ground, forcing out like a centrifuge. It was an ungainly attack, but it had the desired effect of freeing Clarkson from Packard's grip. However, it left friend and foe alike sprawled on the ground, each struggling to get to their feet in readiness for the next attack.

"You picked the wrong side, Jake," hissed Packard, pulling off his suit jacket. "I won't be playing to miss this time."

"At least I've got a side again," snarled Jake.

Clarkson was up. He drove his foot into the back of Packard's knee. The man collapsed forward onto it, but his bent arms were quickly raised up to protect him from the second kick to the head. He drove his elbow into Clarkson's exposed groin. Clarkson coughed out a grunt and toppled onto his back where he was treated to a second blow, this time to the solar plexus.

Jake swung a kick at Packard's head, but the man raised himself back up onto both feet and out of range. Jake stepped back into his fighting stance, looking for the opening he wanted.

Packard rolled his shoulders in a backwards circle a few times, showing he had no fear of the boy before him. "Let's take it up a gear. If you want to play in the Premiership, you've got to play by Premiership rules."

Jake flicked his head to clear some of the rain from his hair that was dripping into his eyes but in that split second of distraction, Packard had covered the distance between them and driven his right arm forward. Jake twisted to avoid the blow just in time, but he felt the burning pain in his ear as the fist ploughed its way along the side of his head. It was quickly followed by a jarring thud at the back of his skull as he was struck by Packard's elbow. He lurched forwards, his eyes closed. A feeling of nausea welled up, heightened by a knee that struck him with such force in the stomach that both of his feet left the ground. Jake landed on all fours, retching up bile that burned his throat.

"Is that it, Jake, my friend?" mocked Packard. He sent a kick into Jake's ribs spinning him onto his back. "I think Humphrey was right after all, you are a waste of space. The Premiership is no place for you. Time you were relegated...permanently."

Jake lay spread-eagled. So much pain shot through his body, he could no longer tell where it came from. He didn't really care either, he just wanted it to stop. Packard raised his foot, 'Leather soles,' noted Jake, almost smiling at the ridiculousness of this thought when it could well be his last.

The shadow fell from his face as Packard was knocked sideways off his feet. "Get up, Highfield," shouted Clarkson. "I can't do this alone."

All Jake could do was roll onto his side and look as Clarkson straddled Packard, pinning him down with his knees. He lay one, two, three left-handed punches into the man's chest. Jake tried to lift his body up off the sodden ground with his arms, but the pain at the back of his head flared once more, blackening his vision and he collapsed again.

Packard reached up, grabbing Clarkson by the ears with both hands. Then arching his back and pushing his hips up, he forced Clarkson over his head, face first, into the grass. Rolling over to his left-hand side, Packard was free of Clarkson's weight and he drove his fist into the boy's midsection before pulling himself away from the tangle of limbs and standing up.

Jake watched as Clarkson staggered to his feet again, despite the obvious pain etched on his face. 'If he can do it...' Jake lifted himself again, and this time managed to get to one knee.

Despite his resilience, Clarkson was getting beaten to a pulp. His one good arm was no match for Packard's relentless assault. Blow after blow rattled across his chin, knocking him back several steps each time. The only thing keeping him standing was determination.

Jake staggered to his feet and tried to call out to Clarkson, to tell him to hold on, but nothing would come out of his mouth. He raised his head as Clarkson was punched back again to slam into the wall of St. Margaret's.

Clarkson began to slide down the stone barrier but at the last second threw his arm out to grab the electric cable that fed the lights of the quadrant to halt his collapse.

Jake was doing his best to cover the ground between him and Packard, but he was weaving wildly from side to side. His legs felt like they were boneless, supported by muscle and tendon alone. He kept his eyes focused on Packard. Nothing else mattered.

Packard stood back from Clarkson, gauging the perfect distance for the killer strike. Jake knew what was coming. He had to get there. He had to. Packard flicked his whole body around, pirouetting on his left foot as his right foot came spinning round at great speed, rising up to capture Clarkson's jaw within its deadly circle. Jake saw the boy's head whip round so hard that it bounced back just as fast with the recoil. Clarkson was lifted off his feet, his supporting hand not given enough time to relax its grip, ripping the cable free from the light-fitting, two metres above his head. He hit the ground and lay motionless.

Jake reclaimed his voice. It was primitive and raw. "No!"

Packard turned. He looked as strong as ever. "Think I've proved a point there, don't you, Jake?" He reached behind his back and produced a knife. "Playtime's over."

Jake heard a shrill voice cry out behind him. "Get down, Jake!" He didn't wait to be told twice. As he threw himself forward the loud bang rang out again around the quad and he heard the whistling of projectiles cutting through the rain once more. He watched another volley of the silver shards of unknown origin as they rattled against the cage around Packard's head. Those that got through the metal latticework buried themselves into the flesh of his face and neck.

Packard was thrown back, cursing with pain, slamming into the ugly sister that stood in the now unlit corner of the quad. He slumped down against the square base of the gargoyle. A sharp crack was followed by the unmistakeable grind of stone moving against stone. The ugly sister pitched forward and Packard looked up. His eyes widened with realisation. Survival instinct overrode any other thought, including the pain in his injured face and he rolled to the side, just as the edifice bit into the grass.

Jake looked over his shoulder. "Angel?"

Angel stood next to a bulky contraption, her hair plastered flat to her head by the rain. "Jake! Look out!"

Jake turned and saw that Packard was back on his feet again, striding forward, knife in one hand, the other pulling fragments of the projectiles from his bleeding face.

"Just so you know," he said, wincing as he pulled another splinter free, "I'm going to kill her too, once I've dealt with you, Jake Highfield."

Pushing with his arms, Jake stood up. His body felt like it was tingling all over. He felt refreshed, strong. He knew it was the rush of adrenaline, he'd felt it often enough on missions, but never to this extent. There was something more too, something he was familiar with: anger. Not the anger he had felt before he'd been dumped at St. Margaret's, the rage that led him to destroy things mindlessly just to vent itself. This was cold, focused anger. He looked back at Angel, her face full of fear, but standing her ground. He looked over to Clarkson, lying face down and motionless, the disrespectful rain bouncing off his back. He looked at Packard, the cause of all this madness, and his veins burned with fire.

"My name," he said, slowly, "is not Jake Highfield.

My name is Chaos." He began to run forward with steady, firm steps, his eyes fixed on Packard, oblivious to the rain that battered against him. Packard mirrored his advance, raising his knife and snarling like a Celtic warrior advancing into battle. They clashed with the force of armies, each determined to fell the other with as much venomous intent as they could drag from their hearts.

The knife swept across, threatening to decapitate Chaos with the force of the blow but he saw it coming and ducked under the swing, rising up again quickly, ready for the return blow. He blocked the attack with his forearm, hitting Packard's arm high above the elbow, forcing the limb to overextend. The shock loosened his grip on the weapon which spun off into the darkness. Chaos then drove his left fist into the exposed floating ribs, causing Packard to wince with pain.

Stepping forward on his right foot, Jake placed his weight on his toes. He spun so he was behind Packard and lined up for an attack on his kidneys. Packard spun in the opposite direction, flailing out with a desperate, but nonetheless effective, back fist. The impact knocked Chaos' head off-centre and toppled him out of his stance; momentarily Packard was lost from his field of vision. Chaos let his body go in the direction it had been forced, bending low and flicking out his leg. As he spun, his extended heel caught Packard low down on his calf muscle, lifting his weightbearing leg off the ground. Packard fell back, his arms grabbing at the air for support he never found.

Chaos raised his foot high to stamp down on the fallen man's chest, but Packard's arm pulled at his supporting ankle and his foot slipped on the wet grass, sending him crashing to the ground too. Packard pounced.

His hands outstretched and open, ready to crush the windpipe they were aiming for, but Chaos curled his legs up tightly against his chest. As he felt the weight of his attacker fall onto his feet he pushed his legs straight up and back, sending Packard wheeling over his head.

There was a wet ripping noise and a loud scream of pain. Chaos rolled off his back and stood over Packard. He looked at the horn of the toppled ugly sister piercing his enemy's shoulder; the tip dyed red with blood.

"Jake," gasped Packard, lifting his hand in a gesture, pleading for help. "You can't leave me like this, can you?"

Chaos stood silent for a moment, his breathing slow and heavy. "You're right," he said. He lifted his boot and placed it on Packard's chest.

"Jake!" shouted Angel and Chaos heard her approaching feet. "Stop it. Doing this will only make you worse than him!"

Chaos turned his head and looked coldly into Angel's pleading face. "Maybe I am. Maybe I always have been."

"Please, Jake."

Chaos turned to face Packard, the anger subsiding. He slowly lifted his foot off the man's chest and placed it back on the ground. Packard gasped with relief and his body slumped.

"Thank you, Jake," said Angel with a faltering voice. "You've done the right thing."

Jake didn't reply. He turned and walked over to where Clarkson lay and crouched down by the still body. He was confused, out of his depth. 'What am I supposed to be feeling?' he thought. 'What am I supposed to do? Is there some kind of ritual I should be performing; some special words I need to say?'

"Jake!"

Jake turned to see Packard, his uninjured arm firmly grasping Angel's chin holding her tightly to his body. "I can snap her neck like deadwood and you know it, Jake."

"And you won't do it if …" asked Jake, calmly.

Packard started to laugh, but the pain in his side cut it short, "As you can see, things have gone a little pear-shaped for me," he panted heavily. "So, I need you to help me make a hasty retreat."

"I see," said Jake, brushing his hand that was on the blind side of Packard, across the grass. "And if I do that you'll let her go?"

"You have my word," said Packard, wincing at his pain.

"Your word," repeated Jake doubtfully, his hand finding what he was looking for and grasping it tightly. "Angel," he said slowly, "do you remember in the Tech department, I said you'd never catch me out the same way twice?"

Angel drove her elbow into Packard. The shock waves it produced juddered through his body to his open wound, his grip loosened and she pulled herself free of his grasp. Jake stood up and twirled the electric cable like a lasso twice round his head before letting go. It snapped forward towards Packard. The black line whipped around the metal frame on his head then the exposed copper core made contact. Packard stiffened as if he had been frozen. Steam started to rise off his head as the rain boiled in contact with the heat surging through his body. Jake found himself coldly surprised by how few sparks there were.

The remaining lights in the quad tripped out.

END GAME

Jake let Angel take some of his weight on her shoulders after she insisted on supporting him. "We'd best check out the Headmaster," she said.

"He'll be alright. I don't think Humpty was in Packard's league...thank God." Jake paused as they drew level with the contraption he'd seen Angel operating. "What the hell is that?"

Angel shrugged. "It's nothing really, just a length of pipe, a bottle of compressed air, a pressure release valve and a handful of snapped CDs."

"Bloody effective for something that's 'nothing really'." Jake limped forward.

"Miss Dunne, Mr Highfield," called the Headmaster's voice out of the darkness. "Much as I can understand your relief at the resolution of the situation, I could do with a little assistance here."

Jake and Angel quickened their pace.

Jake looked down at the Headmaster whose body was still pinning Humpty face down on the grass. "Need a hand, sir?"

"My own two will do fine, thank you, Mr Highfield, once you have released them."

Jake looked at the cable-ties and patted at his various pockets. "I'm sorry sir but I don't seem..."

Angel pulled a pair of long-nose pliers from her pocket and snipped through the plastic binding. She stood up and noticed the incredulous look on Jake's face.

"You never know when they'll come in handy," she said, almost apologetically.

The Headmaster stood up and straightened his jacket. "Is Mr Packard dead?"

"I don't think so, sir," said Jake.

"And Mr Clarkson?"

Jake stayed silent. Angel bowed her head.

"I see," said the Headmaster, softly.

Jake cleared his throat. "He did mention something about more of the Vanished being on the Academy's perimeter."

"All taken care of; they were picked up long before they could be of any help, or hindrance, to anyone."

"What about them?" asked Jake, nodding at the two unconscious figures which lay peacefully oblivious of all the excitement that had happened around them.

The Headmaster looked with some disgust at the man at his feet. "Mr Humphrey found the strength within his character to faint his way out of the situation and as for Mr Routledge, I have a feeling another bang on the head will not have any lasting effect on him."

Jake grinned. 'Could make him less mental,' he thought to say but decided against it. Routledge was staff and the Headmaster did not tolerate his staff being ridiculed by the students, under any circumstances.

"What will happen to them?" asked Angel.

"Happen to whom, Miss Dunne?" asked the Headmaster, without emotion.

"The Vanished. Humphrey. Packard."

The Headmaster didn't answer straight away. "They will be dealt with, Miss Dunne," he answered, eventually.

"Dealt with?" repeated Angel. "You mean killed!" she barked, defiantly.

"What I mean by dealt with is none of your concern, Miss Dunne," said the Headmaster sternly.

"But Clarkson's dead!" forced Angel, her despairing anger dispelling any fear she had for the Headmaster's authority. "And you've used Jake as bait from the start, without a second thought for his safety, as if he was worth no more than a worm on a hook!"

"The Watkinson mission," said Jake slowly. "The dart was defective and you knew it." He looked up at the Headmaster. "It was you who had the dart tampered with."

The Headmaster held Jake's stare, but said nothing.

"It was all false from the start, Jake," cried Angel. "There was no real Watkinson mission. It was a scam set up to guarantee you'd fail. To make you a target for the Void program, to bring you to the attention of the people behind it. He," Angel nodded in disgust at the Headmaster, "knew you would never betray the Academy, whatever resentment you were feeling towards it. And because of that loyalty he knew you would cause all kinds of trouble that would force his unknown enemies out into the open where he could deal with them before their plans were fully formed."

Tears were beginning to form in Angel's eyes as she turned to the Headmaster. "How could you do that to Jake? How could you be so cold? He could have been..." Angel choked on the word, "...like Clarkson. Haven't you got any...any..."

"You must understand, Miss Dunne," interrupted the Headmaster, sternly, "that while you believe you have completed the jigsaw, it is I who holds the missing pieces of the puzzle. Your involvement in this operation is over, and believe me, Miss Dunne, there are times at which I envy your blissful, yet resentful, ignorance of certain matters appertaining to St. Margaret's."

Angel opened her mouth to push further for more information, but Jake could see in her eyes she wasn't sure if she really wanted the burden of that knowledge.

"It's alright, Angel," he said. "We've got through it."

Angel closed her mouth and nodded.

Jake looked at the Headmaster. The man before him was impassive. He could tell by his eyes that he had already moved on from the carnage around him. On to the next challenge that faced him and St. Margaret's. Pushing for answers would be like trying to inflate a balloon with a hole in it.

"Some nice moves you pulled tonight, sir," said Jake. "You took Humpty out, no problem."

The Headmaster didn't reply for a moment, as if silently acknowledging and approving of Jake's understanding of his position.

"It may come as a surprise to you, Mr Highfield, but I was not always the old man you see before you today," he said, digging into his pocket and pulling out his pipe. "I was once an active operative in the field myself."

Jake and Angel looked at each other and then back at the Headmaster.

"Unbelievable, I know, but true nonetheless. I loved my days at St. Margaret's so much, that when the position of Headmaster came up, I jumped at the opportunity; gave me a chance to give something back."

"Did you have a codename, sir," asked Angel. "When you were operational, I mean?"

Jake could almost hear her devious, geeky brain working overtime under all that wayward hair.

"Of course I did, young lady," said the Headmaster, pushing his thumb into the bowl of his pipe. The Headmaster paused, placed the pipe between his teeth and looked up at the stained glass window of his office.

"It was Chaos."

Angel nudged Jake gently in the ribs. He could only surmise she had some dodgy conspiracy theory about this obvious coincidence that she would share with him sooner or later.

"Right, that is enough excitement for us all tonight I think," said the Headmaster, clapping his hands together and rubbing them energetically. "Mr Highfield, eight o'clock sharp for debriefing as usual."

Jake's shoulders dropped "But sir, I'm—"

His protest was cut short. "A student at St. Margaret's, Mr Highfield, that is what you are. One of the chosen, one of the elite."

Jake looked about the window-dotted walls of the Academy as the Headmaster strolled away, then up at the figure of St. Margaret, illuminated like a vision by the light behind her and for a second he imagined he could feel the tug of a puppeteer's strings moving his head to face her.

ALEC SILLIFANT

Alec Sillifant was born in 1965 in Weston-Super-Mare, Somerset but has lived in what he considers his home city, Liverpool, since the 1970s.

He has worked in a number of different jobs, but throughout his life has always been writing. Since the turn of the century, he has settled into a routine of earning his living through the written word; writing short stories, poetry, comedy sketches and in particular greetings cards. Alec Sillifant is the author of nine children's books including picture books, junior fiction titles and for the first time here, a full length novel for young adult readers.

He has plans to write more fiction for young adult readers in the future, and is currently plotting a supernatural thriller set in the dark times of medieval England. He describes his feelings about writing as, 'A slightly masochistic way to have fun,' but, 'the only time I'm allowed to tell long, elaborate lies about stuff.'

He writes at home in Liverpool where he lives with his wife and four sons who he describes as his anchors to keep him in line in the real world.

THE FOLLOWING PEOPLE I OWE A DEBT OF THANKS TO, ONE WAY OR ANOTHER...

The crew from Meadowside: Simon Rosenheim, for the chance, the push, his confidence in me and the stunning cover design; Lucy Cuthew, for her excellent editing, help, patience and the pun which I shall always wish I had seen; Rupert Harbour for getting this book, amongst others, into your hands and the random walking tour of London; Sarah Wilson, for her superb design skills across the years including this book in your hands now which, I'm sure you'll agree, is another fine piece of work; Clare Simms for dropping my name into conversations and generally doing a great job of bugging people with the fact that I am alive; Katherine Judge for hawking my wares across foreign lands and maybe even beyond; Ellie Wharton for her generous, and much needed, help in the past; Alison Maloney, for starting the ball rolling on all of this stuff after rescuing 'Edwin Page' from the depths of the slush pile; Lin Bennett and Charlie Hankers for their much appreciated spit and polish.

Moving away from this book, thus making them blameless for its content, these folk also deserve mention for many a diverse reason: Tracey, my wife, for too many reasons to list here; my four sons, for making me proud and taking part in 'Australian No Rules Boatball' much to my amusement; Mum & Dad, not much could have happened without you two; Pam and Helen for being excellent sisters and not too freaky for being twins. Next a big list of names, they know who they are and why they are here, so in no particular order...Helen and Ronnie Reay; Pam, Kev, Thomas and Damien Sharp; Terry Malone; Jeff, Jan, Elliot and Aiden Gardner; Nige and Diane Sims; Dave, Vicky and Samantha Wright; John and Lily Halvorsen; Mrs M; Rose and 'Orace Gardner; Shaun Taft and family; Mr & Mrs C, Coey and Dave; Milly, Terence and George Johnson; Craig, Trina, Adam and Natalie Pope; the award-winning Daniel Postgate, Mike Spoor, Heather Allen, Uwe Mayer, Joëlle Dreidemy, Barrie Appleby; The Alvos and partners, one and all; Everyone at RYR; The crew from IMI, colleagues and partners alike; and an absolute shedful of people from the greetings card industry who I would like to mention individually but dare not for fear of leaving someone off by mistake. I could go on and if anyone ever wants to publish another book of mine I will but while the word count is just about less than the story I have been told to stop...